D0219552

DEEP IN THE RUSSIAN NIGHT

AARON CHAZAN

CIS

P·U·B·L·I·S·H·E·R·S

New York · London · Jerusalem

„תורת חיים ואהבת חסד וצדקה"

לזכר נשמת

ר' יקותיא-ל יהודה ב"ר יעקב ז"ל

ולז"נ אהרן ב"ר יקותיא-ל יהודה ז"ל

שמחת תורה כ"ג תשרי תש"ה

ולזכר נשמת

מרת חנה בת ר' מנחם מענדל ע"ה

ל' תשרי תש"ה

למשפחת רוזענברג

שנהרגו על קידוש השם הי"ד

Dedicated by

Marcus Rosenberg and Family

Copyright © 1990

C.I.S. Communications, Inc.

All rights reserved.
This book, or any part thereof,
may not be reproduced
in any form whatsoever
without the express written permission
of the copyright holder.

Published and distributed
in the U.S., Canada and overseas by
C.I.S. Publishers and Distributors
180 Park Avenue, Lakewood, New Jersey 08701
(201) 905-3000 Fax (201) 367-6666

Distributed in Israel by
C.I.S. International (Israel)
Rechov Mishkalov 18
Har Nof, Jerusalem
Tel: 02-538-935

Distributed in the U.K. and Europe by
C.I.S. International (U.K.)
1 Palm Court, Queen Elizabeth Walk
London, England N16
Tel: 01-809-3723

Book design: Ronda Kruger Israel
Cover illustration: Gregg Hinlickey
Typography: Nechamie Miller

ISBN 1-56062-030-7 hard cover
1-56062-034-X soft cover
Library of Congress Catalog Card Number
90-82186

PRINTED IN THE UNITED STATES OF AMERICA

Far too much Jewish blood
And spirit mired in crimson mud
Stain the tempestuous Russian night
Trampled by the tsars
Ensnared by commissars
Deep in the treacherous Russian night.

Far too many yearning minds
Drawn into the burning, churning grind
To spark the flaccid Russian night
Dreamed of justice, dignity
But shared the peasant misery
Deep in the rancid Russian night.

Far too long are we in exile driven
Forever, it seems, we are children unforgiven
Condemned to the senseless Russian night
Stripped of self, from cradle taken
On the vast cold steppe remain forsaken
Deep in the endless Russian night.

Yaakov Yosef Reinman

TABLE

OF

CONTENTS

PREFACE

THIS BOOK BRINGS TO LIGHT ONE OF THE MOST
eventful eras of Jewish history, a period that until
now has been closed from view. Noteworthy from several aspects,
this book is a personal account, in English, of the Russian Communist Revolution and its repercussions on Russian Jewry. It is told by
one Russian Jew who not only lived through it but also battled for
half a century against the system to maintain his Judaism.

Numerous volumes dealing with Russian Jewry have been published since the Revolution, but these are generally historical
accounts which concentrate on Jewish social and economic life;
they barely touch on the religious upheaval that occurred. At the
time of the Revolution, the majority of Russian Jewry were strictly
religious *Chassidim*. Immediately after the Revolution, the Communist regime quickly and systematically crushed all signs of organized religion, enforcing a uniform lifestyle of atheism on its citizens.

This book recounts in detail how the cataclysm came about and how it affected the lives of the unwilling but helpless Jews. In addition, it describes events that overtook Russian Jewry in the decades that followed.

Nothing is left out: The Revolution, the Ukrainian pogroms, the persecutions, executions of Jews by the Communists, aided by their Jewish lackeys in the Yevsektzia, collectivization, the Stalin purges, the wave of anti-Semitism that led up to the Doctors' Plot and the resurgence of Jewish identity, beginning in the sixties, of the new Jewish generation. All this unfolds as Rav Chazan sets forth his own compelling story. A person acquainted with Russian history may find his previous conceptions challenged, but he will be amply rewarded by the penetrating insight into the Communists' aims revealed by this work.

Rav Chazan, the protagonist, originally wrote the details of his life as a remembrance for his children and their descendants. He was prevailed upon to release his story so that a wider public might learn how the fiery Jewish dedication to G-d and Judaism still exists in our day. Accuracy is fully assured as Rav Chazan carefully followed every stage of the writing and insisted on twice rechecking the completed manuscript, refusing to include anything that he had not experienced himself. He often tried the writer's patience by changing numerous near-insignificant details to set down the facts exactly as they were.

This is the story of one family's devotion to Judaism in the face of every reason to surrender. It is the writer's hope that this book will inspire in its reader a deeper relationship to their own Jewish heritage and Judaism—as indeed it did for me.

M. Samsonowitz

1 THE RED LAKE

TODAY, A VISITOR TO THE SMALL RUSSIAN TOWN OF Krasnostav could hardly imagine that it was once a vibrant Jewish *shtetl*. Yet, in the early twentieth century, when I was born, over two hundred and fifty Jewish families—artisans and merchants—lived there.

The Jewish population, by and large, consisted of Ruzhiner, Karliner and Czernobyler *Chassidim* whose lives revolved around the *Bais Hamidrash* and their religious duties. They *davened* in *shul* morning and evening. Their children learned in *cheder*. Early *Shabbos* morning, a man used to go around, calling the Jews to read *Tehillim*: "*Shteit oif, shteit oif le'avoidas Haboireh!* Get up to serve your Creator!" Even as late as 1926, there was a man who made the rounds on Friday afternoon, before *Shabbos*, reminding all the people to stop working and close their shops. And close their shops they did.

The name of the *shtetl* was derived from its lake, Krasnostav, meaning "Red Lake." There was a legend that some centuries ago, the Cossacks rounded up the inhabitants of the town and slaughtered them at the edge of this lake. The blood of the corpses turned the lake crimson.

Life in the Ukrainian *shtetl* was simple. Residents dwelt in small one-level houses. They learned to adjust their lives to the climate. Most people worked hard all summer. During the harsh Russian winter families would gather around the oven for warmth, letting business slow down. Drinking and cleaning water came from wells. To wash clothes, a group would go down to the nearby lake, cut a hole in the ice and dip the clothes into the frigid water.

Despite this, or perhaps because of it, our lives were not so much marked by the physical existence as by the spiritual dimension, a dimension that pervaded daily life. The district surrounding Krasnostav evoked the memory of glorious figures in East European Jewish history. Within seventy kilometers of Krasnostav were the town of Mezirich, home of the renowned Maggid, Reb Baer of Mezirich; Anapoli, where Reb Zusia lived and taught; Koritz, from where Reb Pinchas spread the light of *Chassidus*; Polno'ah, home of the Baal Shem Tov's illustrious pupil, Rav Yaakov Yosef Hacohen; Sidilkov, home of the author of *Degel Machaneh Ephraim*, the grandson of the Baal Shem Tov; Zevihl (Novograd Volinsk), where Reb Shloimele lived; Slavuta, home of the children of Reb Pinchas Koritz; and Shepetivka, the home of the Shepetivker Tzaddik.

I was born into a line of distinguished rabbis, a family that had been zealous in maintaining its scholarship and communal leadership for centuries. My maternal grandfather, Rav Moshe Hacohen Rappaport, was an eighth generation direct descendant of the great Shach, Rabbi Shabbesai Cohen (1611-1663), one of the greatest Jewish scholars of Vilna and Lithuania, who wrote the *Sifsei Cohen* on *Shulchan Aruch*. This grandfather was a man whose every action reflected holiness. He had been the Rav of my hometown until his son-in-law, my father, replaced him. He spent his later years in constant Torah study and in teaching Torah to my brother and me. In the turbulent years after the Revolution, he was my primary mentor. It was from him that I acquired mastery in *Gemara*.

My father, Rav Mordechai Chazan, had been one of the eminent students of the Iluy of Zevihl, Hagaon Rav Yoel Shurin, formerly the Poltaver Iluy. For the rest of his life my father looked upon Rav Yoel as his mentor. Appreciating this young man's deep *yiras shamayim*, my mother's father decided to take him as a son-in-law. The couple married, and I was their first born on *Motzei Shabbos*, February 3, 1912. I was named Aaron, because in *Yisro*, that week's *Sidra*, the words "Aaron and all the elders of Israel came" (*Shemos* 18:12) were read. Shortly after my birth, my father became Rav of Krasnostav.

Social structure in Krasnostav resembled that of other Jewish communities. Status tended to be based on the person's degree of Torah learning and devoutness. The most distinguished position was held by the Rav. The community leaders, *shochtim*, Torah scholars and persons of high character were next in the hierarchy. Then came *baalei batim*. Although often unlearned, they carved out a place for themselves in society through their pious deeds.

As the son of the town's Rav, I was inevitably regarded highly. Even as a child, it was taken for granted that I would one day assume my father's position. Little did I know how completely overturned my world would become.

2 THE REVOLUTION

IN MARCH 1917, THE RUSSIAN REVOLUTION BEGAN. At first a provisional government was set up. Seven months later, the Bolsheviks overthrew the provisional government amidst furious bloody fighting. With the entire country in turmoil and the government in disarray, diverse nationalities in Russia tried to assert their rights. The Ukrainians were one such group. They formed a Nationalist Party to secede from Russia. Under various generals, peasants banded together and went marauding from town to town.

The Ukrainian army's avowed purpose was to rid the Ukraine of the Communists . . . and every Jew was considered a Communist. This conception arose from the many renegade Jews who were prominent in founding and joining the Communist Party. In those first years, the Jews held the majority of high positions in the government. Those Jews strongly opposed Judaism, yet ironically, they gave a Jewish connotation to the term Communist, despite the fact that the masses of Jews were loyal to their religion. As late as 1941, soldiers were still being given a free hand to pillage and kill the unprotected Jews wherever they went. Indeed, General Denikin, General Petlura and others even encouraged the murderous excesses as a means of keeping the soldiers content and under control.

The Ukraine was well known for its pogroms against the Jews even as early as the infamous years *Tach-Tat* (1648-1649). Immediately after the Revolution, and for the ensuing five or six years, pogroms at the hands of Ukrainian mobs went on and Jews were killed. I was only a child of seven when Petlura and his gang overran our *shtetl* one *Shabbos*.

Rumors had just begun circulating about the atrocities they had committed, but we were not yet fully aware of their deeds. One day, some wild peasants burst into our house and seized my father, my grandfather and the two *shochtim* who were in the house at the time. I watched as they marched them to the wall of the *shul* across from our home and cocked their rifle to shoot. Fortunately, the rifle jammed, and these Petlurniks had to content themselves with beating them on the head, blow after vicious blow, with the rifle butt.

Finally, my grandfather and father slumped to the floor unconscious. Apparently, the peasants thought their victims were already dead, because they turned their attention to the *shochtim*, and dragged them through the streets by their beards. Mercifully, all four recovered.

We were indeed fortunate; other Jews in our town had not been as fortunate and were killed. Wherever the mobs went, Jews were massacred. Another time, when rumors broke out on a Friday that Petlura was on his way back to our town, my father grabbed the children and our whole family fled. When we returned home on Sunday we found two Jews dead.

Another time we escaped on the eve of *Yom Kippur* to the village of Jablonivka. Together with over a hundred others, we hid in the barn of a non-Jewish farmer. A Jewish maker of groats had arranged this place for us. We stayed there, terrified. On *Yom Kippur*, with no more than one or two *Machzorim*, my father led the prayers. When the fast ended, we still did not go home for fear of the Petlurniks. Fortunately, that night some gentiles brought some potatoes for the adults and milk for the children.

Zevihl, the capital of our district, was located forty kilometers from Krasnostav. In the fall of 1919, the peasants in Zevihl went on a rampage, massacring thousands of Jews. The situation of the remaining Jews was horrendous. Whoever had the means to escape fled. Reb Shloimele, the Rebbe of Zevihl, and his household escaped to Krasnostav, together with hundreds of other Jews. Each of the two hundred and fifty Jewish families of Krasnostav took in two or three refugee families. Many more lived in the women's section of the *shuls* and *batei midrash* of the town for the entire winter, until the disturbances had passed.

It was estimated that at the conclusion of two years of Nationalists battling the Communists, over one hundred and fifty thousand Jews had been massacred in pogroms. Tens of thousands of widows and orphans were without homes or resources.

Finally, the Communists, under the leadership of Vladimir Ilyich Lenin, defeated the Ukrainians. Understandably, many Jews hailed their victory, seeing it as an end to the Ukrainian atrocities. While it is true that the Communists brought a measure of stability, it only served as a platform to promote their ideological atrocities, atrocities akin to and in some ways surpassing those of the Ukrainian mobs.

At the very start of their rule in the Ukraine, the Communists launched a campaign to disseminate their ideology. Everyone had to "voluntarily" contribute toward building the Communist State. The workers, they proclaimed, would no longer be exploited, since everyone would be equal, each a government employee. Understandably, the workers and laborers were quick to join them. In cases where Communists failed to persuade the people with their rhetoric, however, they had no qualms about using other means. Vast segments of the population were declared "enemies of the people," meaning they did not uphold the Communist ideal. Discrimination was sharpest against the religious Jews and against groups with nationalistic goals, like the Zionist and Bundists, two different irreligious Jewish groups who did not subscribe to the

Communist ideals. Only Jews who belonged to the Communist Party enjoyed temporary safety.

The Communists could not tolerate religion; they felt that religious beliefs were a continuing source of hatred and political dissension against Communism. In their view, the unity envisioned by their Communist State could never be realized as long as destructive religious forces were rife. That, at least, was the official line. To convince the masses, they used a different tactic. "Religion teaches that some people have to be poor and others rich, that you must accept your suffering," they proclaimed. "This is only a subterfuge to suppress all the workers, a subterfuge we must abolish! Religion is the opium of the masses!"

At the time of the Revolution, the vast majority of Jews in Russia were religious; the Jews in Socialist, Reform and Zionist movements accounted for a very small percentage of the Jewish population. What these individuals lacked in numbers, though, they made up in zeal, working tirelessly to persuade their brethren to forsake Judaism and join their respective camps. Decades before, the Maskilim — Jews who abandoned Torah in favor of the "enlightened" culture of non-Jewish society — had made a breach in observant Jewish life. They opened Yiddish theaters and published hundreds of stories, novels and plays, all with the theme that religion was antiquated. Only the small towns remained unaffected by the modernist trends.

Both the Jewish labor party (the Bund) and the Zionists established secular schools where Jewish studies were ostensibly taught in a traditional spirit; in fact, the schools brainwashed the children with their ideals. They succeeded partly because of the general low state of formal Jewish education which existed in Russia at the end of the nineteenth century. Also, since Jewish primary education was disorganized, with each parent engaging a private teacher for his son or teaching the child himself, the parents welcomed these schools which seemed to offer the best of both worlds. The general subjects helped their children gain the knowledge necessary for easier, more respectable jobs, while the religious subjects obviated the need for private tutoring. Very few parents grasped the real motives behind the schools' instructors.

My father told me that Reb Yoel Shurin saw some of the pupils of the Jewish school openly desecrate the *Shabbos*, whereupon he assembled the Jewish residents of Zevihl.

"We are placing our children into the hands of devious people who are tearing them away from Judaism," he cried. "Now our children are following in their ways and openly desecrating the *Shabbos*! Our sages declare that such people, while still alive, are to be regarded as dead. We must mourn our children as if they were dead!" His voice broke and he sobbed tearfully in front of the whole assembly.

When the Communists seized power, all Jewish organizations, religious and non-religious, were banned. Conversely, anyone willing to follow the Communist line was appointed to a respected position, granted privileges and publicly honored. The easy life of Communist Party members contrasted sharply with the widespread struggle to survive. Some of the Zionists and Maskilim decided to take the path of least resistance and join the Communist Party. They fawned on the leaders. Indeed, there was nothing they would not do to prove their loyalty, many going as far as to turn on their former friends and associates. These new converts to Communism were taken in by Lenin's promises of equality to the Jews. They felt they could maintain their Jewish identity and still be accepted if they went along with the Communist ideology. It was this group that formed the nucleus of the infamous Yevsektzia, an organization whose aim was to indoctrinate the Jews in Party ideals.

The Communists would probably have been as powerless as the Czars to destroy the Jewish faith were it not for the Yevsektzia. Before long, there were branches of the Yevsektzia in every town and village. In the larger towns, they were headed by the local Maskilim who had embraced Communism. In the villages, they were led by the poorest and lowest workers, whom the Communists had appointed as leaders in implementing their economic policies. The poorer they were, the greater the authority they were given.

These newly empowered Jewish laborers set upon their more wealthy neighbors with relish. Once they were convinced of the righteousness of Communist equality, these Jews began to cherish other Communist doctrines as well. They soon demanded that all traces of the Jewish faith be wiped out.

The Yevsektzia acted with lightning speed. *Chadorim* and *yeshivos* were immediately closed. New Government schools were opened and staffed by Jews who had previously taught in the Jewish Labor schools. Such renegade Jews also headed the local Jewish councils. Rapidly, anti-religious papers and journals were published, with such names as *Emes* (Truth) and *Stern* (Star). One was even called *Apikores* (heretic). Its cover featured a picture of a spear piercing a small circle containing a bearded religious Jew and a Star of David.

These newspapers sounded the same themes being expounded in the schools and councils, that the Jews were not a separate people. The Torah and the Exodus were nothing but a myth. Zionists were thieves who were stealing the land from the Arabs. And so on.

These teachers and newspapers propapagated their ideas in Yiddish which was the only language of most small town Jews. In Orwellian fashion, they created a new Yiddish language with a simplified *alef-beis* by eliminating vowel signs, as well as the letters *veis*, *ches* and *kaf*. All Hebrew words were spelled in this new dehebraized spelling, which was meant to undermine this specifically Jewish language.

In the first years, the Communists' victims were heads of *yeshivos*, rabbis, *cheder* teachers and religious community leaders. The Yevsektzia would find innumerable ways to slander them, and once the victims were brought to court, their fate was clear. Some rabbis were imprisoned and tortured, others transported to Siberia and not heard from again. Terror chilled the community.

Initially, parents who did not send their children to the new schools were fined. If they persisted in keeping the youngsters from Communist schools they were brought to trial and received a harsh punishment. In the end, nearly everyone sent their children to the Government schools. In all towns, separate schools for Jewish children, where the new Yiddish language was taught, were opened in order to infuse Communism among the Jewish population. Some religious Jews preferred to send their children to the gentile schools, where Christianity was denigrated rather than Judaism.

By gaining control of the schools, the Communists managed to convert the Jews as well as the entire populace to their ideals. They simply gained control of the country's youth. It went so far that children would spy on their parents and inform on them to the authorities!

Among the other methods through which the Communists achieved their ends was the institution of a new calendar. Instead of consisting of seven days, a week was changed to six days. Schools and factories were open five days and closed on the sixth. Children, forced to attend school, would thus transgress five out of every six *Shabbosim*. But even on the 'rest day,' adults and older children were obliged to "willingly" help with work in the fields and factories as needed. The name for this compulsory-voluntary duty was Subotnik.

Once their outward actions were under control, the children's inner beliefs were more susceptible to the anti-Torah message they received in the classroom. Daily, the teacher would drill them, "Is there a G-d?"

"No!" the children called out in unison.

Or the teacher would say, "Let's all say, 'G-d give us candy!' "

The children would duly make the request.

"Well, did anyone get candy?" the teacher would ask.

"No!"

"Now let's say, 'Lenin give us candy!' "

The children would say the words, and a bag of candy would be brought in.

Any child who did not join the Communist Children's Movement, the Pioneers, had a hard time. Children were indoctrinated to hate the Capitalists, oppressors and exploiters of the working people, as well as "their servants," the Clericalists, such as Rabbis and religious educators. They were taught that religious people were enemies who prevented fulfillment of the Communist utopia. Were it not for them, everyone would be happy and successful. Thus stirred emotionally, it is no wonder that young people took their lessons to heart.

Anyone who adhered to Judaism was considered an enemy of the people. Parents who wanted their child to *daven* had to keep him inside and close the curtains. Very few families would do it. Not many were prepared to jeopardize their lives and their children's lives for the sake of Torah and *mitzvos*. The one child in a thousand who kept any *mitzvos* had to hide it from his friends who would surely mock him, while his parents lived in fear that they would be informed on.

Every so often, the authorites would take one such parent to court and accuse him of some crime in order to frighten the others. As for those who were merely less enthusiastic about the new ideology, the Communists had Stalin's slogan, "Those who are not with us are against us!"

According to Soviet law, Jews were allowed to keep *mitzvos* because, after all, Russia was by law a democratic land, and keeping *mitzvos* was not inherently seditious. They claimed, in fact, that theirs was the highest democracy. Still, the Communists frequently contended that religious Jews were really Zionists, which was strictly outlawed as a subversive movement, or were spreading religious propaganda, which carried a five year sentence to Siberia.

Thus, in only three or four years, the intensive campaign of terror did away with fully observant Jews, and by the end of the 1930s, virtually no one kept *Shabbos*, the marriage laws, *kashrus* or *bris milah*. People, especially the young, were afraid to pray. They did not resist the new movement and eventually joined the Communists wholeheartedly. As the Rambam says, "It is man's nature to behave as the others do. At first, trangression is involuntary, but if one continues, one relishes the deed in the end."

Parents reacted in various ways to the Communists' indoctrination of their children. There were some who had already been influenced themselves and were quite willing to break away from their age-old traditions. Some even joined the Party actively and became informers. Most of the parents though, were disconsolate at their children's defection, yet felt powerless to curb it. Even at the outset, when the punishment for withholding children from Communist schools was not severe, they sensed that the battle would be lost, if not today, then tomorrow. Only a few children came to learn privately with my father. The other hundreds of Jewish children were firmly ensnared in the Communists' hands.

I remember one *Yom Kippur* night when the school children came around to the *shul* to wait for their parents who were praying inside. Not one youngster went in to pray. Worse, some of the teachers joined the waiting children and made a bonfire around which the pupils danced to disturb the worshippers.

If the Communists made sure to infiltrate the minds of school-chilren, they applied no less effort toward the adults. How could the Jews embrace Communism if they persisted in clinging to their "outdated" religion and, in particular, to their Rabbis and *Roshei Yeshivah*? Accordingly, the Communists devised a cunning plan. Since rabbis, *chazanim* and *Roshei Yeshivah* were considered lazy and unproductive parasites in the new Communist State, they could attain their rights only after openly repudiating their previous work as "useless" and expressing a readiness to begin working for the people's benefit. Moreover, it was not enough for them to tell the local party leader. The *Rav* had to make a declaration in the news-paper or at the weekly council meeting in front of all the city's Jewish citizens. Whoever failed to do this suffered greatly. Thou-sands of rabbis' children were refused jobs in offices or factories, or permission to attend schools where they could learn a respectable profession, until they or their father made this open break with Judaism.

At first, some Rabbis balked at making such a false declaration which the people might view as sincere. Faced with mounting pressure each month, however, more and more broke down. I remember one such man from a nearby town who came to the weekly council meeting with his *tallis* and *tefillin*, saying he did not need them anymore. His son's wish to learn in an advanced high school had finally convinced him to make this move.

For those Jews who tried to adhere to their beliefs, life became bitter. Indeed, not only were they persecuted by the authorities, but their former co-religionists did not encourage them or even see the point of their struggle. Whoever tried to withstand the onslaught was told, "You are crazy. Don't you understand that the Government and the people will not tolerate a religion? Soon they will finish you off. Think about your life!"

In my few years, I had seen life plunge from one extreme to the other. Through it all, though, my parents' and grandparents' faith in G-d was undaunted. Inspired by their strength of character, I also refused to give in to Communist pressure. After all, how could I forsake the birthright of my Jewish heritage? My brother, sister and I never attended the Government school. I stayed at home and learned with my father and grandfather, while my former *cheder* classmates left the religious school one by one. Eventually, none of my former friends wanted to have anything to do with me. I was an oddity to them.

In addition to my having no friends and dreading the future my family was starving. The only thing that kept us alive was our unshakable faith in G-d.

3 THE FACTORIES

IN THE EARLY 1920S LENIN INSTITUTED THE POLICY known as collectivization, whereby all profit and economic proceeds were funneled exclusively into the needs of the State. Private business was outlawed. It was not uncommon for entrepreneurs to be murdered. I remember one man who was sentenced to death for illegally selling salt. Yet even with such deterrents, no one wanted to work without profit, and since there was no incentive, the Russian economy floundered.

In 1922, Lenin came up with the so-called New Economic Policy. The N.E.P. was a nine-year grace period during which people could run their own businesses and farms; it would remain in effect until the plan for nationwide collectivization could be properly implemented. In these nine years, the economy prospered. The peasants cultivated their lands, and trade flourished. Only religion was oppressed. For those who did not care for religion, the nine years

26

were good ones. Thereafter, with collectivization, scarcity of all products and merchandise set in.

However, even during those nine years, the Communists gradually moved in. Factories were appropriated by the Government and new ones were built. Many people had to join these in order to make a living.

The factories became quite a potent Communist tool in getting the people to resign themselves to the government policies. Each factory was run by a party secretary who kept an eye on the workers. The secretary then passed all information to the Ministry of the Interior or G.P.U. This Ministry, which later became the N.K.V.D., thus had a file on everyone—where he lived, what he ate, with whom he spoke and associated.

It was dangerous to be religious. If someone tried to keep *Shabbos*, he would be hounded by the Yevsektzia. His fellow laborers would find ways to make his life miserable, and the foreman, who did not want troublesome workers, would fire him.

The factories had the undeniable advantage of providing lunch at a time when food was scarce. The meals were not kosher, of course, and whoever refused to eat them would camouflage the fact. However, most of the Jewish workers took advantage of the free lunch and ate the food. After eating it at work, they became used to eating it at home as well. At length, those Jews who transgressed *Shabbos* in the factory but kept it at home were just about the most observant who could be found.

Around this time, my father was asked a fundamental *Halachic* question about keeping *Shabbos* under such oppressive conditions. A certain learned Jew approached him and asked, "According to *Halachah*, a Jew is permitted to transgress *Shabbos* if doing so will save his life. However, a clause follows that if a decree is passed against keeping *mitzvos* where the intent of the edict is to force the Jews to give up their faith, then *Halachah* demands even death, rather than transgression of any *mitzvah*. Rav Chazan, does this apply to our situation? After all, in the *Shulchan Aruch, Yoreh Deah* (ch. 157), the Shach comments that this ruling applies only when the decrees are solely against the Jews. If the decree is on all the provinces of the Kingdom, the Jews included, that is not considered a time of forced apostasy. Here in Russia," the Jew continued, "where the Government has instituted a six-day week, it has done away with not only the Jewish *Shabbos*, but even the Sunday of the gentiles. Since this is a decree on the whole population, shouldn't one be allowed to transgress *Shabbos* in order to save oneself from repercussions by the authorities?"

My father did not accept this supposition.

"The words of the Shach," he explained, "refer only to situations that do not involve *Chillul Hashem* (desecration of G-d's Name). If performing the forbidden action were to give rise to a *Chillul Hashem*, that sin retains the status of *yehareg ve'al yaavor*, one must die rather than transgress. The intent of the authorities when they did away with the *Shabbos* and Sunday was to wipe out the Name and Remembrance of G-d. Is there any greater desecration of His Name than that? We are required to let ourselves be killed rather than to passively agree."

My father brought further proof from the episode with Nevu-chadnezzar's idol. It had been decreed (*Daniel* 3:4) that "all peoples and nations of every language" had to worship it. Although it was a decree for everyone, Jew and non-Jew alike, and everyone bowed to it, nevertheless, Chananya, Mishael and Azariah were prepared to die rather than bow, the reason being that the decree's sole purpose was to worship an idol, thereby desecrating Hashem's Name.

There were, in fact, many Torah observers who arrived at the same conclusion as that learned Jew and went to work on *Shabbos*. Moreover, even in those homes where no one worked on *Shabbos*, the day's holiness was marred by the children, infected as they were with the anti-religious propaganda taught in the schools. The frustrated parents did not even try to counter the schools' pernicious effects, considering it a lost battle. Even many rabbis and sons of important families could not muster up the necessary courage to teach their children how to say *Shema Yisrael*, much less to pray.

The individuals who refused to give in were rare indeed. The spiritual fate of those who joined the factories was all too clear. But no one was allowed to refrain from working, by decree of law. There was, however, one occupation a Jew could teach his son that was recognized by the officials as honest and productive. This was the slaughtering of animals and poultry according to Jewish law. Therefore, many G-d-fearing Jews taught their sons to be *shochtim*. Although *shochtim* worked in abattoirs under government supervision, they were at least able to keep *Shabbos*.

The number of *shochtim* multiplied sharply between the years 1928 and 1931, until collectivization began and pressure mounted for them to work on *Shabbos*. At first, these *shochtim* resisted, but the pressure did not let up, and some finally gave in and publicly slaughtered chickens on *Shabbos*. These chickens were, of couse, *treif*.

Most *shochtim* continued to resist, however, and serve the observant public until the Council obliged them to hire women to pluck off the feathers, which were greatly needed for the home market and even for export. Some of the women working in the store were unfortunately gentiles and would often take knives and do the slaughtering themselves, rendering the meat *treif*. It thus became increasingly difficult to determine which meat had been properly slaughtered and which had not.

There are still places today, like Odessa and Kiev, where gentiles come and slaughter purportedly kosher meat, together with the *shochtim*. Reb Mordechai Reshkovsky, a G-d-fearing *shochet* from Odessa, once told me that an old Jew came to the abattoir with a few chickens to be "*shechted*." He gave them to the gentile woman, then turned to the *shochet* and said, "Reb Mordechai, I live among non-Jews and have no one with whom to speak Yiddish. Here, let those gentiles slaughter the chickens, and we'll have a friendly chat together."

4 THE YESHIVOS

IT WAS ONLY A SHORT MATTER OF TIME BEFORE THE Communists turned their campaign against the *yeshivos*. Their tactics were simple—to make life as difficult and untenable as possible. Under this pressure, Rav Yoel Shurin (the Iluy of Zevihl), along with his family, fled to Poland. His *yeshivah* of four hundred students disintegrated. Many other *yeshivos* closed as well. Some tried to reestablish themselves in other areas.

The school of Novardok was one such *yeshivah*. At first, they tried to maintain a foothold in Russia by starting small underground *yeshivos* in many towns. When it was apparent that they could not survive, they decided to evacuate all their students to Poland *en masse*. This was in 1922, when the borders were new and poorly guarded. The Novardokers found courageous, G-d-fearing men in Poland who wanted to help them save these youths from the spiritual destruction in Russia. As the boys were stealing across the border, thez would sing *By the Waters of Babylon* (*Tehillim* 137) which bewails the captivity in Babylon, to the tune of Russian revolutionary songs, in order to fool the border guards into thinking they were Bolshevik soldiers. In this way, hundreds of students were saved.

Krasnostav, which was twenty kilometers inside Russia, became one of the stops for these youths. Boys would arrive and sleep at our house. The next morning, horse-drawn wagons would take them over the border, fifteen to twenty at a time. Approximately one kilometer from the frontier, they would abandon the wagons and continue on foot under cover of the deep red Russian sky. The Russian soldiers thought they had come to guard the frontiers, just as they did themselves. My father knew that if he were caught sheltering these boys he would certainly be put to death, but the urgency outweighed the danger.

I remember when over twenty *bachurim* surprised us one *Shavuos* eve. They stayed in my father's house both days of *Yom Tov*. I was sent to gather *challos*, cake and other food from the neighbors, as it was too dangerous for the boys to step out and be seen. Danger notwithstanding, they danced and sang all *Shavuos*. When the holiday ended, their contacts came and took them across the border. We were not the only family who risked helping Jews escape from Russia. Householders from other towns all along the border also took in boys.

Several times, I begged my mother to let me join these groups, but she replied, "Aaron, you are too young. You're only ten. Who would take care of you in Poland? Where would you go? Wait until you are older and then you'll be able to go." No one foresaw that in a short time the borders would be sealed tight.

Yeshivos in Moscow, Leningrad and Kiev all closed down not long afterwards. Many *chadorim* and *yeshivos* run by Chabad *Chassidim* went underground. They were kept alive by teachers and rabbis with great personal courage, of whose fate I will tell later.

In 1924, my sister became ill and needed medical care. My father wrote to ask advice of his mentor in Poland, Reb Yoel. He was advised to move to Zevihl, the district capital, approximately forty kilometers from Krasnostav, where a good doctor could be found.

Furthermore, Reb Yoel suggested that my father be appointed as the city's *Rav*. Many of Reb Yoel's students still lived there, and they gladly welcomed my father, giving him a writ of *Rabbonus*.

My family moved to Zevihl at the end of the summer. Most of the four years they were there I remained in Krasnostav, learning privately with my grandfather in order to become proficient in large sections of *Yoreh Deah* and *Chullin*. My brother, a year and a half younger than me, joined me every so often in these studies.

My *bar-mitzvah* was held in Zevihl at the beginning of 1925, and the town's *Rebbe*, Reb Shloimele Goldman—of whom my father often asked advice—attended the festivities. But the spiritual life was eclipsed by ominous signs. The *Rebbe* left for Palestine the following year after a gang of boys attacked his grandson and pulled at his *peyos*. These boys had once been his classmates in the religious environment of the *cheder*! It was becoming clear that there could be no future for Judaism in Russia.

When I was fifteen, a Lubavitcher *Chassid*, Reb Mordechai Eliezer, secretly opened a *yeshivah ketanah* in Zevihl. He asked me to come and encourage the students by sharing my knowledge with them. After *Pesach*, a brilliant and dedicated *Talmid Chacham*, Rav Shaul Bruk, took over from Reb Mordechai as *Rosh Yeshivah*. We studied in Reb Yoel's former *yeshivah*, which also had a *shul*. While Rav Bruk lectured, we would take turns practicing precautionary measures. One youth guarded the window facing the street to report the approach of any Yevsek. In that event, the *Rosh Yeshivah* would jump out a back window to the chicken abattoir yard, which was nearby. He would begin sharpening his knife as if he were a *shochet*. The children would pretend to be playing games or learning amongst themselves.

One day, I was reviewing my *Gemara* at home when an agitated classmate knocked on my door. He reported that a well-known Yevsek named Krupnik had entered the *shul* and a policeman was now standing at the door. Fortunately, Rav Bruk was not teaching at the time. I immediately left for the *yeshivah*. When I asked the policeman to let me enter, he contemptuously moved aside. In the study hall, I saw all fifteen students sitting around a table with open *Gemaras*. Krupnik was standing next to them.

"It's good you came," he said to me. "Do you also study here?"

"Yes," I answered.

"Who is the *Rav* that teaches you?"

"We don't have a *Rav*."

"How can you study without a *Rav*?"

"Everyone learns from his father," I said, "and when our fathers go to work, we all come to the *shul* and review the *Gemara*. If we have a question, we ask one of the more learned worshippers."

Satisfied with the answer, Krupnik turned to the students.

"Children," he said, "I see you are learning the chapter *Hakones Tzon Ladir* (One Who Brings Sheep into a Fold, the sixth chapter of *Bava Kama*). Tell me, what practical purpose will you ever have from this study?"

The students sat silent.

Answering for them, I said, "The purpose is that we will be careful not to cause damage to other people."

"That can be understood by itself," he said disdainfully. "That's basic human decency."

"Not really," I countered. "People don't always do what is decent. For instance, when neighbors quarrel, they'll willingly sacrifice what is morally right for what they selfishly want. It's only when we learn from the Torah what is right, and when we appreciate its binding, eternal nature, that we refrain from doing wrong."

"Well then," Krupnik said, "you do know how to learn. Tell me, doesn't the Torah say that you shall incline after the majority (Talmudic interpretation of *Shemos* 23:2)? You are only a few; why don't you follow the majority who are not religious?"

"First of all," I said, "didn't you see the earlier clause of that verse which states that you shall not follow a majority to do evil? Second, you were the minority just a few years ago, and the majority were religious. Why didn't you follow them then?"

"Because we are in the right," he said.

For another hour, Krupnik tried to influence us. His main efforts were devoted to trying to get us to reveal the name of our teacher. Finally acknowledging defeat, he got up and left. The Yevsektzia had lost that battle, but they did not give up. The day finally came when they succeeded in finding Rav Bruk giving his lecture. The youth guarding the window was daydreaming when Krupnik suddenly walked in.

"Aha, my dear *Rav*!" he exclaimed in triumph. "I've finally caught you!"

Rav Bruk paled, but he quickly recovered himself.

"What do you mean, caught me?" he said. "This is the first time I've been in this building. I happened to walk in here to pray and one of the boys asked me to explain the *Gemara*."

The students verified his words. Krupnik, though, was not swayed. He ordered Rav Bruk to come to the police station, whereupon the *Rav* took his *tallis, tefillin* and a slaughtering knife.

What was he doing in Zevihl, they asked him at the station, when his family lived in Ilena? What relationship did he have with the students in the *shul*? The *Rav* answered that he was presently in Zevihl learning to be a *shochet* to be able to provide for his family. As for the children, he repeated the story he had told Krupnik. At the end of the investigation, they recorded his statement as evidence, and ordered him to leave the city within twenty-four hours. If he disobeyed the order, they warned, he would be summoned to court. But the *Rav* protested his innocence and did not leave town. They brought his case to court, and he was released on bail.

After that confrontation, Rav Bruk began to give his lectures in the attic of the *shul*. Its tile roof made it stifling hot inside, and just studying required great effort. Rav Bruk gave one lecture at 9:30 and a second one in the afternoon. He did not leave the attic the whole time in between lectures despite the suffocating heat. After six weeks of this, the increased vigilance of the Yevseks forced Rav Bruk to move the *yeshivah* to a private house where it remained for two months, before moving back to the *shul*.

Following this, my father decided that I should now learn at home. The other children had no choice but to study under risky conditions, he explained, but since I was legally allowed to learn from my father, why should I endanger myself? Also, the fewer students at the *shul* in Zevihl, the better it was for everyone. Shortly afterwards, the increasing agitation against religious people in Zevihl forced my family to move back to Krasnostav.

Up till here I have told Rav Bruk's story first hand. The remainder I heard from other people:

In November of that year (1928), the court convened to hear his case. He hired a non-Jewish attorney who believed in the sincerity of the *Rav's* claim. The fact that the judges were gentiles was also helpful. If they had been Jews, he would unquestionably have lost his case. At the trial, Rav Bruk repeated his claim that he was learning to be a *shochet* in Zevihl and showed his contract from the abattoir. His sentence was unusually light, three months conditional imprisonment.

Despite the apparent victory, the trial attracted unwanted publicity to the *yeshivah*. Studying there became more and more difficult. The *gabbaim* of the *shul* refused to allow them in, fearing that if the *yeshivah* were discovered, they would be harshly punished. In the end, the *Rav* decided to use an abandoned *shul* on the outskirts of the city, but there, too, they were not left in peace.

In January, Rav Bruk was caught teaching and was brought to the police station where his case was reopened. He had to sign an injunction not to leave the city until his case came up in court. For the moment, though, he was free.

He saw that he could not continue his regular lectures, so it was decided that one of the older *bachurim* would teach the youngest class. A few times, the *bachur* was caught with his students, but because he was so young, no one suspected that he was the teacher. As for the highest class, the *Rav* would supervise the lessons from outside the *yeshivah* and give his *shiur* in a private house at night.

Since the danger was mounting, it was decided that the *yeshivah* could not remain in Zevihl. Rav Bruk broke his injunction, and traveled secretly to Constantine, where he contacted teachers of the religious community, asking for their support. They agreed to help, and after *Pesach* of 1928 the *yeshivah* moved to Constantine. The Yevsektzia of Constantine was no better, though. After a few months, they caught wind of Rav Bruk's situation and began to track the students down. Rav Bruk was taken back to Zevihl.

When Rav Bruk's case came up after *Pesach* of 1929, he was sentenced to nine months of labor, followed by confinement in his home town of Ilena. He protested, appealing to the district court in Zhitomir, which rejected his appeal. He then turned to the High

Court in Kharkov, which also upheld the verdict. He was allowed, though, to choose the city in which he would serve out his sentence under supervision of the police. The *Rav* decided to stay with his people in Zevihl. His forced labor was cleaning the streets of the city, which turned out to be easy work. An added advantage was that he could do it in the early morning hours and have the rest of the day to himself.

Rav Bruk continued to study every day with three youths who remained in Zevihl. One of them eventually joined the Chabad Yeshivah in Kiev. The other two were brothers whose parents were murdered in the pogroms. The younger one eventually succumbed to the influence of Communism. The elder, Yaakov Shatz, remained with his *Rebbe*. In time, he married Rav Bruk's daughter and settled with her in Moscow. In 1937, during the terrible Stalin purges, he was arrested together with all the Chabad and Breslover *Chassidim*. It was routine to sentence such prisoners to ten years "isolation," but in fact, they were nearly all murdered in prison. With his death, the last trace of the *yeshivah* in Zevihl disappeared.

This *yeshivah* had been started in the early 1920s. When the Communists started to persecute religion and all *chadorim* were closed, *Rabbeim* were afraid to teach children because the Yevsektzia was familiar with each and every one of them. Reb Shloime of Zevihl, the great *tzaddik*, was ready to give his life to save Judaism, and so he organized a school in his house with about thirty children, mostly orphans. Among these children were four youths from Belo-Tzerkov, Naftali, Yosef, Zvi and Yitzchak, whose fathers had been murdered by Petlura and his bands. There were also two orphans, brothers from Beresdiv, whose names were Yaakov and Moshe.

In 1926, the persecutions got still worse. Reb Shloime left for Eretz Yisrael with his wife and eldest grandson. When he arrived in Jerusalem he did not declare who he was. However, inevitably a Jew who came from America identified him as the *Rebbe* Reb Shloimkella, from which time onward he had a great following, and the line is still going strong.

The *Rebbe's* son and his family remained in Russia. The schoolchildren remained alone is Zevihl as sheep without a shepherd. As their love for G-d was very strong, they did not want to go to the

Russian schools. They searched for a place where they could remain observant Jews. In time, some of the children succumbed to Communism. The others heard that in Oman, near Kiev, where the Rabbi of Breslov was buried, there was a settlement of Breslover *Chassidim*. Those *Chassidim* were concentrated in two streets. They were not influenced by the times; their children did not go to the Russian schools, and in general, they somehow continued their Jewish traditions.

Three of the six orphans mentioned above went and remained there until the beginning of the collectivization in 1929-1930. From those three, two are still alive; Naftali who is now living in Jerusalem, and Yosef, still in Kharkov, both religious *Chassidim*. Yitzchak and the orphans from Beresdiv remained in Zevihl. Those three children were the first students of Rav Bruk when he arrived in Zevihl. When the Yevsektzia got word of this *yeshivah*, Krupnik took away the youngest one, Moshe, who was consequently influenced and lost to assimilation. Yitzchak, under the influence of Rav Bruk, went to Kiev to the Chabad Yeshivah. The last one, Yaakov Shatz, remained with Rav Bruk and as mentioned above, married his daughter. He was executed in 1938 during the purges, together with many other Chabad *Chassidim* and about thirty Breslover *Chassidim* from Oman.

5 IN BRICKS AND MORTAR

AFTER WE LEFT FROM ZEVIHL FOR KRASNOSTAV, I continued studying for three years. My daily learning partners and mentors were my grandfather, until a month before his death in June of 1929, and my father.

The year before I turned eighteen, I was called before a board of doctors to determine my age. The law stated that anyone who lacked proper certification of his birth date had to be medically evaluated to decide his age. I wanted to make use of my youthful appearance to claim a lower age and thereby defer my army duty as long as possible, but I was afraid to lie because former friends of mine were present. I ended up telling the board my true birthday, 1912. The examining doctor peered at me suspiciously.

"I think you're lying," he snapped. "You just want to get accepted early to a university. Well, I'm writing down that you were born in 1914."

Doctors!

Actually, I would not have served in the army itself anyway, being considered untrustworthy for such a sensitive position. Such people had to fulfill their army obligation with some kind of hard labor instead. However, I was saved even from this in the confusion and turmoil of Stalin's rise that very year.

In that year, 1928, Josef Stalin muscled his way to power in Russia, ruthlessly annihilating all his opponents. In addition, all roads and railway lines leading out of the country were cut off. The borders were sealed and guarded with an iron hand. There was no hope of escape.

Stalin raised the Communist ideal to new heights of paradoxical absurdity. He implemented the idea that anyone considered undesirable acquire an official status of being "declassed." A legal term with terrible consequences, "declassed" meant the complete abrogation of not only political and social rights (he could not be elected to public office and he could not vote), but even his most basic human rights. A declassed person could not work in a government office or factory, live in government-owned dwellings or belong to the health clinic. In some cases, he was not even allowed to draw water from the village well or use the wheat mill for grinding flour. Since everyone in the small towns bought his own wheat, ground it in the wheat mill and baked it himself, whoever was forbidden to grind the wheat grains had no bread.

Once, my father was having severe pains in his leg, and the local medic advised him to see the doctor in Shepetivke. He applied to the town council for a permit to travel (one could not leave town without this permit), but he was flatly refused. When he pleaded to the Secretary to relent, the clerk did not mince words.

"We are not concerned with the welfare of clerics," he said coldly. "Who cares if you die? Lenin also died."

My father was thus in anguish for many months, until the pain subsided.

The declassed status extended to all the members of a household. Not only my father, but my brother and I were stigmatized. We could free ourselves of this only if we would "mend our ways," which meant publicly declaring that we severed all ties with our father. This, of course, my brother and I would not do. There was one other alternative to prove our worth to the Communist State, and that was to put in five years of productive labor. Only then would we be given back our elementary rights. But where could we find work? No one wanted to hire a religious youth. And how would we keep *Shabbos*?

When I turned nineteen, I searched desperately for a job. Without one, I stood a good chance of being imprisoned as a useless "parasite" or of even being deported to Siberia. Every day I would set out to find work, but I was always turned down. At last, I was hired at a brick-making factory. Krasnostav had clay suitable for making bricks. In the factory, I would knead the clay with my hands and feet, shape the bricks, bring them to the furnace, and take them out when they were ready. The methods were primitive, the work backbreaking and the wages pitiful. Since almost no one in town would do such work, they begrudgingly accepted me.

I could now understand the bitterness felt by our ancestors in Egypt when they toiled with mortar and bricks. I could not have borne it, if not for the fact that upholding my convictions outweighed any other consideration. How can I describe my mental and physical anguish at this job? During my entire life, it had been ingrained in me that I was the son of Rabbis and heir to a distinguished lineage. I had thrown myself wholeheartedly and deeply into learning *Gemara* and *Shulchan Aruch*, under the assumption that I would carry on the family tradition. Moreover, the only "labor" I had ever done was as a child. My friends and I would go to collect wood and food in the winter and bring it to orphans and widows, or we would ask for a cup of milk from each householder who had a cow, to bring to the needy. Now, instead of learning *Gemara*, I was performing hard, physical labor just to get my daily bread and avoid being deported. Keeping *Shabbos* compounded this already trying period in my life. Every day I had to steel myself against the threats and jeers of my fellow workers and bosses, who glibly foretold that I would soon be on my way to Siberia.

I was a popular topic at the weekly town council meetings where attempts to do away with me were frequently discussed. Every so often, a friend would tell me how he had supported me at such a meeting by claiming that, since I wasn't doing anything actually illegal, I should be left alone. These friends were mostly the children of families I had helped as a child. When they used to come to *shul* as youngsters, I would speak to them about Judaism. Eventually, they stopped keeping *mitzvos* and joined the Komsomol Youth movement, which they were daily pressured to do at school. Now that I was a worker, like them, I continued speaking to them about Judaism, although it was a serious crime. They never informed on me and indeed sometimes protected me against my accusers.

Every *Shabbos*, there was an assembly at which the Communists vented their anger at us. What should be done with such "criminals" who keep *Shabbos*? Our fear was inexpressible. Should we give in? Or should we stand firm?

We fortified ourselves and decided to continue to keep *Shabbos*. They would taunt us that soon we would be in Siberia, where everyone was forced to transgress *Shabbos* anyway. Turning the intent of their words around, we decided that we might as well keep *Shabbos* while we could. There were some people who understood and respected me highly for my sacrifices to keep *Shabbos*. They encouraged me privately, but never in public, lest they be accused of aiding criminals. Most people thought we were mad. They would squint at us in the street and wave their fingers.

"We're telling you this for your own good," they proclaimed. "You're crazy. Why do you want to destroy your lives? What good will all this do you? You'll be brickmakers your whole life, the lowest of the low, and in the end you'll be forced to work on *Shabbos* anyway. So what will you have gained? Wouldn't it be better to enter some university and learn a respectable profession like all those other sons of Rabbis? Too bad for you! What a shame!"

We had no answer to their words, which seemed undeniably based on reality. Once, I was told by Baruch, a friend with whom I had learned as a child, "Look around. You see that no one is religious anymore, especially people your age. Do you think they'll let you be the one religious Jew in the land? They'll take revenge on you! Can't you see how everyone else is trying to get himself a good job? They are accomplishing something. But you!"

"People sacrificed their lives for Communism," I said. "Shouldn't I

41

give my life for Judaism?"

"At least they'll go down in history," he said.

"Well then, I'll also go down in history," I told him, "as the last religious Jew in Russia." I thought a moment, and then added seriously, "But I'm sure, with G-d's help, that there will still be religious Jews, thousands upon thousands, who will keep Torah and *mitzvos*. After all, that is the way of the Jewish nation."

"My father once explained to me a verse from Michah (6:5) in the name of Reb Yoel, the Iluy of Zevihl. 'From Shittim to Gilgal, and you will recognize the gracious acts of the Lord.' Why are those two places mentioned together? At Shittim, the Jews had become so debased that they even consorted with gentile women, whereas at Gilgal, they had entered the Land of Israel and were at the peak of their spiritual greatness, making a new treaty with G-d! The answer is that this is a theme in our unique history. Even from the depths of impurity, we can climb back to our natural spiritual heights. May G-d let us be privileged to see this!"

Baruch only looked away and said nothing, but there was a look of compassion and grudging respect in his eyes. He is alive today, and keeps *mitzvos*.

The following year, my brother joined me at work. Every day we would get up early and *daven* in the *shul*. By now there were only old people attending, and even those were coming less and less. Very often we did not even have a *minyan*.

After work, we returned to the empty *shul* and learned. No one else ever came. We studied as much as our strength allowed and then rested a bit to gather strength for work the next day. It hardly paid to go home, since there was no food there. I had no friends or social life. My only other acivities were occasionally resolving *halachic* questions of acquaintances (those whom I knew I could trust) and teaching a few children secretly. Whenever possible, I would encourage certain friends to keep whatever *mitzvos* they could. Even in that spiritual wasteland, there were unusually determined individuals who would not give up completely.

Newspapers began to increase their tirades against religious people. They ran articles on how religious people were controlled by the capitalists and had ties with rebels outside the country. They the capitalists and had ties with rebels outside the country. They claimed that the Chafetz Chaim and the Rebbe of Lubavitch were sending spies who made secret contact with the religious Jews in Russia.

My brother and I were threatened several times that we would soon be implicated in this alleged conspiracy and that we would get the punishment we so richly deserved. It was obvious to us that our end was drawing near, but we refused to submit. It must have been our conviction that we were right which gave us the strength to survive each day. We reinforced ourselves by telling each other that, since our death was imminent, better to die for the honor of G-d and for the sake of His holy Torah, than to die for anything else. Better to die nobly with the soul pure and the spirit unbroken than to die ignobly like a frightened animal.

Sometimes, the press would invent a "crime" committed by religious people. I remember one outrage reported in the Yiddish paper that was a topic of conversation for days. A famous *shochet* in White Russia, a G-d-fearing man, was reported to have been caught attacking a woman. When I read about it, I thought, "What a terrible *Chillul Hashem*!" Others, of course, were just as shocked. Later, I met some Jews from the *shochet's* town in White Russia and asked them about the shameful incident. They laughed ruefully at my question.

"Didn't you realize that the whole thing against an innocent man was a trumped up charge?" they said. "That *shochet* happened to be travelling to a town in the region, and when he got off the train, he asked someone at the railway station for directions to the address he was seeking. A woman heard him and said, 'I'll show you. I'm also going that way.'

"After walking a few steps, she began to scream, 'Help me! Help me! This man is attacking me! This man is attacking me!' From nowhere, some men suddenly appeared and took him straight to prison where he was sentenced to five years in jail. The *shochet* is conpletely innocent."

This period of my life comes back to me in a haze of overwhelming loneliness. I was a young man, and the constant unbearable fear took away any appetite I had for the future. I just hoped each day to make it through to the next. There were days when I prayed not to wake up the next morning. Better death, I thought, than to fall into their hands. There was no one my family could turn to for encouragement. I did not believe that I would ever get to live openly as a Torah-observant Jew.

6 THE COLLECTIVES

WHEN THE NINE-YEAR GRACE PERIOD ENDED, THE Soviet Government seriously began eliminating private ownership. They extended the declassed status to merchants and artisans, anticipating that the discrimination would force them to bend to the Communists' will. Factory owners had to surrender their industries to the Government, the owners now being retained only as managers. Those with wealth were expected to give it to the Government and take their place as equals with the masses of workers. Well-to-do land owners, known as *kulaks*, had to forfeit their land and possessions and become salaried workers for Government communes called *kolkhozes*, which were formed from their lands. This process was called *raskulachivaniye*, meaning elimination of the kulak class. Of course, there was resistance. No one wanted to be dispossessed of what he had labored his whole life to acquire. The account of how Stalin accomplished this is one of the most brutal and barbaric episodes in history.

In the beginning of the winter of 1931, Stalin ordered all land-owners and peasants to enter the *kolkhozes* of their own volition. Afraid to disobey, everyone brought their tools to the Government warehouses. That way, when spring arrived, they would all begin working together under Government supervision.

In the middle of the winter, a mass demonstration began which spread through the entire Ukraine and other districts in Russia. Peasant women demonstrated in the streets, clamoring, "We don't want *kolkhozes*!" I remember in my own small town, hundreds of women went out screaming. This had the desired effect, and the next day Stalin announced that anyone who did not want to join a *kolkhoz* could take his tools and leave.

"We will not force anyone," he declared. "Only those who want to join of their own free will are to be accepted."

With relief, all the men came to the warehouses and retrieved their tools. In the spring of 1932, everyone sowed his own field industriously, and what a bountiful harvest they reaped! All the landowners gathered large amounts of fruits and vegetables and raised sheep and cattle. People were confident that the Government had learned its lesson and would write *kolkhozes* off their program. But that was not to be.

One October morning, the town was abuzz.

"Do you know what happened? Last night some party members came and took my son. I am worried sick about him. What have they done with him?"

"And me!" said another. "They took my daughter!"

All young people who had disappeared belonged to the Kon-somol, the Communist youth group. No one could understand why. Also, they were all from poor families.

"Maybe there'll be a war, and our children are being drafted," some surmised, "and they're not telling us!"

Next door to us lived a widow with two daughters. When the party men came for her older daughter, the mother asked where she was going. They told her, "Don't worry. It's a secret. Everything is all right."

All that week, people were mystified about where the young

people had been taken. The fog lifted the following Sunday, when the *kolkhozes* began to be organized once again.

There were three classes of people—the rich, called *kulaks*, the middle class, called *sredniaks*, and the poor. The children of the poor were made to feel the most important. They had full rights and were encouraged to express their hatred toward the rich, although some of them were quite incapable and primitive.

The youths that were taken from their homes, it turned out, were placed in the homes of the *kulaks* and middle class people in nearby villages and farms. The Communists stationed one in every house with instructions not to leave it and to take note of everything. Such scouting prevented the farmers from uniting forces against collectivization. Still, no one had any idea of what was yet in store.

Without warning, government officials came and began to confiscate all food products. They had mobilized wagons, horses, and carts to convey all this to the railway station. All items of food were taken away—potatoes, wheat, barley, oats, peas, beans, carrots, onions and every kind of fruit, geese and cattle. They registered all the produce loaded on the vehicles, and explained that they were only checking whether these were home grown or merchandise for speculation. The officials wrote out and signed receipts for all they took and gave them to the confused *kulaks* and farmers. All plunder was put on to freight trains and sent to the north. People's farming tools, wagons, horses, oxen, cars and trucks were also seized.

By trickery, the Government had collectivized the land and emptied the Ukraine. The Konsomol youth, flushed with success, returned to their homes.

In a short time, a famine fell on the land. Fruits and vegetables could soon be bought only at high prices. Those who lacked money began to die from starvation. The famine got worse. The streets were filled with people swollen from hunger. Bread could not be obtained except in Kiev, the capital of the Ukraine, or Kharkov where the big factories were. Those who worked in factories were given bread to eat on the premises. At other jobs, people didn't receive anything. Soon bread could not even be bought. Tens of thousands of people were dying of hunger throughout the Ukraine. In my town, I witnessed the slow starvation of a farmer and his sons.

They were buried together in one coffin.

Farmers were the hardest hit, and then came those who lived in small towns like ours. With swollen legs ourselves, we buried some Jews who died of hunger.

The *kolkhozes* began to operate in full force the following spring. They had cafeterias where food was given to the workers. Not surprisingly, whoever was left alive after the terrible winter of 1933 quickly joined the *kolkhozes*.

Now that the class of *kulaks* was on its way toward extinction, the Government used its momentum to afflict the merchants, who had been allowed to function until then. Since, according to the Communist doctrine, no one should be rich or poor, rather, all should share equally, the well-to-do were accused of undermining the system. Furthermore, since the Government was in great need of gold, silver and foreign currency to modernize Russian industry, it became a patriotic duty to help destroy the businessmen.

At first, the Government achieved this goal by opening *torgsins*, shops where bread and a few other staples could be bought at cheap prices—but only by those who paid in foreign currency or precious metals. Jews brought whatever ornaments they had—a silver *menorah*, *Shabbos* silverware—and exchanged it for bread. My parents exchanged their silver candlesticks for bread. Anyone with relatives outside of Russia had them send dollars so that he could buy food. The Government, however, was not satisfied, and demanded that all gold, silver and foreign currency be turned in.

We began to hear stories of how men came at night, and took people to an unknown destination. No one knew what was wanted of them. After a few weeks, the secret came out. The G.P.U., with its file on every person, had learned that these individuals had silver, gold and dollars. When the owners denied it, they were taken and imprisoned in a small room. A hundred men were packed into a room fit for thirty. A pail was left in the middle to suffice for their physical needs. They were fed starvation rations of bread and water. If the owners did not confess after this treatment, the Communists proceeded to torture them, and many died from these tortures. Others were broken and admitted to their secret reserves. They would take the G.P.U. to their houses and show the authorities their hidden treasure. After this, the owners were permitted to return home. Many went insane or died from these ordeals.

How, though, did the G.P.U. know whom to suspect? In all towns there were two local councils, one for the Jews and one for the gentiles. It was the depraved people at the head of the Jewish council in our town who had informed on their fellow Jews, since they knew who had been rich or even middle-class years before. That people were killed or maimed because of their reports apparently did not disturb their consciences.

I remember one man who had been robbed of everything he owned. He turned to a G.P.U. official and asked, "What else do you want from me? I have nothing left!"

The official answered, "We want to suck the blood of your veins!"

These betrayers were not acting from the desperation of hunger. Quite the opposite, during all the years of famine, they ate more than their fill.

High ranking officials were not ashamed to publish announcements in the papers that anyone having relatives abroad should write them to send them dollars which they were then to turn over to the Government. There were even cases where the Government forced people to write to relatives for dollars, keeping these unfortunates in prison until the dollars arrived.

I remember how they came to a Jew's house one night to take him to prison. They found a visitor in his home, his brother from America. The visitor begged the men to leave and let him enjoy his brother's company a while longer, until he departed for America. They agreed and left. When the visiting brother returned to America, the men showed up again and kept the Jew in prison until he had received his dollar ransom.

That winter, millions of people died. My brother and I continued at our work, making bricks. Of course, we were also starving and swollen from hunger. Probably, the only reason the Yevseks left us alone was because they expected us to die of hunger anyway.

This was a terrifying time. Not only did they imprison and torture the *kulaks* and the wealthy but also anyone who did not adhere to their views. The papers made impassioned outcries against "the enemies of the people," the counter-revolutionaries who, they claimed, were planning an uprising in alliance with forces outside the country. Anyone deviating from the party line was accused of issuing propaganda against them.

Shochtim were afraid to *shecht, Mohelim* were afraid to *malle* (circumcize), and *chazanim* were afraid to *daven. Shuls* and *minyanim* were prohibited. There were those who formed *minyanim* in their homes and paid for it with their lives. Rabbis were thus left without work. In the dangerous position of "parasite," they became candidates for prison and Siberia. Many submitted to the Communists. Those who would not were forced to flee, an extremely difficult and dangerous undertaking during those years of upheaval, hunger and suffering. Fear enveloped the ones who remained.

The director of our brick factory pitied us for our sincerity. Because he held a high rank in the local council, he was privy to some confidential information, which he one day confided to my brother. The next day (it was after *Pesach*, 1933) they were going to arrest the priest of the town, and he assumed that they certainly wouldn't discriminate and leave the *Rav*, our father. If our father didn't flee that night, it would be too late the next morning. My father knew that if he were among those rounded up, he had no chance of coming out alive. In addition to being a *Rav*, he had illegally helped hundreds of *yeshivah* students and their families escape. He had also secretly taught some students during the 1920s. If those "crimes" were discovered, he would certainly be put to death. That night he hiked seventeen kilometers to the train station and boarded the first train that arrived.

This was the beginning of his long exile of wandering. He dressed like an ordinary man, without the black caftan usually worn by Rabbis, to avoid attracting attention. He spent most of the time in large cities like Leningrad, Moscow and Kiev. One of his first stops was Zhitomir, where he visited a Chabad underground *yeshivah*. The Chabad *Chassidim* still had a few *yeshivos* in the cities, each with about fifteen or twenty boys. Their young teacher, Eliezer Pinski, was teaching the boys *Gemara* and *Chassidus* at great risk and self-sacrifice. He made a fine impression on my father, and so he suggested a *shidduch* with my sister Feige. Feige was eighteen then.

Like my brother and I, she was courageously keeping Torah and *mitzvos*, suffering deprivation and contempt for it. Since Eliezer could not travel to our town, which was near the border, Feige went to Zhitomir. The two met and agreed to the match.

It was a bittersweet time for our family. My sister's engagement brought great joy to us, especially as she was fortunate to find a courageous husband who was devoted to the Torah in spite of the dreadful situation that prevailed in Russia at the time. But our fear and hunger and uncertainty about the future weighed on our hearts like heavy stones.

The wedding was held in early summer, around *Shavuos*, and the young couple went to live in Moscow. Since Moscow was a huge metropolis, it would be easier to escape the scrutiny of the authorities.

In the north, where my father was, food was not as scarce as it was in the south, where we lived. My father would stand in line for hours to receive a portion of bread, which he would send us by mail, sometimes once a week, sometimes once a month. Fear of the authorities was so immense that these packets were not pilfered in the post. By the time we received it, the bread was usually moldy. Even so, we ate it with gusto. Anything was better than nothing.

My brother and I continued to work at the factory. We were paid once every two months, although the wages were not enough to provide for even two weeks. It was worth it, though, in that at least the dreaded Yevsektzia left us alone.

A number of times, these officials told us frankly, "We're leaving you alone now, even though you don't go along with our ideology, because we know you don't do anything illegal. But don't breathe too easy. We'll catch up with you one day."

Once, an old gentile, leaning on a crutch, slowly passed by our factory. A fellow worker, a member of the Konsomol, turned to me and said, "Do you see that man? He came out of prison two days ago. Do you know how wealthy he was when they got hold of him? They decided to let him out now only because he's no threat. Look at him. Maybe he'll live another few days. That's what we do to people like you. When your turn comes, you'll get the same treatment."

I was silent but my heart grew faint, and I prayed, "G-d, help me!

Save me from their hands!"

During these years, informing became so rampant that a cynical joke was going around. A man looked in the mirror and said to his reflection, "Tell me, which one is the informer, me or you?"

People informed to prove their loyalty to the Communists and also to destroy their personal enemies. Crimes were sought out. It did not seem to affect people's consciences that others were tortured, maimed or murdered as a result of their words. This continued until the outbreak of World War II. It was a hellish existence.

7 FIGHTING FOR SURVIVAL

IN 1930, OUR TOWN STILL HAD ITS *SHULS, MIKVEH,*
mohel and *shochet*, but it was already clear that
this could not last much longer. The Yevsektzia had its eye on the
largest *shul*, since it was the only building large enough for their
workers' club. Each time they requested it from the town's religious
Jews, we refused even though the building was used only occasionally. How could we give it over for such a sacrilegious purpose? At
the time the law provided that a *shul* could not be expropriated if
there were fifty religious householders who signed an agreement
that they needed it.

Heading the Communists in our town was Batya, a Jewish woman.
She was an anomaly. The daughter of a common worker, she had
risen to power because of her intense devotion to Communist
doctrine. She was chief of the group that helped destroy the wealthy
and considered it her duty to implement all directives. On the other

hand, she respected her devout father and knew quite well that the religious were not the "enemies of the people," nor were they "evil capitalists" bent on destroying the Communist ideal.

One day, we saw her heading toward our house and our hearts began to pound from fear. Batya was not known for her abundance of mercy. What did she want? If she was coming to appropriate items of value, she would be disappointed. The only thing we knew for sure was that she was not coming to the *Rav's* house for a friendly visit.

Once inside, she turned to my father and said, "I have to ask the *Rav* a question." From her bag she took out a slaughtered chicken and asked my father to determine whether it was kosher or not. "I am not trying to ensnare the *Rav*, who is a religious man and is allowed to live by his beliefs, but I cannot cheat my father."

She came secretly several times afterwards to ask such questions. We knew that she was also stringent in not mixing meat and milk.

Nevertheless, it was Batya who was spearheading the drive to take over the *shul* for recreational purposes. Since the law provided that a *shul* could not be expropriated if fifty religious householders signed that they needed it, she came up with a plan. She notified the worshippers that on *Tisha b'Av* night, at the start of the fast, we should meet in the *shul*. It would be determined right then and there whether the requisite fifty men existed.

That whole day, I went from house to house, urging religious Jews to show up and give their support and signatures. I had to work hard to convince them, since so many were afraid of being penalized. Because I did not have time to eat the meal before the fast, I wound up fasting two days in the blazing summer heat.

On the appointed day, right after sunset, Batya arrived at the *shul*, with others from the committee. Going up to the podium, she explained that the workers and youths needed a club and that this *shul* would be perfect for them. This was only an excuse for closing the *shul*, of course; they had enough recreational facilities. The proof is that two or three years later, after procuring the *shul*, they tore it down.

"But," she continued on that *Tisha b'av* night, "we Communists do not believe in unlawful coercion. If fifty religious Jews want to maintain the *shul*, we cannot take it away. So, whoever wants to keep it as a *shul*, come up and sign this paper."

My father and one other man went up. Both signed. (I was too young to have a vote.) The other worshippers sat in fear.

"Nu," she called out. "Who else wants to sign?"

No reaction.

"Look here," she continued in a gentler tone. "I am a Communist who is willing to die for my cause. But you, why are you afraid? Nothing will happen to you if you sign. The Communist democracy allows each man to live according to his conscience. Here, for example is my father. He is a religious man, and he will sign." Her father got up and signed. She then invited each religious Jew present to come up and write his name. In the end, fifty signatures were obtained, and the *shul* remained open for several years.

Despite her devotion to the Communist ideal, Batya had retained her basic human integrity. After the war, I met her. She eventually became disillusioned with Communism and returned to Judaism, keeping *Shabbos* and *kashrus* and going to *shul* regularly.

Around this time, the *mikveh* came under attack. They closed it on doctor's orders, claiming it was not hygienic. Shortly afterwards, the doctor told some men that he personally felt the *mikveh* did not violate health requirements but that he had not wanted to get into trouble with the authorities. If, he said, the regional doctor in Slavita would allow its maintenance, he would not oppose it.

My father immediately set out for the doctor in Slavita, who happened to be a Jew. Explaining the necessity of the *mikveh* for religious Jews, my father pleaded with him to permit its reopening. Although the doctor was sympathetic, he was still not willing to write an official permit, fearing repercussions. He did however, send a verbal message with my father, and the local doctor permitted the *mikveh* to remain in use for another two or three years.

The next target among Jewish practices was *milah*, circumcision on the eighth day. Until 1932, it was relatively easy to find *mohelim*, and a *bris* was still an occasion for public celebration by the average Jew. Only members of the Communist Party were afraid to circumcize their children.

A young couple in our town belonged to the Communist party.

Both were teachers in the Soviet school. When a son was born to them, they circumcized him in secret and took the extra precaution of announcing that they had a daughter. A few months later, one of their fellow teachers came to visit the mother, and saw that the "girl" was really a boy, and that he was circumcized. She told this to the Party secretary, whereupon the husband and wife were fired from work and their party membership was revoked.

In 1932, the oppression and terror reached a new pitch. It became harder and harder to find someone willing to risk being a *mohel*, and people gradually abandoned the *mitzvah* because of the difficulties involved. Thus, it finally came about that the very foundation of Jewish identity—*milah*—was all but destroyed.

Impossible circumstances called for impossible courage. A candle maker called Reb Yudl was a proud, G-d-fearing Jew who possessed such courage. Yudl the *lichtsier* (candle maker) was an experienced *mohel* who, disregarding the danger to himself, continued to circumcize children in our town and the neighboring ones.

"Exile to Siberia does not frighten me," he would say. "In any case, I am already old, and I'm prepared to sanctify His Holy Name."

One day, a senior officer of the Border Guard came and asked Reb Yudl to circumcize his child. This officer lived not far from Berezdiv near the border. He could not bring Reb Yudl to his house, though, for fear of being seen with the aged *mohel*. The only solution would be if the *mohel* would leave his town (which was also near the border) and start walking in the direction of the border. The border guards would surely find him and bring him into headquarters for investigation. Reb Yudl was told to say that he had been trying to go in the opposite direction but had gotten lost. In such cases, it was customary to bring the suspect to the senior officer, in this case, the father of the baby, who would finish the interrogation.

Reb Yudl agreed to this arrangement, although he strongly suspected that it was a trap. He started walking toward the border. The border guards picked him up and brought him to the senior officer. The officer received him with rage and insults and signed the note confirming he had taken charge of the suspect. Once the guards left, the officer secretly took Reb Yudl the *mohel* to his home where he circumcized the child. He was sincere, after all.

Following a warm celebration, Reb Yudl slept overnight at the officer's house, and in the early morning, he returned to his town in the officer's wagon. The officer offered to pay him generously but Reb Yudl refused to take any money for the *mitzvah*.

The year 1932 was marked by intense agitation to take over the *shuls*. A certain fellow named Lioni was put in charge of this cause. In March, on the eve of *Rosh Chodesh Adar*, ten religious Jews in our town secretly declared a fast and prayed that his plans be foiled.

One night, Lioni convened a meeting in the *shul* where he vehemently addressed all the Jews assembled about the need to change the building into a theater. Before the meeting began, I saw him point out to his comrades how the *bimah* and its sides would be suitable for a stage. He received confirmation for his plans from the assembly by a show of hands. How great was our joy when the very next day he was caught in some illegal activity and arrested by the G.P.U.! They placed him on a harnessed wagon in the marketplace for everyone to see. After this disgrace, he was taken away, never to be heard from again. No one questioned how our luck had thus turned for the better, at least temporarily. As I was to learn later however, there was more to the story.

Occasionally, I would go to the cemetery to my grandfather's grave and pour out all the tears bottled up inside me. One day I went and found on his gravestone a brick with illegible words engraved on it. I was mystified. Who had gone to my grandfather's grave? And why had he put this brick there? Later that year, I found out. Rav Moshe Manyatiner was one of the elderly *Chassidim* of the Alter of Trisk. I told him about the brick on my grandfather's tomb.

"Well, I'll tell you the story," he said. "Do you remember when we fasted on the eve of *Rosh Chodesh Adar* and we *davened* in the Stoliner *shul*? Let me tell you what happened. I used to live in Manyatin, three kilometers from Krasnostav, where there was a countess, a woman landowner who would persecute me day and night until I could bear it no longer.

"I travelled to the Trisker *Rebbe* and asked him to daven for me that I be saved from her hands. The *Rebbe* advised me, 'Do what I tell you but do not tell this to anyone. Take a brick, and with a nail, scratch out on it the name of the countess and her mother. On Thursday night, when you heat the oven to bake *challos*, put the brick into the oven, think certain *kavanos*, and Hashem will help you.' The *kavanos* were mystical phrases from *Kabbalah*.

"I followed his instructions. While my wife kneaded the dough, I stood near the oven and kept these *kavanos* in mind. Suddenly, I heard a strong knock on the door. 'Moshkeh! Open immediately!' It was the countess's servant. She was feeling ill. 'Give me vinegar to massage her.' I gave him some vinegar and he left quickly. The next morning, the countess was dead.

"Now, when I saw that scoundrel Lioni, I decided to try it again. I took a brick and wrote his name and the name of his mother on it . . . and you know what happened to him."

The *Rebbe* had told Reb Moshe not to throw out the brick. Rather, he was to place it on the grave of a *tzaddik* or great *Rebbe*. Reb Moshe had done that the first time, but now since no *Rebbe* was buried in our cemetery, he had put the brick on the grave of my grandfather, of blessed memory.

That year, when my father was briefly at home, a young Communist couple came to be married secretly according to Jewish law. They were afraid that if someone were to suddenly come to the *Rav's* house and see them there, they wouldn't have an explanation. They solved the problem by coming with the bridegroom's parents who were prepared to claim that they wanted the *Rav* to arrange a divorce for themselves. The son and his fiancee had only come along to protest his parents' getting a divorce.

In an atmosphere where natural, joyous events, had to be masked with duplicity, another dismal year passed. My father was still on the move but we usually didn't know where. My sister was married and living in Moscow, and my brother and I still worked at the brickmaking factory. We lived at home with our mother. She secretly taught some children how to *daven* from the *siddur*.

I remember an incident that took place one *Shabbos*, as my mother, brother and I were sitting on our porch. Across from us lived a bearded Jew who still kept a few *mitzvos* but whose teenage son had fallen completely under Communist influence. The son had a pig sty at the side of the house, where he raised a pig. That

Shabbos, the swine had escaped to the street and was wallowing in the mud. The old bearded Jew ran out and tried to grab the pig and push him back. It was painful to watch.

"Oh, my children!" my mother groaned. "Look how far things have gone! Will Hashem ever forgive His people for this?"

When my father left, he had given me instructions on how to decide *Halachic* questions. I only answered questions for those people I knew I could trust. To a few former friends, I would speak about keeping whatever *mitzvos* they could. Some even listened and stopped shaving with a razor, using scissors instead.

That autumn, I felt a need to change my surroundings and refresh my spirit. I got permission to leave work and traveled to spend the *Yamim Nora'im* with my aunt, my mother's sister, who lived in Zaslav. Her husband was a greatgrandson of a famous *Rebbe* and made a living as a *shochet*. I came on Friday, planning to remain for *Rosh Hashanah* which fell on Monday and Tuesday.

On *Shabbos* morning, I saw their eight-year-old son take his briefcase, and set off for school. I was shocked.

"What?" I asked my uncle. "Your son goes to school on *Shabbos*?"

"Yes," he answered me dolefully. "Well, what can we do about it?"

"What do we do in our house?" I retorted. "We don't go!"

"But they'll fine me."

"How many times have you paid the fine?"

"I haven't paid it yet . . . and, anyway, if I did, would it help?"

"But at least, by paying the fine, you can prevent *Chillul Shabbos* for a few *Shabbosim* and by that time you might find a way out."

"I wouldn't be able to bear the tension," he said.

With this, our conversation ended.

I went to *shul* to *daven*. When I returned, the child had already returned from school. He went into his room and began preparing his lessons, writing in his notebook. I looked at his father in disbelief.

"What's this? Can't the child prepare his lessons at night?"

"It's a lost cause anyway," he told me. "We won't be able to hold out much longer."

"I am shocked!" I cried. "How can people eat from your *shechitah* or drink the wine you touch?"

For my *Shabbos* meal, I ate only a piece of salted fish and bread. I did not touch the meat or any cooked food. My aunt began to cry.

"I tried to stop the child from going, but it didn't help," she sobbed. "This child is the son of his first wife who passed away, and her mother curses me for what she calls interfering."

I spent *Shabbos* with them, but on *Rosh Hashanah*, I ate with his old widowed father who had once been a *Rebbe*. Even he had a few words of reproof for me.

"Look at you," he admonished. "What future do you have? Who will marry a young man with a beard and *peyos*? Think it over."

I returned home immediately after the *Yom Tov*.

8 THE END OF THE SHUL

IN SEPTEMBER 1934, WE BEGAN A NEW YEAR AT work. I was almost twenty-three and my brother, twenty-one. We often spoke about our future. What did it hold for us? For my part, I had been urging my brother to get married. His constitution was weaker than mine, and the backbreaking labor, combined with constant hunger, was taking its toll on him. A *shidduch* was suggested with the daughter of a distant relative, who was better off than we were. They got married at the end of 1934 and settled in Krasnostav. I had made up my mind, though, that Krasnostav held no future for me, and that I would one day leave it for good. But when? And how?

One day, the Yevsektzia approached the religious Jews in town and made them an offer. If the Trisker *kloiz*, the building in which the Trisker *Chassidim* had their *minyan* and which also housed the Karlin-Stolin *shtiebel*, were voluntarily handed over to them, the

61

Yevsektzia would stop pressing its demands for the big *shul*. Two prominent Stoliner *Chassidim*, both learned and G-d-fearing, were inclined to accept the offer. These men, Reb Mordechai and Reb Moshe, waited until my father arrived on one of his clandestine visits to receive his approval.

My father resolutely opposed the offer for three reasons.

"First of all," he said, "to voluntarily give over the *shtiebel* to wicked people is akin to defiling it ourselves, which is a *Chillul Hashem*. This is prohibited even when one knows that if the object is not given voluntarily it will be taken away."

My father then compared it to the case mentioned in *Terumos* 8:12 that if gentiles tell a group of women, "Give us one of you to defile, or else we will defile all of you," they must all let themselves be taken rather than deliver one Jewish soul to them. Furthermore, if they seize the *shuls* by force, everyone will see them as wicked people and robbers, which would not be the case if it were given to them. Third, one cannot rely on the promises of wicked people. You have no assurance that they will keep their promise."

In the end, these two Jews did not listen to my father. They signed the deal with the Yevsektzia, agreeing to give them the Trisker *kloiz* and Stolin *shtiebel*, so that the big *shul*, about which the momentous meeting had been held on *Tisha b'Av* night two years earlier, should remain. They had apparently forgotten the resolution, that Lioni had obtained by a show of hands, to hand the building over for a theater.

One *Shabbos* morning, the Yevsektzia sent workers to tear down the two small *shuls*. Immediately afterwards, they began to demolish the big *shul*. When neighboring children, in response to the distress of their elders, began to throw stones at the workers, they temporarily stopped their work.

The two Jews who had signed the deal were anguished. They traveled to Kiev, the capital of the Ukraine. There they met with Petrovski, the President of the Republic, and complained about the violation of the agreement. They were promised that an order would be sent to the local Yevsektzia not to touch the main *shul*. When they returned home, they told everyone of the success of their mission. When the local Yevsektzia heard of it, though, they mobilized quickly. In one day they demolished the *shul*, before the

Government order could reach them.

The local Jews were pained by the loss of their *shul*. Even though many had stopped keeping *kashrus* and *Shabbos*, along with most other *mitzvos*, Jewish identity and customs were still dear to them. The destruction of the *shul* symbolized something more basic — that all vestiges of Judaism would soon be destroyed. The *shul* had been razed on the pretext that it was holding back progress, but inwardly, people sensed that their very identity as Jews was being annihilated. A young woman who saw the wreckage sobbed despondently and tore out tufts of her hair, but what was done, was done. The main *shul*, which had stood in the center of our town for hundreds of years and verified our sacred Jewish identity was now gone.

Before they completely destroyed our *shul*, we managed to remove the sacred *Sifrei Torah* and many other *sefarim* under cover of night. A young religious man, Baruch, managed to do the majority of the work that night. He and his father had moved to Krasnostav, when the war against Judaism had been totally successful in their hometown of Berezdiv. He was the only good friend I had at the time, and I learned with him as often as I could. Baruch, unfortunately, was missing a leg and he walked with crutches. But that night, he hopped between the strewn bricks, shattered glass, and broken beams and fished in the debris to find a book, which he would then bring to a neighbor's house for safekeeping. The two of us worked ardently throughout night when the watchmen were no longer there. Only in this way were we able to save the *sefarim*, for the Communists had forbidden anyone to touch them without orders.

The next day the *shul* was razed to its foundations. Under the stairs of the *shul's* women's section was a large pile of *sheimos* (torn pages and worn out holy books, which Jewish law forbids to be thrown away but must be buried in the ground) which the wind had partially blown about. What should we do? We did not have much time, and soon the watchmen would return. We decided that the pages had to be collected from all over the *shtetl* and given a proper burial, as the law requires. I was entrusted with this urgent task and now as the sun was rising, I rushed to go to my job in the brick factory. To my great good fortune, a fire broke out on the outskirts of the *shtetl* that threatened to spread further. The local council ordered all residents to disregard their jobs and come instead to extinguish the fire. I was free! Alone with a wagon driver named Yosef, I collected the *sheimos* and brought them to the cemetery. We made the trip back and forth three times until not another paper could be found.

The two *Chassidic* Jews who were indirectly responsible for the loss of the *shuls* died shortly afterwards, heartbroken, within three months of each other. They were buried in the cemetery next to the burial spot of the *sheimos* of the *shul*. In a way, they, too, had become *sheimos*.

Because we still had many *sefarim* in our house during this period, I feared for their fate, especially the works on *Halachah*. Any day, the police could appear at our door and confiscate them on a false charge.

I decided to divide the *sefarim*, bringing one set to one friend, another set to a different friend and keeping the rest. Thus, I was assured that there would always be some *sefarim* left if ours were taken away.

As the *shtetl* had no *shul* now, we set up a *minyan* the following *Rosh Hashanah* in the home of a cloth painter, Reb Moshe Aaron. About a hundred men attended, including my father. We *davened* the entire morning until it was time to blow the *shofar*. With tears, my father began to read the verse *"Min Hametzar"* ("In distress" *Tehillim* 118:5), the first of seven verses that precede the sounding of the *shofar*. Suddenly, several Yevseks appeared, led by the Jewish mayor. The *kehillah* continued *davening*, unmoved by their presence. When he heard the first *tekios*, the mayor turned aside to the corridor and waited until the shofar-blowing was over. Then he entered and asked, "Whose house is this?" The painter nodded, and the mayor commanded him to send everyone home or he would bear the consequences.

Enwrapped in *talleisim*, we poured out into the street and decided to go to the cemetery to continue praying. We *davened* there the second day of *Rosh Hashanah* and *Yom Kippur* as well. When it rained *Yom Kippur* night, the women entered the adjoining shelter, but the men continued praying in the open. Government officials passing by, three kilometers away, heard our cries piercing the night.

"What is going on?" they asked.

"Jews praying at their fathers' graves," explained the gentiles.

The officials then continued on their way.

9 THE CENSUS

IN 1935, WHEN I WAS "OFFICIALLY" TWENTY-ONE, I became eligible for the draft. The local council wrote a recommendation to the draft board, saying that in their opinion, I was a dangerous risk for the army, since I upheld the subversive ideologies of my father. Because I was not to be trusted, a young Communist in my neighborhood named Motl, to whose poor and sick father I had brought milk a few years earlier, was assigned to come with me to make sure I submitted the recommendation to the draft board. When we got there, thousands of young men were milling around.

After a long wait, we heard an announcement. Anyone with a beard, had to shave it off immediately. It wasn't hard to figure out whom they meant, since I was the only one there who had a beard.

"I'm jealous of you! How can you be so strong?!" Motl exclaimed in Yiddish, seeing how I ignored the orders.

They interrogated me about my religious convictions, to which I clearly stated the truth. The outcome was, surprisingly, that I was sent home in peace. My brush with the military, though, was by no means over.

The same day that we buried the *sheimos*, I was told to come to the local council. I was afraid somebody had seen me collecting or burying the holy scripts, and I would be put into prison. This took place on a Friday morning. I was told to come to the district draft board the next morning, *Shabbos*. As there was only one train a day to the district town, I decided to travel on Sunday and present myself at the draft board on Monday morning.

When asked why I was two days late, I answered that I received the summons only on Saturday morning and had no earlier way of traveling. Surprisingly, they believed me and made no issue. When my name was called, the officer in charge asked me an unexpected question about whether I had a married sister living in Moscow, to which I answered in the affirmative and was sent back home.

Later that summer, although I had been excused from military duty, I was sent to a three-week preparatory militia camp. Since I didn't eat the *treif* food served there, I lived on a diet of bread and water the whole week. I was worried, however, about observing *Shabbos*. My group was scheduled to be sent home each week for one day of rest, but that day, of course, would be Sunday. While I was in turmoil on Friday about what to do, the commander got up and announced that since our group had performed so well, we would be given an extra day off. We were dismissed that afternoon, and I returned home in time for *Shabbos*.

The same thing happened the following two weeks. I fulfilled my army obligations without any problems. Before being discharged, I approached the commanding officer for a confirmation of my army service so that I could be reimbursed for my wages during the time I was absent from work.

He sat opposite me and said, "Who are you?"

He had seen me every day and had read my name countless times during roll call. I thought he was joking.

"Come on, you know who I am."

"What's your name?" he said coldly.

"Chazan," I answered.

"I'll look in the roll call book."

I told him whose name appeared before and after mine in the book. He hunched over the book, keeping it covered from me.

"I don't see any Chazan here. Sorry."

"But you know I was here the whole time!" I protested.

"Are you calling me a liar?" he glowered. Slamming the book, he shouted, "Now get out of here!"

I returned home, disheartened. When I related the incident to the Jewish director of my factory, he only laughed.

"Yes, I know," he said. "But there's nothing you can do about it. Just stay here and continue working. Of course, you understand, I can't reimburse you for the time you were gone."

It took another year till I finally got the money due me. I went back to the recruiting board to request the confirmation of my army service.

While there, I stayed overnight at the home of an elderly *shochet*, a man renowned for his piety and erudition. His son, however, was the *Rav* I mentioned who had handed over his *tallis* and *tefillin* to the Town Council.

The *shochet* awoke after midnight to begin studying Torah. The light in the hall woke me, too, and I decided to join him. After two hours of rapt study, he stopped to have some tea, bringing a cup for me also.

"Aaron, I want to ask your opinion about something," he began. "You know that I'm a *shochet* and a *mohel*. Well, recently, they told me that if I don't stop doing *brissim*, they'll take away my license to be a *shochet* and give me a declassed status. What do you think? Do you really think it would be a *Chillul Hashem* if I stopped being a *mohel*? After all, who says I have to be one? And just because I stop being a *mohel*, that doesn't mean I've actually agreed to the Communist ideology."

"You know," I said, "it won't end with your promise not to do *brissim*. They'll make you sign a declaration in the papers that you finally realize how wrong it was to be a *mohel*! And tell me something, who is forcing you to give up being a *mohel*? Are you so afraid of having your *shechitah* license revoked and getting a declassed status? Why are you so worried about not being a *shochet*? Because you will be left without a living? Then let me give you some advice. Spread the word that because you wouldn't give up being a *mohel*, they took away your income as a *shochet*. You have a fine reputation here in town. Everyone will help you out! And here's another thing you can do. You own a spacious home. You and your wife don't need such a big house. When you get down to your last penny, sell a room and live off that income. Do you honestly think that yours is a kind of life-and-death situation, where you would be permitted to give in to the Communists' demands? I'm sure that even if you didn't have a morsel to eat, you could go into any home here and gladly be given a meal."

He wasn't convinced. Instead, he began to defend his original contention. Almighty G-d, I thought, with a tremor, is this what is happening to the elders, to the best of the lot?

"You know, I saw an interesting explanation," I said. "In an introduction to the responsa of Reb Shlomo Kluger, he quotes the *Gemara* in *Sanhedrin* 52a that a wicked man whose father was righteous can be termed a wicked man whose father was wicked. Reb Shlomo Kluger also cites the *Choshen Mishpat* which explains that if there is a wicked man whose father was righteous and someone calls him a wicked man whose father was wicked, one would normally think the speaker would have to pay indemnity because he shamed the father. But no. He is exempt from paying. Why? Reb Shlomo explains that if a small child rebels against his father, we say that the child has an evil nature, and the father is not guilty. But if the child behaved properly as he was growing up, and then later rebels, then the son's wickedness stemmed from his father, who deserves to be called a wicked man."

"Reb Shlomo Kluger says that?" he said agitated. "I must see it myself!"

I told him the source. We spoke no more about his impending ordeal. Our conversation, however, must have struck a responsive chord. Later, I heard, that this *shochet* was deprived of his right to *shecht* because he stood up for the Torah. He was indeed a very sincere Jew.

Many times after this, until I left for Odessa, I was recalled to the draft board, while other youths my age were left alone. These were special call-ups for the criminals and thieves, in which class I was included, since I was registered in their files as a delinquent. Each time, they brought me into a room, and the same interrogation followed.

"Are you religious? Why? Why would you choose such a life for yourself?"

I always answered openly, "I am religious. I keep the command-ments and believe in G-d." And so on, until they let me go home. Actually I was fortunate. In general, anyone claiming to be religious was sent straight to hard labor, in place of army service.

My brother and I continued working at the brickmaking factory. Time is known to mercifully blur one's pain, but not so with us. Five years of working at the same monotonous tough job, had not dulled the anguish and degradation. Like mannequins, we did our work until the afternoon when we dragged ourselves to our homes.

My only comfort was in my studies. Who was there to understand us, much less encourage us? Everyone thought we were crazy. Everyone that is, until Reb Yosef Kozlik arrived in the late Spring of 1934.

Reb Yosef was an extraordinary man, a Torah scholar and com-munal leader, whose trust in G-d was irrepressible. We had first known him briefly when he fled Zevihl to come to our town during the Petlura pogroms. While living in Zevihl, he did everything possible to uphold religious life. Once, when the authorities had closed the public *mikveh*, Reb Yosef set up a new *mikveh* in a private home. The secret was scrupulously kept by the few who knew of its existence.

One day, though, the woman in charge of the *mikveh* came to tell him that two officials had been to the house and found the *mikveh*. They closed it and pasted signs over it, warning her not to touch the notices. A few days later, the woman came again. The night before, she said, one of the officials had returned with his wife and asked her to open the *mikveh*. He cautioned her not to reveal the visit to anyone.

In Zevihl, Reb Yosef Kozlik had been distinguished and well-to-do. When the authorities were rounding up private businessmen at the end of Lenin's New Economic Plan, he had to flee with his wife and sons. He spent several years wandering, until he arrived in Krasnostav. He, like us, got a job making bricks in our factory so as to avoid desecrating *Shabbos*. Years of suffering and deprivation had not weakened his resolve in the least. He brimmed with encouragement and jokes, and all the brutal power of the Communists seemed like mere puffery in comparison to his strong faith. We felt as precious as gold and silver when we were in his presence.

"Don't let despair get hold of you," he would constantly tell us.

He was the greatest role model of sacrifice for his ideals. Once respected and wealthy, he now could not even buy enough bread for his family, although he worked himself to the bone. But he was happy with his lot. He showed us how to appreciate our own value, regardless of how the world viewed us.

"Even when a dog bites you, you have to remember that you're the man and he's the dog," he would joke. "Imagine a beggar trudging alone, knocking from door to door. One day, he enters a rich man's house, and sees the dog eating a juicy steak. Would it ever occur to him, 'If only I were the dog of this man!' It's better to die like a Jew than to live like an animal."

"You've brought us back to life!" I would tell him.

That *Elul*, the month before *Rosh Hashanah*, I felt a need to pour out my heart at the graves of *tzaddikim*. I gave the excuse that I had to see the dentist in Anapoli and, thereby, I received a few days off from work. I traveled to Anapoli and entered the graveyard where the holy Maggid of Meziritch was buried. His mausoleum was locked, so I looked for the caretaker to open it. In the past, he told me, only distinguished *Rebbes* and leaders were allowed to enter the wooden mausoleum. Lately, however, no one at all came because the town was right at the border.

"But I see that you are a truly religious young man," he said. "You may go in."

Entering through a door in the corner, I found myself in a narrow vestibule and saw the grave through a hole in the wall. I wept and prayed with all my heart. If only this great holy man could see the destruction around him! I left a *kvittel* asking that his merit help me to be steadfast in keeping *Shabbos*, and to soon find a proper mate.

Reb Yosef Kozlik had also sent a *kvittel* with me, asking that he succeed in leaving Russia and merit to live in the Holy Land.

I also made a pilgrimage to Berdichev to the graveside of Reb Levi Yitzchak and repeated my soul's petition. Perhaps it was in the merit of these two great *tzaddikim* that we both had our requests answered.

In the beginning of 1936, all religious Jewry was thrown into turmoil by an announcement from Stalin. A census would be taken of every Russian citizen, without exception. The census consisted of five items—first name, family name, parents' names, nationality and whether or not he believed in G-d. How could we not feel that the purpose of this census was to be used against us? It would provide the Communists with an easy directory of whom to do away with next. On the other hand, if we were to deny that we were believing, G-d-fearing Jews, it would be an undeniable *Chillul Hashem*. We encouraged each other to stand up to this trial, and declare our convictions.

I spoke to anyone who had any connections or feelings for Judaism. I earnestly argued that failing to admit our belief would be tantamount to denying G-d, a clear case of "one must die rather than transgress." But the terror was so palpable that almost no one was able to withstand the test.

In the surrounding *shtetlach*, very few signed that they were religious. Only those rare individuals, whose commitment to Judaism meant more to them than their very own life, did not give in. There was a young girl in town, Rosa, who was a relative of ours, and the only friend my sister had had while growing up. Rosa registered herself as religious. The census taker started to ridicule her.

"Aren't you ashamed, a young girl like you, to state that you're religious? Are you crazy?" He wrote instead that she was an atheist.

She began to shout at him until he finally tore up the form and marked her down as religious. Everyone was sure that she would pay dearly for her temerity. However, there were no repercussions for Rosa or for anyone else who signed. Life continued to be bitter, but no new persecutions resulted.

The majority of non-Jews wrote that they believed in their dogmas. A few days later, however, Lubchinkeh, the Premier of the

Ukraine, declared in the newspaper that the populace didn't really believe in their religion, but only kept it as a tradition.

Reb Yosef Kozlik, for his part, also had a brush with the authorities. When he had first come to Krasnostav with his sons, eight and ten years old, he did not register them in the town's population book. By doing this, he had hoped to avoid sending them to school, which begins at seven years old. After two years, at which time their presence had become known, he asked the local medic to write that they had weak constitutions and needed constant care at home. The authorities soon discovered, though, that the boys were quite robust and that he was teaching them Torah instead of sending them to school. Kozlik was summonned to the town Council and ordered by the Yevsek who interviewed him to explain their truancy.

He demurred with every reason he could think of, until the Yevsek stood up, his face red with anger.

"Kozlik!" he thundered. "We know your true motives! We know you're dragging your children back into the Dark Ages with your religious propaganda! Have no illusions about what your fate will be. If you don't send them to school, we'll bring you to court and make a show trial of your case. Then you'll get what you deserve!"

This was no empty threat. The Communists had no compunctions about killing parents and putting the children into Soviet institutions.

Kozlik exploded. "What! Why can't I educate my children in the way of Torah? I don't care what happens to me, but my children will know there is a G-d in this world! Even if they fall into your hands, G-d forbid, my sons will know what's true!"

The Yevsek carried out his threat and set a date for a trial. When I heard this, I came to Kozlik's house after work and found the whole family desperate with worry.

"Reb Yosef," I said. "What did Yaakov and King David do when they were in tight straits? They fled. That is exactly what you must do, because your lives are certainly in danger. One who changes his place, changes his luck!"

Kozlik agreed, and that night, he and his whole family fled. Their first priority was to escape from Russia. Kozlik brought his wife and sons to Berdichev, where they lived in a tiny vestibule and slept on a fold up table. At least they had friends there who were willing to support them. Kozlik then traveled alone to Moscow, where he joined those who had requests to make of Kalinin, the Soviet Union's President. These people waited on a line that stretched for blocks, and no one left it day or night. After all, who knew when Kalinin would deign to open his door to receive the desperate petitioners?

Kozlik waited there day and night for many months. When his turn came, he requested permission to emigrate, and it was granted! With numerous miracles and great afflictions, he reached the shores of the Holy Land that year. And what blessings he has reaped! His sons Yaakov and Moshe are healthy, successful Gerrer *Chassidim* living in Jerusalem. Both of them are devout and excel in Torah. May Reb Yosef's merit bring about that his descendants always continue to exert themselves in Torah and *mitzvos*.

Kozlik's departure, though, affected my own life for the worse. Once again I was plunged into bitter unrelieved loneliness. That spring, a law was promulgated, abolishing the declassed status and giving all persons equal citizenship. But lest anyone misinterpret this act of benevolence, Kalinin addressed the people and wrote a statement for the press.

"The workers ask, Why should parasites get equal rights with us? They are useless and untrustworthy! I answer our comrades that we are not through with them."

In 1935, Stalin wrote, "We will not sit with clasped hands. We will see to them yet!"

Months later, the terrible purges began.

10 THE FRIEDMAN FAMILY

AS I MENTIONED PREVIOUSLY, I TOOK A VACATION from work during *Elul*. It was to change the course of my life.

I traveled to Berdichev, my intention to pour out my heart to G-d in the ancient cemetery. During the morning prayers at the Berdichever's *shul*, Rav Sholom Freidman approached me and invited me to his home. Although I explained that I had to catch the train back in a few hours, he insisted that I come. After taking a quick dip in the *mikveh*, he came home. I was already there, and he came straight to the point.

"Reb Yosef Kozlik stayed with me when he stopped by in Berdichev, and he recommended you as a learned, G-d-fearing young man. I have a sister of marriageable age, whom I would like to suggest for you."

This was my first encounter with a member of the extraordinary

Freidman family from Odessa. My host in Berdichev, Rav Sholom, was the second son of Rav Zusia, a *Chassidic Rav* in Odessa. Rav Sholom spoke some more, and it was decided to begin a correspondence between my parents and his. My parents found the match appealing, and they arranged the engagement for *Chanukah*.

Setting out from my town for Odessa, I stopped over in Berdichev the first day of *Chanukah*. Rav Sholom greeted me warmly there and together, we arrived in Odessa that evening. My father was already there. I stayed in the Freidman house for six days and became acquainted with Rav Zusia. We spent all our time in discussions. I also met with his daughter. On the sixth day of *Chanukah*, the engagement party was held. I was brimming over with gratitude toward Hashem. He had answered my prayers so swiftly.

My eighteen-year-old fiancee, Leah, was infused with nobility and firmly committed to founding a home based on Torah values. In our short acquaintance, I discerned in her the fine qualities which characterized the whole Freidman family. How fortunate I was to become part of it! And against what odds!

"A match is more difficult to arrange than the splitting of the Red Sea," the Talmud states. In the vast territory that comprised Russia, there were literally only a few dozen Jewish families where the children, like the parents, believed in G-d, and scrupulously kept *mitzvos*. It was almost impossible to find a woman of marriageable age who was a committed religious Jew and, furthermore, who was willing to undertake the dangers and hardships that were certain to be her lot by marrying a religious young man. No *Shabbos* observer could hope to have regular work and a reliable income. Moreover, he was a likely candidate for imprisonment. He would be under constant surveillance by the G.P.U. who lay in wait for their chance to pounce upon a prey. I myself knew of cases where the husband was taken away right after his own wedding. My father-in-law spoke about the wondrousness of our match at our engagement celebration.

I too felt that our match was a virtual miracle. I prayed that my fiancee and I would be given the fortitude and divine aid to overcome the difficult times ahead. Now that I had my ordained partner for life, the loneliness and isolation that had enveloped me all these years would lift. Working together, we could strengthen each other and accomplish what we were meant to.

My father-in-law was a *Chassidic Rav* descended from the Maggid of Mezerich, Reb Dov Baer (1704-1773), who led the *Chassidic* movement after the death of the Baal Shem Tov; through the Maggid's influence and direction, *Chassidism* spread to Jewish communities throughout Eastern Europe. He was also related to the *Rebbes* of Ruzhin, Boyan and Sadigora. He himself was a Boyaner *Chassid*.

Perspicacious and wise, he was sought out by many for his advice. At the same time, he was warm, sensitive and universally beloved. Although he suffered for years from a heart ailment, he always shone with joy, and a smile never left his countenance. Only when it came to matters of Judaism did he show a different side. Then he would thunder out his uncompromising position. Nor was he naive about the consequences of such outspokenness.

"There's not a day we're not in danger," he once remarked to me. Yet, he and his wife continued their activities. They maintained a *minyan* in their house. They made a nice *kiddush* on *Shabbos* and *Yom Tov*, so as to attract more people to prayers. He taught Torah privately. *Shalosh Seudos* was a public affair in their home, where they openly sang and spoke about Torah and *Chassidic* topics. Their house was a veritable hotel where anyone could drop in and stay.

My mother-in-law encouraged her husband in all that he did. All the physical preparations for these activities fell upon her, which she cheerfully and efficiently carried out. She also saw to the thorough education of their children, and her good deeds were surpassed only by her fear of G-d.

Reb Zusia loved his children and their families with a fiery love. They in turn greatly honored him, and every one of them followed in his path. Not one member of his family ever transgressed *Shabbos*, or any other *mitzvah*. The children did not go to Soviet schools, and all the boys wore *yarmulkas, tzitzis* and had *peyos*.

All of Reb Zusia's *mechutanim* were also G-d-fearing and observant. Each one was a rare family in its respective town that had not given in to the Communists. One law Reb Zusia had determined for all his children was that sending their children to Soviet schools was something for which they must die rather than transgress. In matters involving the sanctification of G-d's name he was unyielding.

His oldest son Reb Avraham possessed fear of G-d on par with his father. Indeed, such was the conviction of the whole family. Shortly after I arrived in Odessa, I remember a visit Reb Avrohom made to his father who was sick in bed. The son began relating all his sufferings on account of not sending his sons to the government schools. His father raised himself up and embraced him. In a voice shaking with emotion, he said, "I and my sons will let ourselves be killed before we give over one child to the Soviet schools!"

This scene was etched indelibly in my heart. I knew that every member of the family was indeed prepared to die to sanctify G-d's Name. A week after my engagement, Reb Zusia died. However, all his activities continued to function. The *minyan* in his house still met on *Shabbos*. There were three other *shuls* and several secret *minyanim* where men prayed regularly. These *minyanim* were kept up principally by the Rabbis and learned elderly Jews, because among the youth there were only a few individuals who were still observant.

There was one other family, that of the Turover *Rav*, who equalled my father-in-law's in adherence to Torah and *mitzvos*. This family had come to Odessa from Poland in the wake of World War I and had steadfastly clung to tradition. They lived in dire poverty, and not one member of their family had left the path of Torah. His sons and sons-in-law all wore *peyos*. When I passed their street, I could not help but drop in to visit them. Each time I would leave their house fulfilled and inspired. Unfortunately, the entire family was later wiped out by the Nazis, except for his oldest son-in-law, two grandchildren from another son-in law and his youngest son-in-law along with the young man's family. To this day, all of them are without blemish in their adherence to *mitzvos*.

It was in such an environment that I finally began to "breathe." Our lives, of course, were fraught with danger, but we were buoyed by each other's support. During my youth, my family had preferred to stay in a small town, assuming that the Yevsektzia would concentrate their destructive efforts in the urban centers. I now discovered that we had erred. In the large cities, Moscow, Leningrad, Odessa and Kiev, religious Jews had united to maintain their Judaism. They were thus able to keep *Shabbos, kashrus* and other practices; everything in fact, except withholding their children from the Soviet schools, albeit the key to assimilation.

Religious Jews were not conspicuous in the huge metropolises. They could find a variety of jobs that did not require desecrating *Shabbos*. And in cities, the Yevsektzia did not wield the total power they did in the small towns and *shtetlach*. Border *shtetlach,* like Krasnostav, it turned out, had fared worse than anywhere else in Russia, since the Communists' policies were the most strictly enforced at the frontiers.

My wedding took place on June 14, 1937, at a time when the Rabbis of small towns were being sent into exile and Jewish weddings were clandestine affairs held in basements. Yet not one of the guests—and there were hundreds—suffered consequences for the celebration. My parents enjoyed a rare and precious spark of happiness.

Our wedding was held on the street, and among the guests, were many G.P.U. agents. Because the G.P.U. kept a constant watch on visitors to the Freidman house, they no doubt felt themselves acquaintances from afar, entitled to attend the family celebration.

11 YEARS OF TERROR

AFTER THE WEDDING, MY WIFE AND I MOVED INTO my mother-in-law's apartment in Odessa, away from the brick factory in Krasnostav. Once again, I had to start looking for work. A *Rav* who lived in the suburb of Maldovanka, Reb Yoel Gyrshowitz, suggested I become a *Rav*, as my appearance would surely prevent me from finding a job. But I refused.

"I've been working as a laborer for six years now, and they haven't bothered me yet. They know I'm not involved in anything forbidden, and I was never caught trying to teach Judaism. But if I become a *Rav*, that would be the end of me."

He disagreed. "Everyone knows you're the son of a *Rav* and strictly religious. If you become one, too, your situation won't be that bad."

I did not accept his reasoning, since I knew the Communists looked upon a *Rav* as an outright enemy. G.P.U. officers continued to terrorize all levels of the population, and Rabbis were among their prime targets. In fact, I had firsthand experience of discrimination. The week I arrived in Odessa, I had gone to the police to register as a new citizen. Taking note of my un-Soviet appearance, the clerks looked me up and down and confiscated my documents, including the important army service book. It took a full year until they returned them.

For six months I looked for work, although I knew that even if I found a position, my chances of keeping it were slim because of *Shabbos*. I trudged from one office to another, asking, "Do you need a worker?"

The answer was always, "No."

My appearance proclaimed that I was religious, and no one wanted such a worker. When I saw I wasn't getting anywhere, I began to learn bookbinding, a job with which one was able to keep *Shabbos*. Since no one government office could provide a bookbinder with more work than a few days a month, the bookbinder had to work for about ten offices simultaneously. He made his own schedule and could come to each office when he chose. A number of religious Jews I knew were in this profession.

A new government office that dealt with matters of housing had just been opened. They had branches all over the city and accepted me for work. Every month, I had to report two days to each of the twelve branches of this office. No one knew that I kept *Shabbos*, even though they knew that I was religious because of my *peyos* and beard.

Once an employer asked me, "Why do the bookbinders all have sideburns? You're the third bookbinder I've met who has them!"

"This is the uniform of workers in the bookbinding trade," I said smiling.

He took my words in good humor.

I was able to continue this work for three years, until the outbreak of World War II. Even with a regular income, our sustenance was still meager. From 1937 until the second World War, there was a famine in Odessa. During the four years I lived in Odessa, we had very little to eat.

During this time, in March of 1938, our first child was born, a daughter. Our joy was very great, but we trembled at the thought of the terrible world into which she had been born, a world filled with physical and spiritual peril.

The privations were endless. There was no meat, and only rarely did we have chicken. Even though we were right near the Black Sea, the only fish available were small bychkies. There were days that I stood in line for eight hours to get one hundred grams of butter for my child, only to reach the counter and find none left. Bread was even more difficult to obtain. I would get up in the middle of the night to join the line in order to get one loaf. Every so often, my brothers-in-law in Kiev would send us a small package, since food was more plentiful there.

Only once did I have a frightening experience as a bookbinder. Working one day in the cellar of one of the offices, in the Kulikova-Poli Place, corner of Sverdlov, I was suddenly surrounded by fifteen directors, my employers, all Jews.

"Why do you have to go around with *peyos* and a beard?" they interrogated me. "It's unbecoming for a young man, and it's no good for us either, having a non-conformist working for us. You know how tense things are these days. There are a lot of enemies of the people whom they've thrown into jail, and a lot of them are religious. Comrade Stalin says, 'Whoever isn't with us is against us.' We must be crazy to keep a worker like you! The authorities will ask us, 'If you're all Communists, how do you allow this insurgent to work for you?' What can we answer? And here you are, working for us, making a comfortable living!"

The longer they ranted, the more incensed they became. One of them had clippers with him and offered to shave off my beard.

"What do you want from me?" I answered them. "It's true that I'm religious, but I've never done anything against the government. I'm not involved in any political activity. I'm only a simple man, trying to provide for my wife and child. I'm so busy working for you, I can't even go to *shul* every day. I've never shaved my beard in my life, and I'm not about to do it now."

They continued arguing and threatening me while I sat silent, terrified. No doubt, they had received an order from above . . . and soon I would be taken to prison. They left but I was sure they were watching me, planning my imprisonment. I thanked Hashem daily for giving me strength, otherwise I surely would have gone out of my mind from fear. I already had despaired of remaining alive, but miracles continued to follow me at each step.

In 1937, Stalin's purges began. Led by the arch-murderer Yezhov, the G.P.U. machine was accelerated for greater effectiveness in spying on and terrorizing the people. Everyone lived with the fear that he would soon end up in prison. More than any other group, the religious were in grave danger. Hundreds of people disappeared daily, and the charges were always the same. Terrorists. Enemies of the people. Trotskyites. Zionists. Counterrevolutionaries. Spies.

Along with countless others the authorities deemed too powerful were many members of the fawning Yevsektzia. Ironically, they were dealt with the same fate as their victims of a decade before. They were accused of Zionism and conversely of helping Hitler by spying on Russia. Thus were fulfilled the words of our sages (*Sota* 41b), "One who flatters a wicked man is destined to fall into his hands."

We went through each day, hungry, thirsty and racked by fear of what the next day would bring. At night, we slept alert for the knock on the door. Every day which we survived unharmed was a miracle. We were even afraid to walk in the street.

One day, I was traveling home on a bus. During the ride, a middle-aged man with a red star of distinction did not take his eyes off me. When I left the bus, he followed and confronted me.

"Do you believe in G-d?"

"Yes," I answered.

"Fascist!" he shrieked. "In your prayers you say, 'Who gives salvation to kings'? Do you want a czar in Russia again?"

He continued to rant as inquisitive passersby congregated around me.

"Why did you start up with me?" I asked him. "What do you want from me?"

I turned away trembling. Would he order me to follow him? Luckily, he left me alone.

When I got home, my wife asked, "Why are you so pale?"

"I'm not feeling well," I said to spare her unnecessary worry.

I got used to people deriding me in the street. One night, while sitting at the station waiting for a bus, a gang of Jewish youths fell upon me and pulled my beard, leaving me a souvenir of painful wounds. Thank G-d, the bus arrived and I was able to escape.

Life lacked all joy. *Shabbos* meant being imprisoned in the house. At work, keeping *Shabbos* became a terrifying ordeal. What excuse could I give if my employers found out I didn't work on *Shabbos*? Should I forestall their anger by admitting to it now? What if they informed on me?

The number of worshippers who regularly attended *shul*, dwindled to almost none. In the Prevozna and Kehilas Yaakov *shuls*, only elderly people came. No one dared to start a conversation. We went to *shul* to daven, but we always knew there were spies there. In a way, talking to another worshipper wouldn't matter, since they knew the business of everyone who attended, anyway.

I remember coming to *shul* once, and seeing Reb Pinchas the son of Reb Moshele Twersky, a great *tzaddik* and an old friend of my family. He sat a couple of benches away, opposite me. I snatched a few minutes of conversation with him by lowering my head and pretending to read the *siddur*. All this, just for a few words!

The day we dreaded arrived.

In February 1938, we heard the news that Sholom, my wife's brother, had been arrested in Berdichev. A few weeks later, on March 4, *Rosh Chodesh Adar Sheni*, his brother Avraham was celebrating a *siyum* on *Mishnayos*, as he did once a month, with more than forty elderly people attending. He was the only young man among them. That night he was also taken away by the G.P.U.

The next day at work I heard two workers talking.

"Did you hear what happened last night?" one said.

"They rounded up the Rabbis of Odessa and took them to the G.P.U.!"

"Why?"

"Because they're really counterrevolutionaries. Those hypocrites go around like holy men, while in reality they're spies working for England. Now they'll get what they deserve."

I was sitting apart. In my heart, I wept, "Master of the World! Please forgive me for not saying a word to defend the honor of those holy and righteous men!"

Those workers did not know that one of them was my brother-in-law. I often heard people abusing religious Jews, but I never spoke up. By being silent, I hoped to gain another day or two of not desecrating *Shabbos* or another few days of life itself. Although we all knew how precarious our situation was, when Avraham was taken, it shook the family deeply.

12 SANCTIFYING THE NAME

AVRAHAM WAS AS WISE AND BELOVED AS MY FATHER- in-law. He had followed in Reb Zusia's path, maintaining an open house. He spoke beautifully and had a handsome, royal bearing. When he had reached marriageable age, he was offered dozens of *shidduchim* with the daughters of wealthy and Rabbinic families. He rejected them all. He married the daughter of a merchant of average means, who had steadfastly observed Torah and never sent his children to Soviet schools.

Avraham had six sons, the oldest being Aaron Nachman, whom his father and I dearly loved. The pleasant-mannered Aarele was brilliant and carried himself with grace and refinement. In addition, he was strikingly handsome. Avraham had invested time and effort into educating this son particularly, bringing him to a level of learning and fear of G-d rarely found in youths his age, anywhere. I heard that at his *bar-mitzvah*, he had delivered an outstanding discourse. I used to learn with him frequently.

While growing up, Aarele and his brothers accepted the fact that they were different from other children. Until age six, they would play in the courtyard with everyone, but afterwards, they knew they had to begin learning Torah seriously. From that age onward, they stayed in the house and learned secretly. Their parents almost never let them leave the house and courtyard. The dangers from outside were too real to be taken lightly.

Aarele and his brothers were infused with an indomitable trust in G-d, and were completely dedicated to Torah and *mitzvos*. Although the older ones were only in their early teens, they did not swerve an inch from the path of Torah. They had *peyos* and would not walk four steps without wearing *tzitzis* and a *yarmulka*; and they put on a *gartl* every time they *davened*. They never missed praying, morning and evening, and they would go to *shul* with pride. Everyone eyed them, including the malicious agents of the G.P.U. Jewish children in the street would taunt and throw stones at them. I saw some of the incidents myself. One child threw a stone at Aarele and blood gushed from the wound. We passed a group of girls in the street, one of them spat in his face. All the sons suffered such abuse.

Even after their father was seized, they didn't change. They continued to *daven* in *shul* morning and night and, without their father to teach them, they still learned Torah as much as possible. Avraham's wife Sarah got a job in a factory, spinning threads, to bring some food into the house. Almost no one dared to visit them, since everyone in Odessa knew that the G.P.U. kept a strict watch on their house. I decided, though, that come what may, I would visit them. I came as often as possible, to speak with them and keep their spirits up, but it was too dangerous to teach them there. The law prohibited teaching religion to anyone under the age of eighteen except for one's own children. Therefore, they would come to my house, ostensibly to visit their grandmother, and then I taught them *Gemara*. My mother-in-law would lock the door of the house and sit next to it outside. If an unwanted guest came, she would tell him that the house was locked and the key was with her daughter who had gone out and had not returned yet. Sometimes, we put dominoes and dice on the table. If the doorbell rang, we would hide the

Gemaras immediately, and the children would begin playing games.

The same night that Avraham was arrested, eight other religious communal figures in Odessa disappeared, including Rav Fishman, Rav Shmuel Dembo, Chazan Tevel and the *gabbaim* of several *shuls*. We had no illusions that we would ever see them again yet our spirits were completely shattered when we heard the outcome a few weeks later from someone who had ties with the G.P.U. The Rabbis had officially been given lengthy sentences in Siberia, but in fact, the authorities had decided to stand them in front of a firing squad. None of us had the heart to tell this to the children.

After both my brothers-in-law were arrested, one of the Rabbis began to rebuke us for the untenable position we had taken. He pointed out that by remaining so stubborn, we would only incite the G.P.U. to further action against us. One man who kept *Shabbos* expressed the opinion that my brother-in-law should not have risked his life by witholding his children from the Soviet schools. He had forfeited his own life by this action, he said, and it was about time we learned our lesson and enrolled them. "All the Jews have submitted," argued another. "Why should your children be any different from the children of other Rabbis?"

Another man approached me and said, "Let me tell you a parable. Once a Jew in a small town wanted to show everyone that he was very devout. What did he do? He sat on a stone, fasted and afflicted himself day after day. Everyone who passed by saw him and exclaimed, 'What strength he has! This must be a holy man!' These people strengthened his resolve to continue. Then along came someone practical, who admonished him, 'Are you crazy? Why are you doing this?' Everyone praised your brother-in-law for his self-sacrifice over his children's education. That's why he stuck to his wrongheaded ways. It's too late for him, but don't you be foolish too! Forget all these ideals of yours. Don't you know everyone is laughing at you?"

I heard this kind of criticism countless times, often from very learned people. My brothers-in-law had not maintained their convictions for their own glorification. Quite the contrary, they simply refused to bow to the idol of Communism, whatever the cost would be. Raised by unflinching ideals, their children never left their path, even in the most harrowing times.

I could not escape this kind of demoralizing talk, even in *shul*. Once I went to *daven*, and I saw Aarele standing in a corner of the *shul*. He was speaking with an elderly Jew who had come to Odessa to collect money secretly. Drawing near, I heard the man say, "Why do you carry on like this? You grow *peyos* and wear a *gartl* during prayers. Don't you see what they did to your father? Look, you're already an adult. Who will want to marry you the way you act?"

In the midst of his tirade, he turned and saw me standing there, whereupon he began to berate me as well.

"Let me tell you an insightful interpretation that I heard years ago in the name of Rav Yoel Shurin, the Iluy of Zevihl," I answered him. "It's on a passage in *Malachi* (3:14-16). 'You have said, It is useless to serve G-d. What have we gained by keeping His charge and walking in abject awe of the Lord of Hosts? And so, we account the arrogant happy, they have indeed done evil and endured, they have indeed dared G-d and escaped. In this vein have those who revere the Lord been talking to one another. The Lord has heard and noted it, and a scroll of remembrance has been written at His behest concerning those who revere the Lord and esteem His Name.'

"The meaning of these words," I continued, "is that a time will come when men will ask, 'What's the use of keeping *mitzvos*? Why should we endure so much for them?' Now, if ignorant people say this, the situation is still bearable, but if 'those that fear G-d' speak to each other in this fashion, then 'G-d will listen and hear,' and He will surely have mercy on those who mention Him and hold His Name in esteem. If even people like you talk this way, then surely my nephew deserves great credit for his steadfastness."

The man had no answer and left. He did not mean harm; he only pitied us. He thought we carried the ideal of *Kiddush Hashem* too far.

On one side we were attacked by the non-believing, and on the other side, even the religious would not support us. Reality, of course, seemed to be undeniably against us. What hope could we have for the future by clinging to Judaism? Who was left in Russia that believed as we did? Indeed, from where would Aarele and his brothers find their partners in life?

It was our deep trust in G-d that made us stand firm. We knew we had to learn Torah and keep *mitzvos* right now. Hashem would take care of the future as He saw fit. It was those who lacked or fell short in this conviction who yielded to the Communists and became lost to Judaism.

After my brothers-in-law had disappeared, the entire family suffered repercussions, including myself. I remember returning home once to hear two neighbors talking, "Is he still walking around free? When will they finally take him to prison?" I knew they were talking about me.

My brothers-in-law in Kiev went through worse. Reb Yaakov, who was my father-in-law Reb Zusia's third son, lived in Kiev. On the record, he worked a knitting machine in his home. Actually his wife did the work, while he was an unofficial *Rav*. He answered questions and made his house open like his brothers-in-law. When Sholom and Avraham were seized, he was afraid the G.P.U. would discover what he was doing and arrest him too. Since, officially, he was not a Rabbi, he looked for a job at which he would not have to work on *Shabbos*. He found a cemetery job in Kiev. My second brother in law, Mordechai Sternberg, a very learned man, also lived in Kiev and worked in a knitting factory. Thank G-d, he now lives in Israel together with his family.

We, in Odessa, kept in contact through my mother-in-law, who corresponded regularly with him. Once I saw her receive a letter from Reb Yaakov and write an answer with bitter tears. I thought she was crying because of the family's recent tragedies. Three years later, when Reb Yaakov and I were together, he told me what had happened. He had been writing weekly but, with the pressures of his cemetery job, he found time only once every two weeks. He excused himself, writing that he was so busy that he didn't have one day to himself. His righteous mother misunderstood that he was working on *Shabbos*, and immediately sent off her anguished reply, "My dear child, why do you no longer keep *Shabbos*? How is it that you've become afraid? Your brothers weren't afraid to die for the sanctification of G-d's Name! Your father, who loved you and took pride in you, made countless sacrifices for Judaism! And now you're afraid? You've begun to work on *Shabbos*? I will never forgive you."

Reb Yaakov answered, "What is my sin? Why do you suspect me? I would never work on *Shabbos*. I've corresponded less only because of the pressures of my job during the week."

The G.P.U. did not leave Reb Yaakov and Reb Mordechai alone. In 1939, the two were summoned and threatened that if they wanted to live securely, they had to become informers, reporting every word they heard in *shul*, and from their friends . . . or else. Both men answered that they had to think it over, but of course, they did not submit. Reb Yaakov assessed his perilous situation and fled. He traveled south to the Georgian Republic and wandered for a year. Finally, worn out and sick, he came back in 1941, not to Kiev, where he was a wanted man, but to Odessa.

"If they take me, they take me," he told us. "I can't bear it any longer."

Reb Mordechai remained in Kiev. One night, he woke up suddenly and heard men in the courtyard asking, "Where does Sternberg live?" That was it. In his pajamas, he jumped out the back window and spent the next year and a half in hiding in Kiev. The danger was so great that he would not go outside to use the common bathroom.

We had another brother-in-law in Odessa, Reb Dov Slabodianski, whose father had been a *Rav* in Chmelnik. Married to Reb Zusia's oldest daughter, he made his living as a watchmaker and, fortunately, was left alone.

As the days went on, we heard more and more reports of terror against religious Jews all over Russia. There had been a large Jewish community in Uman consisting of about a hundred Breslover *Chassidic* families, whom the authorities inexplicably had not bothered all these years. Indeed, when police found a Jewish man wandering in the fields, engrossed in solitary meditation, they would leave him alone if he identified himself as a Breslover *Chassid*. They all wore *peyos* and *Chassidic* garb, never sent their children to government schools and maintained all the facilities necessary for a religious congregation. But now their hour had also come.

In 1937-38, Stalin appointed Yezhov as the Minister of the Interior (i.e. head of the N.K.V.D.) and charged him with eradicating Trotskyites and other "counterrevolutionaries." Yezhov particularly persecuted the few Jewish communities that still remained religious on the grounds that their activities were counterrevolutionary.

All the Rabbis who registered as such were arrested as spies, since in the "Soviet Democracy" a person could not be arrested for being a Rabbi. They also arrested the Chabad and Breslover *Chassidim* for teaching Torah, in spite of the fact that only a few very brave individuals were involved in the teaching effort and even these did it only on a very small scale.

They also arrested professionals of all kinds, even generals in the armed forces and people who had devoted a large part of their lives to fight for the communist cause. Officially, the sentence was ten years in prison without permission to communicate with their families. In truth, however, all of them were killed in prisons and camps and were never heard from again.

Providentially, Rabbi Levi Yitzchak Bender, the head of the Breslover *Chassidim*, and his friend Rabbi Elie Chaim Rosen were arrested two years earlier for disseminating religious propaganda and were thus unexpectedly saved from execution during Yezhov's purges. At the time of their arrest, they were taken from Uman to Kiev by the N.K.V.D. in a sealed van, and a heavy dossier of charges as counterrevolutionaries was levied against them. However, the chief prosecutor in Kiev had more than an inkling about the actual nature of the Breslover activities. He knew full well that these were very humble people who lived in dire poverty and knew nothing of politics, and thus, he decided to let them go.

"Do you have any relatives in Kiev?" the prosecutor asked before releasing them.

"No," they stammered, thinking that this was a most dangerous question, aimed at getting more people implicated.

"But do you know where the Kiev synagogue is located?"

"That we do know," they admitted.

So he ordered them to stay overnight at the *shul* and to come back the next day for their identity papers.

As they walked down the long corridors on their way out of the building, they were beset by the fear that they would be shot from behind, but to their astonished relief, they were actually allowed to go free. They stayed the night in the *shul* and in the morning, they mustered enough courage to return to the prosecutor's office.

"Here you are!" he said good-naturedly as he handed them their papers. "You can go home."

They did not, however, dare return to Uman and were, therefore, absent at the time of the purge. Rabbi Bender learned about the fate of the Uman community from its two surviving members, a shoe-maker and another man, both of whom had "proletarian" occupations which made them innocent even in the eyes of the N.K.V.D.

The shoemaker was Reb Nachman Stracks, who later gained notoriety as the grandfather of Yossele Shumacher. From his meager earnings, he supported starving *Chassidic* Jews at the risk of being accused of supporting "counterrevolutionaries," a capital offense. Many years later, in London, I met one of his grandchildren, who serves as a teacher of Talmud in a Jewish day school.

The two sole survivors of Uman reported that Reb Yaakov Kaufman, one of the leading members of the Breslover group, was tortured in an attempt to force him to sign a statement that the entire group was engaged in a conspiracy against the government. Of course, he persistently refused to sign anything that would implicate his beloved brethren. His interrogators lowered him bare-foot into a freezing cellar for several days, until his feet froze solid. Not surprisingly, his feet became infected and were amputated in order to keep him alive and continue torturing him to confess.

Reb Yaakov Kaufman did not survive his ordeal. He departed this world as a saint, just as he had lived in it. It was said of him that when relatives from abroad used to send him money, he would give it away to others. One snowy Friday afternoon, he came upon a funeral of a woman who had died of starvation and was about to be buried without a burial shroud. Disregarding the freezing weather, he took off the clean undershirt which he had already put on for *Shabbos*, so that the woman could be buried according to the Jewish custom.

My sister and her husband Lazar, who lived in Moscow at the time, also had their lives ripped apart during those years. Some men came looking for my brother-in-law, but getting wind of the "visitors", he fled and spent a long time living as a hunted animal. He could not even risk visiting his wife and children, let alone come home.

In 1939, after the purges had let up because of the war in Poland, my father finally returned to our hometown of Krasnostav. He took my sister and her children home for *Pesach* to alleviate her pain. She agreed to stay on for a while.

In 1940, I suggested that she go back to her home in Moscow to be nearer to the places where her husband was hiding and closer to the friends and relatives who could help her. Unfortunately, she ignored my advice and was still in Krasnostav when the Germans invaded. She lost her life together with all the Jews of Krasnostav, who were all murdered on the same day, the sixth of Elul, 1941.

In light of such fearsome persecutions, almost no *yeshivos* still existed. There was one small underground Chabad *yeshivah* in Berdichev that held out somehow. In 1937, the Communists uncovered it and exiled its eighteen-year-old *Rosh Yeshivah*, Rav Moshe Karelevitcher, to ten years in Siberia. Its twelve students, who were thirteen and fourteen years old, were placed in a non-Jewish Soviet orphanage. The boys refused to eat anything besides bread and water, and they steadfastly kept *Shabbos*. The director of the orphanage relaxed his guard over the boys on *Shabbos*, because he understood that they would not run away or travel on *Shabbos*.

One fifteen-year-old boy, Chanoch Rappaport, had been absent when the Communists took the *yeshivah* students into custody. He returned to Berdichev with a plan. He lay in wait one Friday night when the boys were taking a walk. When he saw no one was with them, Chanoch slipped out of his hiding place. Their rescue from the Communists was unquestionably a matter of life and death, he told them, which permits desecration of *Shabbos*. They fled to the train station, where a train was preparing to leave for Kharkov. Each boy entered a different coach, and when they reached their destination, all went into hiding, leaving no trace behind. After this *yeshivah* was disbanded, only one *yeshivah* was left in all of Russia, a small Chabad *yeshivah* in Georgia, which lasted until World War II.

This story was told to me by Rabbi Chanoch Rappaport. A few years later he was also arrested and imprisoned for fifteen years, which left him as an invalid. He came to Moscow after the war ended and later was allowed to leave for Israel together with his family.

13 SERVICE IN THE ARMY

A YEAR AFTER MY WEDDING, SHORTLY AFTER MY daughter Devorah was born, I was ordered to go into the army reserves. On Sunday, July 1, 1938, I arrived at the training camp. We, the soldiers, spent the morning doing calisthenics and then returned to the base for lunch. I spent the lunch break walking around from room to room, so that no one would notice that I was not eating. Suddenly I heard a shout.

"Chazan!" an army officer called out. "Where are you going? Why aren't you eating?"

"I am eating."

"Where?"

"I mean I already ate."

His lip curled. "You did not eat. Now you'll come with me, and we will eat together."

We were served two hot dishes of *treif* meat. He sat opposite me, took a spoonful and began eating.

"Take your spoon," he ordered.

I sat silent, not knowing what to do. I prayed, Hashem save me!

"Come on," he barked, "Eat! Eat! Are you trying to get out of the army? You will get the punishment you deserve! Eat right this minute!"

I decided that come what may I would not eat. "I don't feel well. I have a stomachache, and I can't eat."

"Oh, really? You're sick, are you? You're not sick!" he thundered. "Eat!"

I was silent.

"All right, what hurts you?" he said.

"My stomach," I said.

He saw that I was adamant. "Very well, we will have your problem checked out. I'm sending you to the hospital. If you are healthy, I will bring you immediately to court. And you know what that means."

"Fine," I said, inwardly terrified.

He finished eating and wrote me an application to the hospital with a closed letter. He glared at me as I left.

"Bring me an answer," he said.

The hospital received patients in the late afternoon. The entire afternoon I did nothing but run and drink gallons of water. When I entered the hospital, my heart was pounding.

A Jewish doctor checked me and asked in alarm, "What's wrong with you? Where do you live?"

I answered him and he gave me a closed note. When I went back to the army, I found out that it said that I was unhealthy and unfit for army duty. I was sent back home.

That was only the beginning of my encounters with the army.

When Germany invaded Russia in June, 1941, Stalin commanded all eligible men to register for the draft, on penalty of death. My brother-in-law Reb Yaakov Freidman and I registered, and we were drafted on July 6. Most men who reported to the draft board were dispatched to their battalion after a day, but I was held at army headquarters in Odessa for two weeks.

During this time, a number of officers had been pressuring me to shave off my beard, but of course, I would not consider it. Then one day, I was ordered to appear at an office. Two burly soldiers forced me into a seat and held my hands down, while a third sloppily cut off most of my beard with a scissors. Then they let me go. If they thought I would even out the scraggy edges afterwards, they were mistaken.

Then the officer in charge said, "Now you look like a real good fellow."

I answered him, "I did not do it. It was done to me by force."

On *Motzei Shabbos*, July 26, we left from Odessa to the Black Sea in three big ships, the *Gruzia* with seven thousand soldiers, the *Voroshilov* with six thousand and the *Lenin* with three thousand. On our way through Sebastopol in Crimea, where the three ships rested through the night, we suddenly heard a loud noise. The *Lenin* had been sunk and only two-hundred-fifty soldiers survived.

Yaakov and I traveled on the *Gruzia*. We landed in Mariupol on the sea of Azov. There were only two or three religious Jews on the ship, and we *davened* in the bow among seven thousand soldiers, wearing our *tefillin*. No one bothered us. In Mariupol, we had to camp under the open sky. That night there was a heavy rain, and the ground became drenched, while the dew covered us in the morning. A miracle occurred, though, and not one of the thousands of soldiers became sick.

During the next few weeks, we were moved from one camp to another in preparation for the front. All this time, I tried to think of ways to get out of army duty. Since I was drafted, I had eaten the barest minimum of bread and water (not touching the *trief* meat), hoping that my thin, weak appearance would exempt me. I did not understand why I should be separated from my family, be forced to live on a starvation diet, only to face almost certain death at the front. And all this for a "homeland" that was oppressing me!

The menace I faced was that I might be forced to eat *treif* in order to stay alive and then, only to die at the front with a mouth defiled by *treif* food. For the same reason, I wore a big sized *tallis katan*; if I were to fall at the front, then let me at least be laid in the earth with a properly sized *tallis*.

I knew that Krasnostav was already in the hands of the Nazis, being close to the border. I did not yet realize, however, how extensive their mass-murder plan for Jews was. Our memory of Germans from the First World War was of saviors from pogroms. This time around, however, and three months after the Nazi entry into Ukraine, the Krasnostav Jews were, in fact, murdered *en masse*.

A few weeks before *Rosh Hashanah*, our platoon was moved to another camp in Mariupol. Our commander told us he had to go and would return in a few hours. In the meantime, we walked about the town. As I passed a street, I noticed a health clinic. Entering, I asked to be checked by the doctor of internal medicine, a woman about thirty years old, who looked Jewish and whose name also was Jewish.

"What's your problem?" she asked.

"I have pains in the heart."

She took her stethoscope and examined me. "I don't find one thing out of order."

"But if I'm healthy, why am I so thin?"

"Maybe," she said, "the problem is with your lungs?"

"When I was a child, I had trouble with my lungs, but for many years now they haven't bothered me."

She then asked, "What do you want to achieve? To be cured or to be exempt from the army?"

"I am not trying to get out of the army," I said. "I am all alone here and have nowhere to go. But since I am weak, I would like not to have to do the strenuous exercises. I'd like to do lighter duties."

"If that's the case, I'll send you for a lung examination in the opposite building."

"Take off your shirt," the next doctor, a woman in her forties, ordered. I removed my shirt together with my woolen *tallis katan*. I did this in a manner attempting to hide the *tallis katan*, so that the gentile lady should not ask questions.

"What's that?" the doctor asked.

"I wear this for added warmth."

"You do not! This is an *arba kanfos*." The second doctor was Jewish, too!

"Excuse me, you're right," I said. "That's what it is."

The doctor examined me with a stethoscope and an X-ray machine and said, "Your breathing is perfectly fine. I can't find anything wrong with you."

"But my heart bothers me," I complained.

"Enough!" she snapped.

I was about to go, when she told me to wait, because she wanted to do an X-ray. She and another woman took the X-ray, and then checked the results carefully.

I heard them whispering, "He is in perfect shape." I started to go, but she told me, "Wait a minute."

My mouth went dry. This doctor understood that I was looking for an excuse to get out of army duty. Maybe she would inform on me to my commander and tell him I was trying to desert!

She wrote out a note and gave it to me. I walked out disappointed and worried. I sat down on a wooden platform in front of shops, peering at the note. Unaware to me, a non-Jew was reading over my shoulder. He called out in wonder, "You're sick?"

He had spotted the word "tuberculosis."

"Yes," I answered ecstatically.

The note declared that I was sick with a latent case of tuberculosis. I walked down the street greatly encouraged. In the merit of my *tallis katan* the Jewish doctor had given me a note that might yet save my life.

The next day, all the draftees had to line up.

The commander called out, "Whoever is unhealthy, raise your hand."

I raised my hand, as did tens of others. All of us were brought to a new camp. After three days, a commander from the previous camp showed up to look over the "invalids."

"You're all draft evaders," he shouted at us. He asked each of us what our problem was. To all our symptoms he gave a uniform diagnosis. "Liar! Deserter!"

Anyone who lacked conclusive proof of his malaise was put on one side. Nearly everyone ended up there. When my turn came, I showed him the note that the doctor had given me. He looked at it and sent me to the doctor-in-command in the camp. He arranged for a young army doctor with X-ray equipment to examine me. This doctor pronounced me completely healthy.

I had to deliver the results of the examination to the doctor of the camp. I decided to wait a few days. Perhaps the commanding doctor would forget the details of my case, and to which X-ray doctor he had sent me. Meanwhile, I went back to the health clinic in town.

"Comrade doctor," I said. "Please do me a favor and give me another note. My commander took away the note you gave me."

The doctor complied and wrote me out another one.

After a few days, I went to see the doctor of the camp. Before knocking on his door, I ate a sharp onion and smoked a few strong cigarettes. I felt nauseous and looked ashen. Just as I entered his room, I began to vomit.

"What's the matter?" the doctor asked with concern.

"I'm sick and cannot digest my food," I explained weakly. "I tried to drink some milk and eat a piece of bread, but even that won't go down."

I showed him the note from the doctor of the tuberculosis unit. As I had hoped, he forgot he had sent me to the army doctor. Owing to the note and my sorry appearance, he sent me to a medical board who heard the details of my case and granted me a month's vacation. The papers confirming the vacation were not given to me, but I was told they would be sent straight to my commanding officer. This made me uneasy, since every day troops were being sent to the front, and soon it would be my platoon's turn.

Every day I went to the office to inquire if the papers had come, but the answer was always, "No."

The day arrived when my troop was to be sent to the front. We lined up and a new officer took command. It was getting dark when we began to march to a depot to receive new uniforms. On the way we met a few captains who had just come from the depot. They told us to go back because the electricity could not be used after dark and it would be impossible to distribute the clothes in the dark. We returned to our base.

The next morning we were lined up again to begin the march. In the last few minutes that we had, I decided to try again and see if the office had received my confirmation for a month's vacation. I knew, though, that my commanding officer would be unsympathetic. How could I leave the line?

"Comrade officer, I need to use the bathroom."

"Go quickly", he commanded.

I ran to the office and asked the clerk if permission had come through for those who were supposed to get vacations. It had just arrived that morning! I asked him for the document confirming my vacation. The rule, however, was that the papers could be released only if the commanding officer requested them. My officer who had made sure my army stay wasn't overly comfortable would certainly not go out of his way to help me. He would only push me off with an excuse, like "Come with us now and when I get the notice personally, I'll bring you back from the front." In that case, all would be lost.

I thought fast and told the clerk, "Comrade, my commanding officer says he doesn't know how to phrase the request. Please write down the proper formula, and I'll give it to him."

The clerk obliged. I took it and went to my commandant. At that moment, he was speaking with another officer.

When I came close, the second officer snapped, "What do you want?"

I gave him the note. He did not understand what was written inside.

"What's this?" he asked me.

"I don't know. They gave me this in the office."

The second officer told my officer, "Listen, go to the office and find out what this means."

My officer took the note and ran to the office, while I followed close behind.

He asked the clerk, "What did you give him?"

"Comrade officer," said the clerk, "Chazan has a month's vacation. He is sick. Let him rest."

The officer glared at me suspiciously over his shoulder.

"Since when are you so sick?" he growled.

I told him indignantly that I had tuberculosis and had been suffering for years.

Suddenly, he had pity on me and said, "Don't worry. You'll get your month's vacation, and if you're still feeling bad, you can ask for an extension until you're healthy. Afterwards, you can come back to us."

As I was leaving, he warned me to report back to the base after the month's vacation was over.

What a turnaround. A week before, I had discussed with Yaakov what to do with the two hours we had off every week. *Rosh Hashanah* would soon be here. Should we use those precious hours to hear the *shofar* on *Yom Tov*, or go into the nearby city to make *hataras nedarim* (annulment of vows) before *Rosh Hashanah*? Now I had a month's vacation! When I left, Yaakov wept bitterly, and I also wept at leaving him. It was the last time I saw my brother-in-law. Shortly afterwards, he was killed at the front.

I wanted to use this month to return to my wife and children in Odessa, but the area was closed off because the Germans were advancing toward the city. I decided to travel to Saratov, far from the front lines, where I knew Jews were. Boarding a freight train filled with Jews from Odessa who were fleeing from the Germans, I found a person I knew among them, a G-d-fearing, learned Jew. Since it was Friday, we began to discuss whether travelling on *Shabbos* was permitted under the circumstances. I concluded that the need to desecrate *Shabbos* was not that pressing.

The train had just stopped at Lisk and was beginning to pull out, when I jumped off the coach. I had been considering spending *Shabbos* in the train station and resuming my journey Saturday night but the unbearable crowding in the station made it impossible. Many refugees had been milling around, waiting to squeeze themselves into the few meters of empty space available on each train. I already regretted having left my place on the train. Just then, German planes appeared from nowhere and bombed the city, many bombs falling nearby. The refugees ran for cover.

Two minutes later, a small train rolled in, whose destination was Voronezh. I recalled that a family named Shiff, related to the Iluy of Zevihl, lived in this town. The father, a *shochet*, had been visiting the Iluy when World War I broke out and had found a job through my father. He also lived with us until the war ended. I decided to travel to Voronezh.

Arriving half an hour before *Shabbos*, I hurriedly squeezed off the train. I immediately gave my small bundle to the station's package department. I spent the night in the station, going to town in the morning.

In the street I saw a religious Jew.

"Good *Shabbos*," I greeted him.

"Good *Shabbos*," he answered. "How are you?"

"Tell me, where is there a *minyan*?"

"There is no *minyan* here. I've been here for three months, and there is absolutely no *minyan*."

"Would you please let me *daven* in your house? I just arrived in the city. I have my own food. I just need a place to *daven* on *Shabbos*, and to say *Selichos* tonight."

"I-I'm living with a relative who has a very small house," the Jew stammered. "I myself take up too much room."

He quickly walked away.

I understood his fears. I was still dressed in my army uniform. Later I met more Jews and received the same type of terse response. Finally, I saw an old Jew with a flowing beard and *peyos*. His coat was so bulky around the neck that I knew he must be wearing a *tallis*. I had no doubt that he was on his way to some underground *minyan*.

I approached him and said, "Good *Shabbos*."

He answered my greeting and asked, "Where are you from?"

"From Krasnostav."

He broke into a smile. "I'm from Luber!" This was a town not far from us.

"I'm the son of Rav Chazan from Krasnostav."

"Why, I knew your father and also your grandfather!"

We began a friendly conversation.

Finally I asked him, "Where is the *minyan* here?"

"There is none."

"Look," I spoke earnestly. "It's been six weeks that I haven't prayed with a *minyan*. And tonight we begin to say *Selichos*. Do me a favor and tell me where everyone gets together to *daven*. I know there must be a *minyan*."

This time he couldn't refuse. "All right. Follow me at a distance, and watch which door I enter. But don't come in right after me, or I'll be blamed for divulging the secret. Very few people know about this *minyan*."

I entered a few minutes after he did. All the worshippers stared at me in fear. "Who is this man? How did this soldier find us? Who told him about our *minyan*?"

"Don't worry," I assured them. "I'm a Jew who follows the Torah. I saw religious Jews entering here, and I realized that there must be a *minyan*."

"Don't tell anyone about us," they pleaded. "We only organized this *minyan* for a few days, that's all."

The room was narrow and dark. I asked for and was given a *tallis*. It was wonderful to be able to *daven* with a *minyan* after all this time.

After the service, an old friend whom I found there, Reb Yochanan, invited me to his house for the *Shabbos* meal. I spent all of *Shabbos* there, and my host went out of his way to make me comfortable. He told me that my father's friend, Shiff, was still alive, almost ninety-years-old. I went to visit him on Sunday. After introducing myself, he fell upon me emotionally.

"Thank G-d that your father merited such a son!"

We spoke for a long time, and I explained what had led me to him. The major problem before me was to get a complete army exemption. He advised me to speak with his nephews Tzvi and Zev Slavin. They outdid themselves in doing good deeds and favors, and they had influence with government offices.

"Maybe they can help you out."

At eight o'clock that evening, I set out for their house. Bombs were falling all over the city which was in total blackout. All I could hear was the thunder of the bombs and fire crackling. There was smoke in all directions.

I managed to find the Slavins' address. They opened the door and brought me to an inner room where a faint light flickered. Before me was an elderly Jew and his two young sons sitting and learning *Sanhedrin* (a tractate of the Talmud). I felt transported and spoke at length with the elderly man and his two sons, as they listened carefully to my problem.

"We will look for a way to obtain your complete release," he said, "and until we find it, you will live with us."

I accepted his hospitality, slept and ate at their home. I continued to eat minimally, though, in case I should have to undergo new medical examinations. The few weeks I spent at the Slavins, enabled me to witness their exemplary good-heartedness and fine qualities. During the war years, many Jews were wandering from city to city. These refugees had been forced to flee on the spot, and had nothing but the clothes on their backs. The Slavins used to arrange places for them to eat and sleep and tried to provide for their other needs as well. I remember one *Shabbos* night, when the old man was at the table about to make *kiddush*, when suddenly he put the cup down.

"I can't make *kiddush*," he said, "until I know that those refugees in the basement nearby have food."

We left the house to attend to them. Only after all the people were taken care of did he return home and begin the *Shabbos* meal. His wife was his helpmate in all he did, and her care of me and countless others was outstanding.

His tremendous trust in G-d was expressed in his resourcefulness. Since it was impossible for government employees to keep *Shabbos*, the Slavins had set up their own weaving factory, which was overseen by the authorities. The family employed Russian workers all week, but on *Shabbos*, no one worked—not even the gentiles (as required by Jewish law)—because every week the Slavins blew the fuse. Although the workers had to be present, in actuality they did no work. They always had an excuse ready should a supervisor show up and see their inactivity.

As the war continued to rage, I finally received my precious exemption from the army. A relative of the Slavins, who had graduated from medical school, had begun to work in the tuberculosis department at a clinic. He wrote out a confirmation of my unhealthy state. I needed a second confirmation from the army doctor in the draft board. The Slavins found the way to this doctor, too. Undoubtedly, he had to present the doctor with a generous gift, but ordinarily even that would not have helped, since doctors, like everyone else, were afraid of being caught doing illegal activity.

It happened, though, that the government offices received instructions from Moscow to evacuate the city, which seemed likely to fall to the Germans. Since the draft board had to liquidate its records, the army doctor felt safe enough to oblige us. The exemption he gave me saved my life and enabled me to return to my family.

Behind me lay a period where, in quick succession, G-d had led me from one miracle to another. The doctor in the clinic who had seen my *tallis katan*, the blackout in the depot just before we were sent to the front, the train that just happened to be heading for Voronezh, the miraculous events that had led to my exemption from army duty, all had saved my life. Hashem, who had protected me from countless dangers, continued to sustain me.

14 SURVIVAL IN UZBEKISTAN

I HAD NO IMMEDIATE HOPE OF RETURNING TO MY wife and children, as Odessa had fallen to the Germans. My next consideration was to keep myself out of the grasp of the army. Hundreds of thousands of refugees at that time were streaming to the eastern Asiatic provinces of Russia. Besides being remote from the battlefront, the milder climate there improved chances for survival.

I boarded a freight train overflowing with refugees, which chugged onward for several weeks to Uzbekistan, a Soviet Republic north of Afghanistan. Regular passenger trains were all appropriated for army use. The congestion and inhuman conditions of the ride, however, didn't bother me as much as the idea of traveling to a strange destination, far from all the people I loved.

The train arrived in Tashkent, the capital of Uzbekistan. In the central station, I met a Jew from Odessa, who gave me news that made my heart soar. My family had left Odessa for Uzbekistan, although he did not know their exact whereabouts. One avenue I could try was the evacuation units, the Evakopunkt. This was a government office established to attend to the needs of the onrush of refugees. Its facilities, though, were not nearly adequate for the mountain of relief work required. Housing, jobs and food were in dire short supply. The native population was itself suffering from famine, and at the start of winter, it was hard to get a loaf of bread.

Seeing the long lines, all hopes sagged, since the amount of bread sold sufficed only for the lucky few at the beginning. Presently, however, food distribution became more efficiently organized and monthly ration cards were allotted to each inhabitant. The daily bread ration was only six hundred grams a worker and four hundred each for women and children. Furthermore, this was only given to a person who had living quarters. A person without official housing did not get anything, and it was impossible to buy other staples.

The problem of housing was just as acute. A man was considered lucky if he was able to get a room in a broken-down hut. Given these conditions, the Evakopunkt was certainly unable to keep a registry of refugees' whereabouts, and my visits to them yielded nothing.

I decided to try another city that had drawn thousands of refugees, Samarkand. Around *Chanukah* time, I found my brother-in-law, Reb Mordechai Sternberg, whom the N.K.V.D. had tried to arrest in Kiev, but he too did not know where my family was. He had been in hiding, but when the war broke out and refugees streamed to the East, he and his family fled with them.

After further searches, I heard that my wife was in Jizak. It seems that when the Germans arrived near Odessa, the Jews there were in a dilemma; they did not know whether they should remain in Odessa, in the belief that the Germans could not be much worse than the Russians, or to flee and not know where the next loaf of bread would come. Most Jews, hundreds of thousands, remained. My brother-in-law, Reb Baer Dov, who was exempt from the army, was terrified by the Germans' heavy bombardment of Odessa and decided to escape with his family. He took along with him my mother-in-law, my wife and our two children.

And then, I found her! But living under what conditions! Lacking medicine and living in an unhealthy lean-to, my son had succumbed to measles with complications and died. It was a crushing blow, and I was overcome with a terrible guilt and sadness. The news that I had a new daughter, Chaya Sarah, who was three weeks old, did little to ease the pain.

My mother-in-law was helping my wife, but after months of struggling for food and housing, they were no better off than when they had first arrived. It was winter, bitter cold, and they were housed in inhuman conditions, in a shed without windows, with an earthen floor on which the bedding lay in a corner.

Now I heard what had befallen our family since Yaakov and I had been drafted. My oldest brother-in-law Reb Dov, fearing the bombardment, decided to flee with his family to Uzbekistan. His wife refused to go without her mother, and my mother-in-law would not go since that would mean leaving my wife—pregnant, with two small children—alone in Odessa. My mother-in-law's youngest daughter and husband also journeyed to Uzbekistan, joining Reb Dov's family. Reb Mordechai was hiding underground in Kiev and decided he would be better off in the East. Yaakov's wife also came with her children, seeing that her brother-in-law was leaving Kiev.

Most of the family had left Kiev and Odessa. Only Sholom's wife had decided to remain in Berdichev, since it was too difficult to travel alone with her five children. Avraham's widow with her six boys also remained in Odessa. Her father had heard that many refugees were dying from the unbearable living conditions, and he did not want her to take the risk of traveling. Furthermore, they believed that if they remained, their husbands would come back home. All of them perished with the arrival of the Germans.

Finding no way to earn a living in Jizak, I decided to go to Samarkand myself and try to find a job and a small apartment. I arrived after *Purim*, 1942. There I met a man who promised to give me a job in the city of Tashkent that would provide me with an army postponement. A law at the time stipulated that if a person had an army exemption, and he went to another place, he had to do all the checkings with the draft board doctors all over again.

After we arrived, though, the man's plan fell through, which left me in a precarious position—a young man of draft age, without a job or an exemption. True, I had received an exemption in Voronezh, but the authorities were constantly having new call-ups, and exemptees had to appear for each examination. Worse yet, a law was passed that week stipulating that any man traveling between two cities had to get a permit from the G.P.U. If I applied for a permit, they would demand a new examination, from which I would probably be sent straight to the front.

I found a job in Tashkent making dishes for army use. Since I had experience with clay from my years in brickmaking, I was considered an expert in the field, which would entail registering my new address with the authorities. I worked at this job for a few months, too afraid to travel to my family and too poor to send them the fare to join me.

The day before *Yom Kippur*, I stepped out of my factory, heading for a room in which to *daven*. I walked straight into a police search. The police were combing the area for deserters, and they rounded up any man in sight. One ordered me to go with him, demanding to see my exemption. It was a year old.

"Aha!" he said. "Come with me to my commanding officer."

"I can go myself," I protested. "I have nothing to fear."

On my way to the commandant, I passed the door of our factory. The manager had been stationed there to prevent anyone from slipping in, but he recognized me.

"This fellow works for us," he told the officer, who then let me enter. I waited inside until the police had pushed the crowd past my factory. Heaving a sigh of relief, I dashed back to the room and started a heartfelt *Kol Nidrei*. How Hashem was continuing to watch over me!

After this brush with the police, I was more determined than ever to find work that would provide an official army exemption. A friend who was an engineer advised me to apply for a job at the huge Stalin Coal Industry, built on the Angren Shachstroy Mountain, one hundred and twenty kilometers from Tashkent.

Ever since Germany had seized the Russians' coal mines, Russia had been feverishly mining the Angren for its newly discovered coal reserves. An enormous complex of mines and factories was erected there, with tens of thousands of men and their families living and working on the premises. Someone was needed now to produce the huge quantity of dishes required by the workers. In Tashkent, I was merely one of many who knew how to make dishes, whereas, this friend argued, in the Stalin Coal Mining Complex, located in Angren, I would be considered a highly skilled worker filling an urgent need. He was in good position to know this, since from his Tashkent office, he was responsible for all that went on in Angren. Armed with his recommendation, I set out for Angren.

During the journey, I had to go out of my compartment for a moment, and when I came back to my seat, all my belongings were gone. These included my *tallis* and *tefillin*, from which I had never been separated since my *Bar Mitzvah*, some books and a loaf of bread. I was heartbroken at having lost my most precious belongings.

I arrived in Angren in the early afternoon with about fifty other people coming to work. The first thing on my mind was getting a pair of *tefillin*, and I pestered every Jew I met to find out whether he might have a pair. Soon, I was the laughingstock of the town with people inquiring derisively if I had yet found a pair of *tefillin*. It was therefore natural that, when an elderly lady made such an inquiry that I said, "Are you also making fun of me?"

"No," she said. "I am trying to help you. An old man died recently. His *siddur* was buried with him, but his *tefillin* remain with the family." She gave me an address in a nearby village, where I found a woman with two daughters.

"I'm sorry to hear you had a loss in the family," I began, "but I understand the *tefillin* remain with you. Can you please sell them to me?"

They firmly refused to part with this memento for any money in the world.

"I will leave you my identity papers as security," I said, "if you just lend them to me until I get a pair of my own."

"No!" they replied adamantly.

I pleaded that they would let me *daven* with them just once, on the spot. They became quite apprehensive and defensive, afraid to pass the *tefillin* into my hands. They called in a neighbor, also a Jew, who said to me, "If that's how they feel about their fond memento, then there is nothing that can be done.

As I began walking away, I heard them say to this neighbor, "This young man must be batty! Whoever needs *tefillin* nowadays?" It was a severe disappointment.

The dishwares workshop was located in a village called Ablik, about twelve kilometers from the Angren Works. It came together with a small dwelling which I could use all by myself. Since my boss let me set my own hours, I could keep *Shabbos* undisturbed.

Among the tens of thousands of laborers in the Angren Coal Works there were a number of Polish and Romanian Jewish refugees. All of them lived and worked in Angren, none in Ablik. There were not even any gentile Russians with whom to exchange a word in Russian. The people of this little village spoke only Uzbek.

On a Sunday, which was the market day, I strolled to the market where I spotted two men with heavy coats lying on the ground. After walking past, I glanced back at them. One of then winked and asked me in Yiddish whether I was a Jew. I was happy to meet them. One of them was from Tarnopol, an ex-merchant named Yosef Margulies, the other a baker from Lodz. I told them I was from Odessa.

"How are you getting along here?" Margulies asked.

"As G-d willed it," I replied.

"Are you really from Odessa? Does a Russian Jew speak about G-d?"

"Well," I said. "The same G-d who is over Poland is also over Russia."

Hearing this, Margulies pulled out a pair of *tefillin* from his coat pocket and said, "You see, I also believe in G-d."

I rejoiced, since for the previous two weeks I had been without *tefillin*.

The two men then told me that they had served in the army and contracted typhus. By the time they recovered and were dismissed from the hospital, they were discharged from the Russian army, because of an agreement with the Polish government in exile to form a Polish Army. However, when they reported to the Polish Army Headquarters they were sent away with some excuse I no longer remember. The truth was that the Poles did not want Jews in their army.

They found jobs guarding a bridge, which entitled them to a worker's ration of eight hundred grams of bread per day, but they had no place to stay. They were outdoors in the cold and snow, day and night. I was happy to let them share my premises at the shop.

To them, I was a life-saver. To me, they provided genial company and, most important, I could use Margulies's *tefillin*. After a while, Margulies, who had a travel permit, went to Tashkent and got me a pair of *tefillin*. I could have gone myself, but in order to return, I would have had to apply to the Tashkent N.K.V.D. I did not enjoy the prospect.

Next thing on my mind was saving enough to pay for train fare so that my wife and children could join me. My salary was barely enough to buy daily rations. My boss suggested I make a thousand dishes to sell on the black market. He would write off the missing materials as failed experiments. I took his advice and soon had the necessary money.

With the money in my pocket, I travelled to Tashkent, hoping to transfer to the train to Samarkand, where my family lived. As I got off in Tashkent, I began to feel feverish. Soon, my whole body was shaking. I could hardly walk. An elderly couple I knew from my youth took me in. I was very ill with high fever for a week, and I used up my entire savings on food and medicines.

I now had to decide whether to spend the little money I had on the ticket to Samarkand or to go back to Ablik and save up again. I went to the Machnovke Rebbe for advice, and he told me to go join my family. Unfortunately, I did not follow his advice and decided to go back to work, not wanting to come to my wife penniless. I was also afraid the Samarkand draft board, to which I was obliged to report, might reclassify me for combat. I went back to Ablik.

I subsequently regretted my decision not to obey the Rebbe's advice. As I later learned, the Chabad *Chassidim* in Samarkand had found a way to counterfeit Polish citizenship papers, and most of them left for Poland in 1946. I also firmly believe that had I followed the Rebbe's advice I also would have found a way out of the draft.

Four days after I returned to my job, a draft board visited the works to check worker's credentials. Although I was exempt from combat, they drafted me into the Labor Army which meant that, although I still had my job, my status was different. As a serviceman, I was now tied to my place of work and forbidden to travel.

When *Purim* came, the bread supply ran out and rations were not distributed. We had to borrow some bread (there were always "well-connected" people who had extra bread) for the *Purim* meal.

On one of his journeys to Angren, Margulies made a detour to the town of Akhangaran, the regional center. He met a Jew there and begged him for a *sefer* which would provide us with much needed food for the soul. The Jew gave him a little *Sefer Torah*, printed on paper, such as is held by children on *Simchas Torah*. The gift was on the condition that, should a *minyan* become possible, it would be read there. We rejoiced at having it, we could now sit after work, read from it and quote such commentaries as we could remember.

We now had to make preparations for *Pesach*. Margulies found seven hundred grams of flour with which we baked *matzoh* on *Erev Pesach* for the *Seder*. I made an earthen jug for a wine bottle and small earthen receptacles for glasses. Two weeks before *Pesach*, I set raisins in water in the jug to make wine for the *Seder*. We managed to get some potatoes, sugar beets and horseradish for *marror*. We also found some peas (which can be eaten on *Pesach* when other food is not available). I soaked the peas overnight after shelling them. To my great anguish, the next day I found a grain of wheat which had also soaked the whole night among the peas, making them entirely unfit for *Pesach*, and we threw away the whole lot. The three of us sat together at the *Seder*, saying whatever we remembered of the *Haggadah* by heart, since we did not have one.

On the second day of *Shavuos*, some sixty Jewish draftees were brought over by Margulies to be with us on the *Yom Tov*. They brought their own food, and we stayed together in the backyard of the shop. They left after *Shavuos*.

The problem of bringing my family to Ablik remained unresolved while another year passed; 1942 became 1943.

After saving all I could, I set out for Samarkand. My boss provided me with my travel documents. In Tashkent, I found out that tickets to Samarkand had to be ordered in advance. Unwilling to wait, I climbed onto the roof of the coach, ready to ride all the way, about six hours, hanging onto the smokestack. For this "luxury" I had to pay the conductor thirty rubles.

The train stopped in Jizak, where I met a Jew and asked him if he knew my brother-in-law, Reb Dov Slobodansky.

"Reb Dov?" he asked. "The one who just passed away?"

I was shocked. He was just thirty-three years old. "No!" I cried.

A third Jew saw my agitation. "It's nothing," he said. "He's lying."

In the meantime, another Jew passed by, and I inquired again. This man said softly, "He's dead. I was at his funeral two weeks ago."

I jumped off the train and rushed to my sister-in-law's house. My sister-in-law confirmed the sad news. I wept, completely heartbroken. I had loved Reb Dov so much! What a wonderful man! His kind deeds and good heart were unparalleled. I later heard that he provided food for students of a small Lithuanian *yeshivah,* who found themselves in Jizak, from his meager earnings as a watchmaker; otherwise, they would have starved. Now his thirteen-year-old son worked as a watchmaker to support the family.

I stayed that day in Jizak and then boarded the roof of another train to Samarkand. At long last, I was reunited with my wife and children, whom I brought back to Ablik with me.

Margulies, who worked in Angren, came to sleep in our premises at night. When the next *Purim* arrived he told us that a Sephardic Jew in Angren had a *Megillah.* We went to Angren to see this person, and a *minyan* was organized. We let the others put on our *tefillin* and said *Shema,* and we donned them ourselves during the service.

One man in his fifties refused to put on *tefillin.* He proclaimed that not having worn them for forty years he was not about to start now. I said to Margulies in a loud whisper that most likely the man did not know how to put them on and was ashamed to admit it. The man heard me and reacted, "Do you think I can't put on *tefillin?*"

I asked his forgiveness, but I still felt that I was right.

"What will you give me if I know how?" the man said.

Margulies had a bottle of vodka all ready for *Purim.* "I'll give you a bottle of vodka," he said.

The man took the *tefillin* and Margilies put the vodka on the table.

"But," I said to the man, "you must also make the blessings."

The man agreed. Margulies offered to buy the *mitzvah* of *tefillin* from him. "How much do you want?" he asked.

"Not for any price," the man replied. "Nor do I want vodka."

"And how long is it since you last put on the *tefillin*?" I asked.

"Haven't I told you?" he replied. "For forty years."

"Not true," I said triumphantly. "You have now broken your record. And if we make a regular *minyan*, will you join?" The question was hypothetical; it was impossible to organize a *minyan*.

"Yes," he said. "I'll come."

Following the services, Margulies gave each of us a drop of vodka.

Rosh Hashanah loomed next on the horizon, and I prepared a *shofar* from the horn of a ram. The Day of Judgment arrived and I blew for the nine of us who came. A tenth had also promised to be with us, but when I called at his house his wife said that on *Erev Rosh Hashanah* he'd gone off to Tashkent on business!

Erev Yom Kippur, I walked twelve kilometers to Angren, where one hundred Jewish families lived, and *davened* with the refugees. There was only one *machzor* and a paper *Sefer Torah*. I led *Kol Nidrei* and *Neilah*, the congregation repeating after me.

On *Yom Kippur*, I suggested to the Jews that they set up a secret *cheder* in Angren. They were willing, and the *cheder* was in action the next day. Reb Yosef Margulies taught the students at night.

All through 1943 we heard that the Russians were slowly driving the Germans from Russian territory. Nevertheless, rumors and exaggerated reports were so rife that no one was sure what they could believe. Living in Oblik, one heard virtually no news at all.

On *Shavuos*, Margulies received a two-week leave to Tashkent. When he returned, he related some shattering news.

"I went to *shul* in Tashkent," he said, "and there was a general who had taken a leave of absence from the battlefront; he had come to *shul* to say *Kaddish*. I asked him what was happening at the front. He said, 'We're advancing; we're pushing the Germans back.'

" 'How did the Jews fare in those parts?' I asked incidentally.

"He stared at me and then told me slowly, 'There are no Jews anywhere, my friend. Don't you know that the Nazis hunted them down and killed every single one? Millions of Jews are dead, murdered and shot down in death pits! Don't hope to find one relative alive! I'm saying *Kaddish* now, *Kaddish* for two million Jews!' "

My heart turned to stone. My parents. My brother and sister and their children. Aarele and his brothers. Sholom's wife and their children. I simply would not believe his report; the pain would be too much to bear. But then, my thoughts gradually warmed to the hope that some of them might have escaped the cruelty. Their likely fate, though, preyed on my mind for months. Fortunately, work occupied me.

I was able to avoid the army for a long time. Finally, one day, it caught up with me. They ran a check on all the factory's employees when my boss was not around, and this time, they found me able bodied. They immediately drafted me to the front. This occurred in the main office in Angren.

"Give me a short exemption," I begged them. "Just one day to bring my wife here to Angren and get her settled. She does not know a soul in Oblik, and right now the children are sick. How can I just leave them in such a condition?"

The officer was unsympathetic. I continued to plead, until he finally agreed to let me have one day off, on the condition that I sign a promise to return that same day to Achengaran. I signed and he let me go. I then brought my wife and children to Angren where we rented a room with the same Jews who had promised to help her go to Tashkent. From there she could easily travel to Samarkand to all her relatives.

That same evening, I went back to the draft board in Angren instead of Achengaran. I wanted to try my utmost to find a way out of the draft. I went to the factory's personnel office; perhaps they could pull some strings. But they said that once I was written down on the army list, they were powerless.

While I was at the office, a soldier came to pick me up and bring me to the train station to Achangaran. He had been sent by my untrusting officer. By the time we arrived at the depot, however, the group of soldiers destined for that day's transport had already left. The soldier brought me to the room of the officer who roundly cursed me for being a deserter. He called over an Uzbek soldier and shouted, "You are a criminal and I'm placing you under guard."

He gave instructions to the Uzbek soldier not to let me out of his sight and to shoot me if I made the slightest move to escape. The next day, I was to be escorted on a train to Tashkent, taken straight to the draft board and sent to the front or court-martialed.

We had a whole day and night to wait, so the Uzbek, the guard and I went to a cafeteria and made ourselves comfortable. The Uzbek was simple and uneducated but had strong religious feelings. (The Uzbeks were generally Moslems.) We began talking.

"I see you are a religious Jew," he commented. (Jews from Buchara lived among the Uzbeks.) "Why did you want to desert the army? Don't you believe that if G-d wants you to live you'll live, and if not, no matter where you are, you will die? Every bullet has its destined address."

"My friend," I answered. "I believe as you do. I am not a deserter, and I'm not afraid of the army. It was bad luck that made me miss the transport that went out this morning."

I continued speaking in this vein until he was thoroughly convinced.

After a while, he gave me my file and said, "I see that you're an honest man. You can have your own papers for the trip tomorrow. I'll also be traveling with you tomorrow, but in case I'm not there, go by yourself." Then he left.

The next morning, he didn't show up. I took the train to Tashkent and arrived at the draft board. It was completely empty, since a large transport had gone out just the day before. Only a tired supervisor sat at a desk. I put my papers down, but he didn't open them.

He looked up wearily and murmured, "Oh, you're one of those Polish refugees drafted for labor."

He put aside my file, filled out a form and sent me to a factory for three days of work, instructing me to return after the three days to be assigned a new job. He gave me a food ration card, and I left.

Instead of treating me as a deserter, he had miraculosly mistaken me for a refugee and given me papers as such. This was Friday afternoon. With three days to search for a permanent way out of army duty, I planned to look up my friend the engineer; perhaps he would be able to help me now.

While riding on the bus, I heard someone cry, "Aaron! What are you doing here?"

It was an elderly Jew who recognized me. I explained my predicament to him. "Go to Rav Twersky, the Machnovke *Rebbe*," he advised me. It was the same *Rebbe* whose advice I failed to take two years earlier.

The Machnovke *Rebbe* had led hundreds of *Chassidim* from his hometown of Machnovke. In the 1930s, when he saw that the Communists were getting the upper hand in Machnovke, he moved to Moscow. Then, during the war, he fled to Tashkent. He maintained a regular *minyan* in his sister's house, and many Jews sought his help and advice. I changed directions and headed for the *Rebbe's* house. I arrived *Erev Shabbos Hagadol.*

He listened to my problem and arranged for his wife to take me at six in the morning to a Communist Jew who directed an entire district of army factories. It normally took a week or more just to get an appointment to see this man.

The director had a warm Jewish heart despite his party affiliation, and upon hearing my story, he said, "If you have a note that you were sent to the labor division, that's good enough for me to employ you. I'll fix the rest. Remember, if you meet up with a draft or army official just say you live with me and that I have all your documents."

I went to his factory at nine o'clock and applied to personnel. They called in the director, who signed that he had already taken charge of my documents. This was a dangerous move on his part, but he made it anyway. This man and his wife, who still reside in Russia, went out of their way for many other Jews as well. In their eyes, no sacrifice was too big when it came to charity and good deeds.

When the director asked me what type of work I wanted, I told him it made no difference, as long as I could keep *Shabbos*. One week after *Pesach* 1944, he got me a job as watchman in a warehouse of army tools. My family and I moved into a small hut where we remained until the end of our stay in Tashkent, in 1946. Our neighbors were the Slavins, who had also fled to Tashkent.

My daily schedule changed. I worked the nightshift in the factory, coming home in the morning. I stayed with my two daughters, by now six and three years old, while my wife saw to the shopping and other needs.

One winter morning, I fell asleep while watching the girls. Instead of letting me have a peaceful nap, they began to cry and wouldn't stop. "Why are you making such a racket?" I shouted groggily. "Let me sleep!"

But they kept crying. My head was aching from fatigue, but when I saw they wouldn't be quiet, I had to get up and see what was wrong. I rose, but my head began to ache terribly, and I fell to the floor. I felt as though someone had hit me on the head. I tried to get up, but fell down again. This time I couldn't even get up. I began to crawl to the door, feeling as if smoke was choking me. I didn't even have the strength to grab one of the girls.

I was barely able to crawl to the door, open it and tumble out into the snow. Cold air rushed into the house, as smoke billowed out. I sucked in the brisk air while hugging the snow. Summoning all my strength, I shouted to a passerby to enter the house and see if my daughters were all right. I asked a second man to knock on the door of my neighbor Reb Zev Slavin, and have him take care of the girls. Reb Zev and his wife ran out and took charge of the girls. Thank G-d, we were saved.

My wife had lit the winter heater, but the charcoal had burnt badly, causing smoke to fill the house. The smoke had entered my lungs while I slept, and the lungs of my daughters. It was their crying which saved us. Hashem had pulled us back again from the abyss of death. He had saved me from human enemies and was guarding me from every threat to my life.

My life now took a new turn. Tashkent was a metropolis where thousands of native Jews lived. The Chabad *Rebbe* had sent emissaries years before to educate these Bucharan Jews. They had full community facilities—a *mikveh, shochet* and Rabbis—and they openly kept the kosher laws as well as all the Jewish holidays.

I remember how, on *Pesach* night, they would go out after the *Seder*, in all their finery, and dance in their yards. This Jewish environment made things relatively easier for the hundreds of thousands of Jewish refugees who had fled there. We shared whatever food we could. By 1944, we had bread and could even get hold of vegetables and some fruit. Occasionally, there was rice and even chicken for *Shabbos*.

After four months as a watchman, I had to leave my job. The Jewish director had gotten into trouble causing him to flee. Without my protector, remaining in that factory was a senseless risk.

I continued to feel Hashem's presence wherever I went. A friend paid off an army doctor to give me an exemption from combat duty, but was again drafted for work in the war industries. With this new exemption, I was able to get a position in a factory producing knitwear for the army. Another friend, Reb Pinchas Sudak, helped me buy a machine for knitting socks. The directors were Chabad *Chassidim*, Reb Moshe Sudakevitch and Reb Zusia Rivkin. They employed many *Chassidim* and religious Jews in their factory, who of course, did not work on *Shabbos*. They had even organized a daily *Gemara* class in the evening, taught by Reb Moshe Shalit.

15 THE TASHKENT CHASSIDIM

REB MOSHE SUDAKEVITCH AND REB ZUSIA RIVKIN were part of a community of Chabad *Chassidim* who had become wealthy during the war years in Uzbekistan. These middle-aged *Chassidim* had previously lived in cities and towns throughout Russia and had fled to Uzbekistan when the Germans were advancing. Like all the other refugees, they had arrived penniless and starving, but at that time when industries were springing up to supply the army's needs, the government was looking for efficient and reliable directors. Because educated, Westernized *Chassidim* stood out amid the primitive Asian populace, and because they did not refrain from bribing officials, they attained prominent positions.

Since obeying the law meant living in abject poverty, people began to turn to illegal activities. The black market flourished, maintained by all levels of society. At the same time, directors were discharging their official duties; be it in the local government, police courts, or factories, they were manufacturing and selling numerous items illegally. Bribery was a way of life.

Nor did the attainment of wealth satisfy people's ambitions. They continued their black marketeering, until some of these directors eventually amassed huge fortunes. They knew the grave penalty incurred by such illegal activities, but the situation was such that everyone felt his life in danger no matter what he did.

These wealthy *Chassidim* formed a close, friendly network. They were ready to help anyone in need. They paid off bribes, helped arrange work and made sure that religious needs were not forgotten either. A Chabad *minyan* was set up, where *kiddushim* on *Shabbos* and regular get-togethers were held. A secret Chabad *cheder* and *yeshivah ketanah* were established to educate their children. Once their own religious facilities were established, they threw their energy into supplying the religious needs of their fellow Jews. Their plans were fraught with danger, but they were resolved to be as zealous for Judaism as they had been to attain material success.

In the winter of 1944, one of these *Chassidim*, Reb Elie Lipsker, visited me, asking me to start a *cheder* for refugee children in Tashkent. He promised that I could remain a worker in Reb Moshe Sudakevitch's factory, so that I would have no problems with the draft. I took the challenge. As for the salary, I wanted nothing more than the amount I would lose from missing hours at work.

In the month between *Pesach* and *Shavuos*, I set up three *chadorim* in different parts of the city. After *Shavuos*, I set up the fourth, with twenty children studying in each *cheder*. Years later in Israel, I met some of these children who remained religious. The families of these children were Ashkenazim, originally from Russia and the Ukraine. The fathers were in the army, and the mothers and children had fled to Uzbekistan when war broke out. They knew nothing of Judaism. Some of the boys were not even circumcised.

The *chadorim* formed an underground network of Torah. On Uktchi Street, Reb Moshe Nosson Gorelick, a Chabad *Chassid*, taught; Rabbi Zalman Leib Estollin, a man handicapped by the war, who is now my neighbor in Bnei Brak, taught in Sotzgorodok, next to the Textile Plant; Reb Asher Zelig taught on Novaya Street. These teachers were elderly men devoted to their students. They tried to imbue them with a love for Judaism. They taught all levels, from reading in the *siddur* to studying *Gemara*. One *Shavuos*, I visited Rav Nachum Lifkovsky, with whom I had consulted all along.

"I really should say the blessing *Shehechiyanu vekiyemanu vehegiyanu lazman hazeh* (Who has kept us alive, preserved us and allowed us to reach this occasion, a blessing said on festivals and when performing certain *mitzvos*)," I told him. "The last two words, *lazman hazeh*, contain the initials of Zalman Leib (*zayin, lamed*), Moshe Nosson (*mem, nun*) and Asher Zelig (*zayin*). Without them, the *chadorim* would not exist."

After *Shavuos*, I organized one more *cheder*, on Profsyozny Street, taught by Reb Moshe the Litvak. When he left, Reb Chaim Binyamin Brod took over.

Supervision and maintenance were entirely my responsibility. I planned the studies, tested the children, arranged lunch and paid the teachers, as well as the monthly rent for the rooms. In order to insure security, the teachers did not even know where their money came from.

The expense of running these *chadorim* was enormous. The teachers' wages alone amounted to twenty thousand rubles a month. At that time, the monthly wages of a worker in Russia was seven hundred rubles a month. The daily lunch and the monthly rent for the four rooms also cost tens of thousands of rubles. This huge budget, covered primarily by rich Chabad *Chassidim*, cut deeply into their income, but at times, they were able to influence Jewish acquaintances, even those far from Torah observance, to donate generously for the upkeep of the *chadorim*.

The hardest task lay in convincing parents to allow their children to attend. I would start by visiting the parents at night, trying to persuade them that their children should know something about Judaism. This education would cost them nothing; I always emphasized that I was doing it to attain merit for my parents and not for any monetary gain.

If they agreed, I took out a notebook, wrote down some large-sized letters of the *alef-beis* with vowel signs, and taught them to the child using the phonetic equivalents in Russian. In a few days, after the child had learned the complete *alef-beis* at home and could even read complete words and lines, I told his parents that they could broaden their child's Jewish knowledge in a special school that had recently been set up. Would they agree to send their child to this *cheder*? This was no easy decision, as it meant taking their child out of the Soviet schools. The majority did not agree, linked as it was with the danger of teaching the child religious "propaganda" and withholding him from the Soviet schools. This was tantamount to counterrevolutionary activity or spying. In the case of the few who were willing, I brought the children to *cheder*.

It was highly dangerous work. If I had feared for my life before, now my fright increased a hundredfold. With these activities, the authorities had an undeniable "crime" with which to accuse me. Officially, I was an army recruit assigned to work in a vital military textile industry where parachute cords were manufactured. I made token appearances at the factory morning and evening, but the entire day I was out working for the *cheder* network. If I were caught, then not only I, but the works manager named Moshe Sudakevitch would have faced a capital charge, something of which he was acutely aware. Still, I felt it was my responsibility.

The *rebbe* and children knew full well that teaching and learning in a *cheder* was strictly forbidden and were prepared in the case of an unwanted visitor. Each *cheder* had a secret place to stack the Jewish books and a place where toys were kept should they be needed. One winter day, a clever fourteen-year-old lad spotted N.K.V.D. officials heading for their building. In a flash, the *Gemaras* disappeared. The boy dragged a withered yule tree from the corner and when the officials walked into the room, he found a crowd of children pushing Reb Zalman Leib to a yule tree, mocking, "Look! We found a Santa Claus!"

"Shame on you!" the officials reproved them. "Do you have nothing to do but torture an old man? Leave him alone!"

They stopped their show, and the officials left, satisfied.

It once happened that the *Rav* of Charkov and his son-in-law Reb Yaakov Freidman sent us the child of a friendly neighbor. The next day, the child brought a friend with him.

A few days later, the grandmother of the second child, a woman from Poland, came and asked Reb Asher Zelig, "Did the government give you permission to teach in such conditions? Look at this room! It's unhygienic! And look! These texts are old and moldy. Is this how you teach young children? If you don't show me your teaching license, I will have to tell the authorities about you."

Reb Asher Zelig was frightened and told her that he was closing the *cheder* in a few days anyway. He stopped teaching and reported to me, "I am afraid we will soon be informed on!"

"Wait a bit," I told him. "We'll straighten things out."

I told Reb Yaakov to tell his neighbor's parents that the *cheder* had closed and not to send the two boys anymore. A few days later, we opened again and kept it in operation until the refugees left after the war.

In the *cheder*, there was a youth from Russia named Kogan. His mother was a sister-in-law of Aaron Kaganovich, the brother of Lazar Kaganovich, one of Stalin's chief advisors. Her husband had been a famous Communist leader, but Stalin had brutally murdered him during the purges in 1938, and she had fled with her son to Tashkent during the war. Considering her family connections, we were afraid to admit her sixteen-year-old son to our *cheder*, but our fears were groundless. After this woman had seen how her own brothers and sister had done nothing to save her unjustly condemned husband, she became bitterly disillusioned with Communism.

In the *cheder*, her son advanced rapidly, and he quickly reached the level where he could study *Gemara*. Immediately, he decided to circumcize himself. Seeing him in such pain during the operation, his mother started to cry. He shook his hand at her, though, and said, "Whose fault is it that I have to go through this now?"

This youth continued learning with Reb Zalman Leib for a long time. To test the children's progress, I frequently came to the *chadorim* armed with a bag of candy. Once I visited the *cheder* on Sutzgorodok Street where Reb Asher Zelig taught. Being the grandson of the *tzaddik* Reb Shmuel of Kaminka, Reb Asher happened to know Russian very well, a considerable advantage since the children of six to eight did not know Yiddish. He had begun teaching the children the *alef-beis* and had advanced to the study of *Chumash*.

I asked the children in his class, "In how many days did Hashem create the world?"

"Six!" they called out.

"And when did He rest?"

"On the seventh day."

"Very good," I smiled. "Now who can tell me what was created on each day?"

The students began to count on their fingers while reciting, "On Monday, Hashem created the heavens and the earth, and light. On Tuesday, He created the waters."

Something was wrong. Sunday, Hashem created the heavens and Earth; Monday, the waters, etc. They had pushed up the weekday count by one.

Then I asked them, "And when did Hashem rest from all His work?"

"Sunday!"

I was shocked. What had these children learned? I turned to their teacher.

"Reb Asher," I said. "What did you do? Are you teaching them Christianity? What's happened here?"

We soon figured it out. Since he had not taught them the Russian names for the days of Creation, the children had assumed that the first day of Creation was the first day of the week in Russia, which is Monday. In Russia, the last day of the week is considered Sunday, the official day of rest.

I was relieved to have discovered this mistake, which might have remained with these little children for the rest of their lives. That entire month, Reb Asher reviewed with them the days of the Creation in Russian, also discoursing with his boys about the holiness of *Shabbos*, and how one must desist from work on that day.

I was working on a different front as well, entering children into the covenant of our forefather Avraham. For generations, *bris milah* had been one of the few Jewish practices that even assimilated Jews would not renounce. Only during the years of Communist terror had this *mitzvah* been abandoned because of ignorance of Judaism, the fear of being accused of anti-Soviet activity and the difficulty of finding a *mohel*. Now that the country was preoccupied with the war effort, however, and religious persecution had temporarily eased up, we saw our chance to rectify the situation.

A few community-minded individuals and I, began to educate the Jewish refugees on the importance of this *mitzvah*. We circumcized tens of children. The parents were often afraid to let a *mohel* do the operation unsupervised and would demand the presence of a doctor. In response to this, Reb Gershon Richter, one of the well-to-do *Chassidim*, would dress up in a white coat and be the "doctor."

The *chadorim* lasted until September of 1946, as long as the Chabad *Chassidim* and I remained in Tashkent. Never did we have an unpleasant incident. This was because of the strict security measures we took. It is also likely that the authorities chose to close their eyes as long as there were still Polish refugees in Russia, thinking, "Those are not our people, they are Polish."

Many of the children who learned in our *Chadorim* were still keeping whatever *mitzvos* they could when they emigrated from Russia thirty years afterwards. Some of those who settled in America and Eretz Yisrael even sent their children to *yeshivos*.

In 1945, after the Russians had advanced into Poland, we met a few Jewish survivors of the Nazi murder camps. They had gruesome tales to tell. I could have no doubt now as to what befell the members of my family.

One night, I dreamed that my mother stood before me. Trembling, I asked her what had become of my brother?

"He was killed," she answered and disappeared.

In another dream, in 1945, I saw myself sleeping in an empty *cheder* room. My father and brother were lying behind me. I longed to talk with them, but I could not get a word out.

Finally, I forced myself to ask, "What happened?"

"They tortured us."

I asked, "When?"

"*Rosh Chodesh Elul.*"

"In the day or at night?"

My father said, "In the night."

But my brother answered, "It was still day."

I woke up shaken and went to the Machnovker *Rebbe*, Reb Avraham Yehoshua Heschel Twersky, to whom I had gone for advice before.

"Should I keep *Rosh Chodesh Elul* as the *yahrzeit*," I asked him, "even though I have not heard any definite report of their death?"

The *Rebbe* felt that it was still too early to set a date. I decided to keep *Rosh Chodesh Elul* as their *yahrzeit* provisionally, with future *yahrzeits* conditional on the news I would hear.

When I came to Moscow at the end of the summer in 1946, I met friends from Zevihl who brought crushing news. The whole Jewish community in Krasnostav had been wiped out on the sixth of *Elul*. Only two young girls survived, the daughter of Velvel Kelrich and the daughter of the *gabbai* Yerachmiel. They had fled to the nearby forest. The eight hundred and fifty Jews of our town were murdered in one pit. Even a family that had converted before the war was killed along with the rest. Years later, the Kelrich daughter told me that just before the shooting, my father had feelingly addressed all the Jews and that he was the first one hit by the bullets.

The anguish I felt pained my heart for months on end. I had already learned that Lezar Pinski, my brother-in-law, succumbed to typhus in Moscow. Of my entire family, I was the only one left.

In the middle of the winter of 1945, I answered a knock on the door. Before me stood a weary stranger, gaunt, pale and sickly.

"Aaron!" he said. "Thank G-d, I've found you!"

I gazed at the man who was utterly unrecognizable to me.

"It's me, Yisrael Freidman, your wife's brother's son," he said.

"Yisrael! Wh-where is your mother . . . Aarele . . . your little brothers?"

"Aaron . . . I'm the only one left."

Though only twenty, he looked like thirty-five; he was so worn.

The two of us, each the only survivor of his family, embraced and wept.

16 YISRAEL'S STORY

I BROUGHT YISRAEL INTO THE HOUSE WHERE MY wife served him food. Both of us wept for him. How bad he looked, how swollen from hunger, and what horrors had befallen his family! His terrible sufferings had aged him. He was weak from lack of food, hard labor and beatings.

Yisrael related that shortly after the Germans took over Odessa, partisans had blown up the Central G.P.U. Building, which was serving as German headquarters, killing dozens of Nazi soldiers. In retaliation, the Germans had rounded up tens of thousands of Jews and slaughtered them *en masse*. Aarele had died in this massacre.

The Germans then began to make house searches to recruit young men for forced labor. Yisrael, who was sixteen, was taken, together with a neighbor's son and fifty others. They performed hard labor for the Germans that entire day. That fateful first afternoon, however, it was discovered that one youth had escaped. The

Germans decided to punish everyone in the group. They brought them to a narrow ditch and had the boys crouch on their knees inside the pit. Yisrael had prepared himself and was already saying *Shema* and *Viduy* when the shots rang out. Blood began to gush and soon filled the canal reaching to the boys' necks. Then the Germans came to the corpses and bashed each head with the handle of a rifle to see if any were still alive. Satisfied that their work was done, they moved on.

Yisrael was miraculously untouched, but he was too frightened to move. He waited a few hours before cautiously poking his head out of the ditch. The field was completely deserted, except for something very far off. The Germans were emptying a volley of bullets into another group of victims. He quickly lowered his head and remained in the ditch until no German could be seen. Finally, he got out slowly and checked the other bodies in the ditch. All were dead, except for one Jew who had been seriously wounded. Yisrael helped him out and supported him while the man limped home.

On the way they met a gentile woman and begged her to give them clean clothes, since theirs were soaked with blood. But the woman fled. There was not one person on the street. Yisrael dropped the man off at home and then walked back to his family. Coming into the courtyard, he met the mother of the other boy who had been conscripted with him.

"Where were you?" she asked fearfully.

"I was at the abattoir," he murmured evasively. "They didn't let everyone go home."

"If I bribe them," she said, "do you think they will let my son come home?"

Yisrael had no words for her. He had been her only child.

Yisrael was careful to avoid being caught in other house searches. His younger brothers stayed on the outlook, and when the Germans approached, he would hide behind a closet. Finally, the day came when the remaining Jews were all rounded up and forced to march on a seemingly endless journey. With pitiful food rations and no medical aid, the physical strain proved too much for the emaciated, weak prisoners. One by one, Yisrael's brothers died. Yisrael was the only survivor.

131

He was taken into Romania and made to labor for the Germans for one and a half years until the Germans began their retreat. Then they herded all prisoners onto a freight train and fled. Yisrael was packed together with numerous prisoners, some of whom had collaborated with the Nazis. They somehow found a saw and cut a hole into the floor of the train. Many of these former Nazi collaborators were afraid that even if they escaped the Nazis they would be made to pay for their anti-Jewish activities by the Russians. They helped Yisrael escape, hoping this deed would count in their favor. He lowered himself through the hole under the train and lay between the tracks in deserted terrain. The train disappeared behind him. He was a free man. But now what?

He started walking toward Odessa, hoping to find his father but the city was empty of anyone he had known. Finally, upon hearing he had relatives in Uzbekistan, he came, hoping to find us. At the end of 1945, he reached our home.

We took him in immediately, and my wife slowly nursed him back to health. The strong faith that had maintained him before the war now helped him recover from his harrowing experiences. Since he was already twenty, without family or home, we all agreed that the time was ripe for marriage. We knew a fine religious girl who was also an orphan. Yisrael married her and established his own home.

Towards the end of the war the Jewish refugees from Poland began to leave Russia. They traveled back to Poland, and from there many went to Palestine and America. Many Russian Jews, the members of our family included, tried to get out as well. My brother-in-law had pretended all along to be one of the Polish refugees. The Russians had no record of him, since he had gone into hiding, and he was able to blend in with the many religious refugees. Once the N.K.V.D. caught him and demanded to see his documents, but a generous bribe enabled him to escape. At the end of the war he bought forged Polish papers and entered Poland without difficulty.

About this time, my mother-in-law joined us. She had spent the war years with her youngest daughter. Now, however, the daughter fled across the border. Her mother, being ill and weak from a stomach ailment, could not risk such an arduous journey.

As for me, I could see no way out of Russia since I was officially registered in all their books. As a last resort, I decided to go the way of many Chabad *Chassidim* — travel to Lemberg (Lvov) at the Polish border and bribe agents to secretly cross over. It seemed like the only solution. Yisrael Friedman and his wife decided to accompany me.

To my great sorrow, I had to close down all the *chadorim*, because with the Chabad *Chassidim* gone, I had no funds to keep them up. I had no choice but to run away because had I been caught, I would certainly have been put to death as a deserter and counter-revolutionary. This was true even when the *chadorim* were operating, but at least then I was risking my life for a cause.

We all left Uzbekistan, the home of our extended family for five years, with a heavy heart. Our brother-in-law Reb Dov Slobodiansky, to whom we all owed our lives, was not with us. He was the only family member in Uzbekistan who did not survive the war.

17 LIFE IN MOSCOW

OUR DESTINATION WAS LEMBERG, BUT ON THE WAY we stopped in Moscow where I rented one room of a house in the suburb of Reutovo for a week. It was before *Rosh Hashanah* of 1946. With me were my wife, mother-in-law and three daughters. I was about to buy tickets for Lemberg, when the Chabad *Chassidim* in Moscow received a telegram from Lemberg that "Relatives in Lemberg fell sick." This was a coded message that meant the authorities had caught *Chassidim* trying to slip across the border. Now security would be tightened, and they would be on the alert for religious Jews.

With Lemberg out of the question, we had no choice but to remain in Moscow. Thus began a twenty-year period of fighting to keep *Shabbos* and educate our children amidst privation and great personal risk.

The room we had rented was actually the hall of a house, about two and a half by three and a half meters square. It was bare. The owners, a widow and her two children, had to walk through the hall to leave and enter the house. When we decided to remain in Moscow, the owners gave us two closets, a portable oven and a kerosene heater. We needed the heater desperately, since the room was poorly insulated. Even in September we were suffering from the cold gusts blowing in through the cracks. By the time winter arrived, the cold was unbearable, but I could even not think of moving out. Although I soon found work, I barely made enough to buy food.

At that time, the authorities were rationing out six hundred grams of bread to each worker and four hundred grams to every other Moscow citizen. Just to get Moscow residency took me several weeks of pleading with the local municipality and supplying them with bribes. Even after we became residents, though, we still did not get the portion of bread due our two oldest children, since we did not dare write their names in the registry book of our building. Once a child's name appeared there, he automatically was registered for the local school. We could not take the risk of having our children attend school, as we had no excuse that would exempt them from attending on *Shabbos*. Furthermore, if our *Shabbos* observance was discovered, we would immediately be imprisoned and our children taken into custody by the Communists. Thus began our stay in Moscow, hungry, cold and not even receiving the scant portion of bread everyone else received. (I could not dream of buying bread from the black market, since a one-kilo loaf cost a hundred rubles, and I was making between seven hundred and eight hundred rubles a month.)

Before *Rosh Hashanah*, I heard that a neighbor, an old man, had a *Sefer Torah* at home. I had the *shofar* I had made in Oblik, and in my one room, we got together a *minyan* on *Rosh Hashanah* as well as *Yom Kippur*. I led the service for *Musaf* and read the Torah both days. Then *Sukkos* arrived.

Never had I been without a *sukkah*, but now I totally lacked resources. *Erev Sukkos*, I noticed that my Jewish neighbor was building an extra room for his house. The walls were already up, and the ceiling was missing—perfect for a *sukkah*. I asked this neighbor

135

if I could make a *sukkah* in one corner of the room, at least for the first evening of the holiday, but he refused.

When his wife heard us talking, she said to me in Yiddish, "Tell me what you need."

I explained to her the *mitzvah* of building a *sukkah*, and she said generously, "Why settle for that corner for just a day? I'll give you whatever you want! There's a place on the other side of the house perfect for putting up your *sukkah*, and you can use it for the whole holiday."

Investigating the spot, I found two walls protruding, and a door lying on the ground. Within half an hour I had attached the door to form a third wall, and my *sukkah* was complete. She helped me with the construction and added, "You can even hold your *minyan* in my house."

There was an elderly Jew in the neighborhood with whom I had become friendly, Reb Yeshaya. He couldn't believe that I was planning to build a *sukkah*.

"What! A *sukkah* here in Reutovo near Moscow? How many years has it been since anyone made a *sukkah*? For so long, the most we've been able to do has been to go to the Great Synagogue on *Chol Hamoed* (the intermediate festival days) to make a blessing on the *sukkah* and the *lulav* and *esrog*."

I could not convince him to enter our *sukkah* and make *Kiddush* the first night. But the next day he ate there with us, and the following year he made one himself. With time, word got around that building a *sukkah* was indeed possible, and others also began to build *sukkos* of their own.

Right after *Rosh Hashanah*, I found a job weaving shawls in a factory. The director was Jewish, and he accepted my stipulation that I could not work on *Shabbos*.

"You can stay here as long as no one realizes what you're doing," he told me frankly. "When you're found out, you'll have to leave, but you can resign. At least, by not being fired, your chances of finding a new job won't be so bad."

I took work from the factory to do at home, to bring in whatever extra money I could. By the time *Yom Kippur* had passed, we felt somewhat settled. I was making a living. The sense of fear that had dogged me all my life still accompanied me, though, and the danger now was greater than ever, for I knew when I had left Tashkent that the authorities had begun investigating clandestine religious activities. I had been principal of four *chadorim*, a criminal offense that carried a heavy punishment. My eighty pupils, their parents and many others, had all witnessed my "illegal" activities. All it would take to cause my arrest was one of these people informing on me, informing being almost a Russian pastime.

Acquaintances would exacerbate my worries by telling me to shave off my beard; I was inviting catastrophe, they said, by just walking in the streets. It came to the point where should some stranger look at me twice I was convinced that he was watching me. If, while walking, I felt someone's eyes on me, I would turn down a different street and return home by a twisted route. I was haunted by these delusions. Although I knew that most of the time no one was actually there, my fears were so overpowering that I could not help reacting as I did. This is the way I lived for the next twenty years.

My typical parting from my wife was, "May Hashem help me return home!" Because of my worries, I was afraid to do anything illegal. I feared that if they found me guilty of one crime, they would also uncover all my other illegal activities. And if convicted, a terrible fate would certainly await me. What would become of my children and their education? Without me present, what chance did they have to grow up to be G-d-fearing, learned Jews? Thus, although everyone in Russia was involved in some illegal speculation to help him survive the inflation and low wages, I kept away from even the slightest illegal act. Acquaintances would laugh at my fears.

"You're torturing yourself and your family," they told me.

It was true that we were always hungry. The entire time we lived in Moscow, we had to measure out the food to each mouth. During the years we were "well-off," we would divide one chicken among thirteen people.

Actually, in the long run, the poverty we suffered was beneficial. All our non-Jewish neighbors saw how impoverished we were and pitied us. Even when they saw I held a *minyan* in my house, baked *matzos* for *Pesach*, and committed other questionable deeds, they never informed on me. My situation illustrated tne words of our Sages, "Poverty is becoming to Jews." (*Chagigah* 9b)

It was from my father and grandfather that I learned to shy away from illegal gain. Since we had lived by the border, many townspeople traded contraband to make large, easy profits, until the borders were sealed in 1928. But my father and grandfather kept away from anything illegal. They knew that if they were caught, keeping Judaism and educating children would be impossible. Better to curb our desires for the sake of Judaism, they had decided. My parents suffered terrible poverty because of their attitude, but they never regretted it.

Hundreds of Jewish families lived in the Moscow suburb of Reutovo, but only one of them was fully religious, although a few others did keep *kashrus*. Nevertheless, most had some kind of Jewish feeling, particularly in the wake of the horrors that had been publicized concerning our people.

Winter set in. I gradually became acquainted with Jewish life in Moscow. The Great Synagogue, the only Synagogue officially recognized in Moscow, had been left open for publicity purposes. It was thirty kilometers (almost nineteen miles) from us. The Synagogue provided religious services to Jews who were interested, proof to the world that the Russian democracy allowed freedom of religion.

A *mikveh* was maintained for the use of Jewish families. Out of a Jewish population of hundreds of thousands, only about twenty-five families used it, though. A *shochet* and a *mohel* were available upon request, and classes were occasionally held in the Great Synagogue. Of course, only elderly people attended. Keeping kosher in Moscow was no problem; our greatest "sacrifice" for *kashrus* was the thirty kilometer ride to the *shochet* and back . . . during the years we could afford chicken.

There were many elderly religious Jews in the city, whose children had forsaken Torah observance. Nevertheless, there were a few families like us, who would not yield an iota of their Judaism and whose children, also, kept *Shabbos* and *kashrus* and learned Torah secretly. These families were, generally, Chabad and Breslover *Chassidim*. One or two belonged to the Boyaner *Chassidim*, my nephew Yisrael Freidman being one of them. Like me, he had been stranded in Moscow. He remained as uncompromising in his Torah observance as his father and grandfather had been.

How did these families and their children manage to keep *Shabbos*? Yisrael Avraham Mahzel was a *Talmid Chacham* and a descendant of the Rebbe Reb Zusia of Anapoli. The Mahzels solved the problem of keeping *Shabbos* with a ruse. After the war, when they moved to Moscow, the wife claimed she was a widow, and her husband claimed he was her brother, having settled with his sister. Since the law made provisions for widows, she was allowed to take home work from a factory. They sent each of their three children to different schools, far from home. The children did not attend school on *Shabbos*, the excuse being that they had to bring the completed work back to the factory for the mother. So it was for years, and no one caught on. Their children attended high school and university and graduated with professional degrees—never once transgressing *Shabbos* at school.

Reb Chaim Heschel was the head of another family whose children did not succumb . He made sure that his daughter and son never violated the *Shabbos* throughout their school years. Also, Reb Yaakov Ornstein of the illustrious family of that name—a Boyaner *Chassid* and a *baal tzedakah* (generous giver to causes)—married off his daughter, an only child, to a religious young man Reb Gershon Michlin, an engineer who kept all the *mitzvos*. The only child of this couple, Yoel Michlin, grew up and went through school and university without ever writing on *Shabbos*. Thank G-d, all the members of these families are now in Eretz Yisrael and adhere faithfully to the Torah.

I became acquainted with the illustrious Rav Yitzchak Kresilschekov, author of one of the only religious texts published in Communist Russia, *Sefer Tevunah* on the Rambam, printed in Poltava in 1926. His commentary on the Jerusalem Talmud was printed years later in Eretz Yisrael. During my frequent visits to him to discuss Jewish law, he often tried to persuade me to become the *Rav* of Moscow. However, as Stalin was still in power, I turned down his proposal each time.

The last time I visited Rav Yitzchak, he was sick in bed, but even so, he tried to convince me again. This time, I felt I could not refuse. He would give me *semichah* (ordination) and secure my appointment, he said, after he recovered. However, he did not recover. He was rushed to the hospital, where he breathed his last breath.

In recalling distinguished Jews of that period, some mention should be made of the *Rebbe* of Machnovke, who had settled in Moscow during the 1930s. Reb Avraham Yehoshua Heschel Twersky, descendant of Reb Mordechai of Chernobyl, was the *Rebbe* from whom I took advice constantly when we were evacuated in Tashkent. Upon his return to Moscow after the war, the Communists repeatedly visited him and talked with him. Finally, they invited him to become one of their men. They offered him the office of Chief Rabbi of Russia, with a motor car and chauffeur, but he firmly declined.

"I am not really a rabbi," he said. "Not a rabbi for an official post. Even if you were to threaten shooting me, I will never sign a paper saying that I will cooperate with you."

He knew that signing was tantamount to becoming an arch informer. The *gabbai* of the *shul*, Chobrutsky, a known informer, also came to him.

"You will become great," the *gabbai* said. "You will not live in a hovel, but a big comfortable residence like the heads of the Christian Church!"

"I will have nothing to do with politics," the *Rabbi* replied.

Thereafter, the N.K.V.D. came in the middle of the night and banged on his door. When he did not open it, they broke in. They made a search in the small dwelling but found nothing incriminating. He had in fact maintained himself as a laborer, making socks and handbags on a small spinning machine. Indeed, he always came to *shul* on weekdays with greasy hands. What they did find was his bread ration card. They tore it up, as if to intimate, "No bread for the likes of you!" Then they took him away.

For several weeks it was not known where they put him, until the news came that he was in Yeniseysk, Siberia. He was sentenced to five years exile as an undesirable. He was known to be a *Rebbe* who never forsook his holy ways. During the worst times, when he had to run his activities from his small house, he did not change his manner. Even five years in Siberia had not broken him; he had come out with body and spirit intact. His influence extended over many Jews, and his talks attracted many people.

During the war and afterwards, he helped countless Jews. Because he was friendly with doctors, professors of medicine and many other irreligious Jews, they stood ready to help anyone for whom he needed a favor in all matters of health. His good deeds and charity were famous throughout Moscow. His influence over people was immense, and it would have all been lost had he accepted the eminent position so enticingly offered him.

18 MILAH IN MOSCOW

ONE MORNING, I WENT TO THE GREAT SYNAGOGUE. Many worshippers were there, and Reb Zalman Nosson, an ex-Rabbi of a *shtetl* and a *Talmid Chacham* was giving a *mishnayos* class.

I sat down at the corner of a table, next to some elderly men. The *gabbai* Chobrutzky eyed me from the side. It was no secret that he was an informer. The lecturer was reading a passage from the *Mishnah* which states that women are disqualified as witnesses.

The *gabbai* interjected, "That was in the past. Nowadays, in Soviet Russia, there is equality between men and women. Men and women both study and are represented equally in the professions."

Everyone was too afraid to speak up. I felt it was a *Chillul Hashem* to dispute the Torah's ruling, no less in the middle of a class.

"Comrade Gabbai, tell me," I said. "How many ladies are there in the Politbiuro? Not even one. Right?"

He did not reply.

"Why didn't even one reach such position? Don't the women in Russia go to universities as the men do? The difference between men and women is obvious in all aspects. In making decisions in law, one needs a person who would be inflexible in his ideas. That's a man. As a witness one also needs a man who is better able to stand his ground firmly. The Talmud says that women are light-minded. Understandably, being a judge or a witness are not tasks for women. Their tasks are running the home and educating their children."

The gabbai had no argument to refute me, and the incident passed without further complications.

One day, a Jew from Perlovke visited me. Perlovke was a small town near Moscow, with a sizeable Jewish population including a number of learned Jews. They had a regular *minyan* and a Jewish cemetery. This man had a question.

"Do you think that two people are sufficient to do *taharah* (ritually clean and purify) on a corpse? How can they pour the designated amount of water by themselves? After all, according to one view, the minimum number of people needed is three."

I went to check this *Halachic* problem in the sources and verified his assumption that the pouring of water was being done improperly. I consulted with Rav Sandler, the *Rav* of the *shtetl*, saying that in such an important place as Perlovka, they were not doing the *taharah* as the law demands.

"What can we do?" he replied. "The authorities don't allow more than two people to attend to a corpse."

After discussing the problem, we decided to stand a board upright and bind the corpse against it. In this vertical position two people could sufficiently pour the water over the corpse two times.

The situation regarding *milah* was no better. Even though a *mohel* was readily available, only an extremely small percentage of boys were being circumcised. Of those few, many had not had it performed properly.

One day, I was attending a *bris*, and the *mohel* was Reb Yitzchak, an elderly Jew originally from Kiev, the best *mohel* in Moscow. After he made the incision, I noticed he did not perform *metzitzah* with his mouth but just wiped off the blood with cotton wool.

"Why didn't you do *metzitzah*?" I inquired.

"This is considered *metzitzah*," he replied.

"This is wiping, not suction," I told him. "And our Sages say that if sucking is not done, the child remains in danger, and the *mohel* should be removed from his profession."

Nevertheless, he held firm in his view. At the end of *Birchas Hamazon*, Rav Yitzchak began to sing the verses that are added at a *bris*. "May the Merciful bless the one who cut away the foreskin and sucked the blood."

"There was no sucking done," I interrupted.

"Yes there was," he maintained.

He continued with the blessing, "The man who is afraid and weak-hearted, his work is disqualified."

"Our Sages explain this phrase to mean, the one who is afraid of the sins he has done with his hands," I told him. "In your case, doing the *metzitzah* with your hand instead of your mouth."

This time Rav Yitzchak accepted my words, promising to do *metzitzah* only with the mouth. Whenever we met, he would remind me of what I had told him, typifying the words in Proverbs, "Rebuke a wise man and he will love you." We remained close friends.

On a different occasion, I was present when another *mohel* did not do *metzitzah*. Reb Yitzchak Mintz, a devout and learned Jew, offered to do it instead, but the *mohel* would not let him.

"Why won't you do *metzitzah*?" I asked the *mohel*.

"Nowadays, one just doesn't do it," he answered.

Stalin was still alive, and the *mohel* was afraid that if anything in the *milah* went wrong, he could be sued and severely punished. Upon hearing my words, he stopped to reconsider.

An elderly *Rav* spoke up. "There is no obligation to do *metzitzah* with the mouth."

Many old and distinguished rabbis were present, but they did not reply to his words. I could not listen passively to this wrong ruling.

"It is *chutzpah* to overrule our Sages! Who allowed you to decide like this?"

He looked at me angrily, but Reb Simcha Schechter laid his hand on the *Rav's* shoulder and said firmly, "Here you must keep silent."

A few weeks later, I met the *mobel*. He told me that the *Rav* had shown him a *sefer* recently printed in Paris, where they had ruled that *metzitzah* need not be done with the mouth.

"I cannot believe that reliable Rabbis would decide against our Sages," I said. "Maybe they mean that *metzitzah* can be done through a tube, which in any case involves the mouth."

The *mobel* went to check the *sefer*. When I met him again, he told me that the ruling was exactly as I had surmised and that he would do *metzitzah* according to *Halachah*. I was thankful to have been able to correct the error.

Reb Mordechai Reshkovsky, a Skverer *Chassid* and *shochet* from Odessa, once told me an amazing tale.

"One evening I came home and found a young woman waiting for me. 'I must ask a favor of you, but it must be kept completely secret,' she said. Then she related her story. She was an orphan whose religious parents were murdered by the Nazis. Alone in the world, she began to study in the university in Odessa, where she became friendly with a Jewish student who wanted to marry her. She would only consider it, she told him, if he agreed to a Jewish *chupah*. The young man knew nothing of Judaism, but he agreed to her condition. His father, however, being an avowed Communist, would not hear of it. The son disregarded his father's feelings and held the wedding as his fiancee wanted. His father gave the young couple a room in his house.

"After the wedding, her husband confessed that he was not circumcized. She was aghast; she told him that under no circumstances would she live with him unless he circumcized himself. She would not desecrate the honor of her religious parents who had fallen martyrs in the war! This time, the young man refused, and his wife kept her word. She returned to the university dormitory, and he remained in the house.

"After half a year, he broke down. He agreed to circumcize himself, but not in Odessa. He traveled to Bessarabia and had his *bris milah* performed there. His wife returned to him, and they resumed living with his father. They lived together in harmony, until a son was born. She invited a *mobel* to their home and they scheduled the *bris* for a time when her father-in-law would be out. Unfortunately, the day before the scheduled *bris*, the *mohel* came by to check the baby's health. Suddenly the father-in-law walked in. Finding the *mohel* there, he began to scream, threatening to turn him over to the N.K.V.D. The *mohel* departed in haste and refused to perform the *bris*.

"When she came to my house," Reb Reshkovsky told me, "she asked me to help arrange her son's *bris*. 'What will you do,' I asked her, 'if your father-in-law throws you out of the house?' She told me, 'That's our business. My husband and I have decided to go ahead with it, no matter what.' When I saw her strong will, I took upon myself to see to it that her son be given a *bris*. And her father-in-law? In the end, he caused no problems."

The months were passing. At the end of 1947, my family had our first *simchah* in Moscow; my son Moshe Mordechai was born on *Shabbos*, November 22. A small crowd of thirty people attended the *bris* which was held in my house. I had decided that I would openly perform *mitzvos*. It was senseless to try to hide every deed. There were so many informers around anyway that, no matter what I did, word was bound to get out.

Our family was growing, but we were still living in that crowded hall. I could not dream of moving out, though, because the situation at my job was so precarious. My boss knew that I kept *Shabbos*, but every week I would carefully assess my co-workers' knowledge. Did they figure out why I did not show up on Saturday? Was anyone complaining or jealous of me?

After a year, I began to hear grumblings. I was pulled aside by my employer who asked why I didn't come in like everyone else? By the summer of 1948, the risk had become too great. I left that job.

I then began to work in a factory that employed blind people. They needed a skilled sighted man to lay out the warp for the blind workers, who then wove the woof by sense of touch. Few people were interested in such work, so my new boss was willing to close his eyes to my strange hours.

On August 27, 1949, Chaim Meir, my second son was born. A year later, after *Sukkos*, we finally left our tiny hall. It was not the desperate living conditions that propelled us to take this step, however. We were fleeing to save our lives.

146

During the four years in Reutovo, our daughters had not gone to school. We had tried to keep their existence as inconspicuous as possible, but neighbors began to notice. Finally, we were reported to the school authorities, and an official visited us, grimly demanding that our daughters attend the Soviet school. We did not even offer an excuse. That night we decided to flee.

We packed and moved to a distant suburb called Kliazma. Once again, we were faced with the task of finding inexpensive accommodations in unfriendly surroundings. We were grateful that our new home was roomy, a one-and-a-half room apartment, with the added advantage that we had our own entrance. It did not look like a proper house to live in, so the gentile neighbors could not possibly envy us there. They even pitied us, as did those of Reutovo.

"How can you live so poorly when the other Jews are so well housed? You must be genuine people!" they concluded.

Kliazma had a small Jewish population. There was even a weekly *minyan* kept up by some elderly men. Unfortunately, whatever *mitzvos* these men kept were not done properly. The one who recited the Torah reading in *shul* used to say some words from memory instead of reading word by word from a Torah scroll. When I asked him why, he said that it was the only way he could do it, and that if I knew better, I should do it. So I did. There was even open desecration of *Shabbos* in this *shul*.

By 1951, my oldest son Mordechai was already four. He knew *berachos*, and could tell stories from the *Chumash* and name the *Sedra* of the week, which he had heard from my wife and mother-in-law. It was time for his formal Jewish learning to begin. Obsessed as I was with the fear that I could be taken away one day, I felt compelled to begin my children's education as early as possible. For this reason, too, I had them begin studying *Gemara* at the age of six. I soon found a teacher for him.

Reb David Honigman was an elderly man who had lost his job during the wave of anti-Semitism that erupted in Russia in the years before 1953. He agreed to become the teacher for my son and other religious children. As a precautionary measure, he taught each of his students in their homes.

All the parents, however, were impoverished and unable to pay for Reb David's tutelage. I turned to a well-to-do friend, Dr. Shlomo Yosef Steinberg, for aid. He was a young doctor whose trust in G-d was sincere; he was strictly religious and scrupulously kept *Shabbos*, even though he was a public employee. He willingly agreed to pay the teacher's full salary. Imagine my distress then, when this beloved friend died a few years later of a heart disease, at the age of thirty-eight. He was the only son of Reb Michael Steinberg of Berdichev. Reb Michael had truly educated his son, for Shlomo Yosef graduated as a doctor without desecrating the *Shabbos*. In fact, while in university, he influenced other students, boys and girls, to keep Torah.

Reb Michael Steinberg was a learned, distinguished man, one of the few in Moscow who was strictly religious. After his son's death, he and her other grandparents, Rav Yitzchak Mintz and his wonderful wife Chava brought up his granddaughter Miriam. Many years later, Miriam emigrated to Eretz Yisrael with her husband and established a home in Bnei Brak, raising children who followed in their families' ways.

Even after Dr. Steinberg died, the teacher continued to educate our children. The Machnovke *Rebbe* and others offered to cover the expense.

On February 20, 1951, Batya was born to us. We were three adults and six children in a one-and-a-half room flat, and the children still did not go to school. The longer we were in Kliazma, the more frightened we grew of being found out. At the end of 1951, I had other worries on my mind. I had no choice but to leave work; it had become too noticeable that I was delinquent on *Shabbos*.

It took me months to find appropriate work. I spent these months at home, educating my children, and other children at their homes. Yitzchak was born during this period, in February of 1952.

It was quite dangerous to be unemployed for any length of time. I began my next job in the summer of 1952, again as a weaver who specialized in laying the warp of a weaving loom. My Jewish supervisor knew that I would not work on *Shabbos*. It would be hard to conceal this from the other workers, he said. He suggested that we wait to see how they would react. If no one objected, he would keep me, on the condition that no one found out he knew I kept *Shabbos*.

Actually, my work demanded that I keep different hours from the other workers. I would set up the warp of the loom, and then ten other workers would weave in the woof. They could not work until I was finished, and frequently while they were weaving, I had finished my work. The other employees got used to seeing me absent a good deal of the time, which helped me conceal my *Shabbos* observance.

In my initial talk with the supervisor, he told me that the director of the factory came to check up twice or three times a week, and I should not mention my absence on *Shabbos* to him.

"He's an elderly Jewish man in his sixties and he's likely to be unsympathetic," he warned me.

To arrive in time for my job in this factory, I had to leave home at six in the morning. First I had a fifteen-minute walk to the train. Then I commuted for forty minutes before reaching downtown Moscow. Once there, I took two subways, getting off at the Kiev Terminal. About this time, the sun rose. I took a bus and got off at the last stop where the Bisk family lived.

The Bisks were religious Jews who outdid themselves performing good deeds for others. I knew people who would have starved to death if the Bisks had not helped them with food. In addition, Reb Yitzchak Bisk was a studious and very learned *Talmid Chacham*.

I stopped every morning at their house to put on *tallis* and *tefillin* and *daven Shacharis*. When I finished, I took the bus to Kunsova, a large suburb. After riding a second bus five stops and walking forty minutes to Zarechi, a secluded village, I arrived at my factory to begin work at nine. I would thus traverse the sprawling metropolis of Moscow twice a day.

On the way home, I would stop in Moscow to buy bread and other staples—sugar, barley, butter—which were not available in Kliazma. Indeed, at times even the bread in Kliazma was barely edible. Of course, this meant waiting in line for hours, and I sometimes returned home at ten or eleven at night. Nevertheless, I tried to help out however I could, since my wife had more than enough on her hands.

Every morning, before setting out, I had to fetch the daily supply of water. I made a cart on which I placed a vat that held six pails of water and went to the well at five in the morning. In the winter, a sleigh replaced the cart.

I had undertaken this job despite the arduous traveling conditions because it gave me a plausible reason to demand an extra day off.

"If you want me to come," I told my superiors, "you had better give me flexible hours!"

Since not many were willing to trek out to that isolated village, they agreed.

A year and a half passed uneventfully, but a storm was brewing on another front. All over Russia, a wave of anti-Semitism was building up. This time, every Jew, even the non-religious, was as much a target as I was.

19 THE DOCTORS' PLOT

ANTI-SEMITISM IN SOVIET RUSSIA, OF COURSE, WAS nothing new. It had erupted in 1936, gaining momentum with each passing year. Thousands of Jews disappeared in the years 1936-38, many of them influential Communist Party members. Although such wholesale persecutions had ended during the war years, Jews were still hated. A Jew who managed to escape from the Germans to the Russian side was shown little sympathy. Frequently, he was accused of the ludicrous crime of spying for the Germans and punished with imprisonment or death. They would demand of these refugees, "Why have you remained alive? You must have worked with them!"

Nothing exemplified this national sentiment better than the law Stalin promulgated after the war, forbidding Jews to take revenge on Russian and Ukrainian Nazi collaborators. Anyone caught killing these savage murderers would himself be shot to death.

This law was passed at a time when Jews were thirsty for retributive justice. The Ukrainian people, largely rabid anti-Semites, had been restrained during the beginning years of the Communist reign when so many prominent leaders were Jews. When the Nazis overran their land, however, these gentiles took part in the Jewish massacres with abandon. The Nazi murder troops rarely had more than nine hundred German soldiers at their disposal, but they were able to kill tens of thousands of Jews at one time because of the zealous participation of the local Ukrainians. Even when the war was over, these peasants thirsted for blood. They did not refrain from killing those broken Jews who managed to make it back to their homes in an effort to start their life afresh. Over one and a half million Jews died through their complicity.

A bitter denouncement fell upon the remaining Jews. Although the "utopian Communist democracy" proclaimed that all nationalities were to be equal, Jewish blood was revealed to be cheaper than others. Right after the war, Stalin heaped praise upon the Russian generals and people, declaring them to be foremost among all the nations which comprised the family of Soviet peoples. He knew well how the Jews had fought like lions. By deliberately ignoring their courage and dedication, his statement bespoke the undisguised Russian animosity towards Jews.

Most of the Jewish members of the government, who had despoiled their compatriots of their Jewish heritage, were long dead, victims of the same political maneuvering they themselves so often employed. They were acting on the hope that once Judaism was suppressed, the Jews would attain equality with all other peoples. This was shown to be nothing but wishful thinking. Here they were, Russian citizens loyally following the Party line, but they were still discriminated against and despised by their countrymen.

An entire generation of Jews had been educated in Soviet schools. They had believed the Communist propaganda against religion, that it was only a myth created by primitive peoples which could not sustain itself against modern, rational thought. They were taught that the terms "Jew" and "anti-Semitism" were anachronistic racial words that could not be applied to devoted Russian citizens like themselves, particularly since anti-Semitism was a ploy of the former

Czarist regime to divert the peasants' minds from the struggle for emancipation.

Now, suddenly, they discovered that Russian citizens hated Jews and that the Russian soldiers hated their Jewish comrades. The Germans were annihilating the Jews, and the Russians, who were fighting the Germans, also hated the Jews. Bewildered Jews were forced to admit that Jewish destiny was unique. What is a Jew? Why is he despised more than any other nation?

This revelation led to a gradual revival of Jewish pride and identity, as Jews began to realize how they had been taken in by the Communists' empty promises. The tragedy was that no one was left who could give these Jews the guidance they sought. As long as Stalin was alive, the Jewish outcry was stifled. But it survived as a seed, waiting for a chance to break through the hostile ground.

Immediately after World War II, punishments against Jews accelerated. The few prominent Jews who remained were killed or sent to Siberia. The next ones to suffer were the Jewish masses. Jews were fired from their jobs for no reason—whether professionals or workers. Jews were imprisoned on trumped-up charges, to the point where jails were bursting with them. In one Jewish neighborhood, Davidkova, the Jews were evicted on *Yom Kippur* and ordered to leave Moscow. There were even times when Jews were thrown out of trains and autobuses. It became common for them to be insulted by hooligans.

Daily, the newspapers published articles laced with lies and accusations against Jews. They ranted against Jews who had dared to adopt Russian names and alerted the public to the danger of Jewish spies and traitors. There was no one to take up the side of the Jews, and their situation steadily deteriorated.

I remember when people were waiting in a long line at a grocery store. Tea kettles had arrived, and everybody wanted to buy one. An elderly Jew asked the saleslady if he could pay for a box of candles while everyone waited, since he did not want a kettle. She refused.

"Let the poor old fellow have it," someone snickered. "He won't be around in Moscow much longer. In a few days, they'll all be expelled."

By this time our situation was precarious. How and from where would our salvation come?

Then, in March 1953, the papers unveiled the notorious Doctors' Plot. Stalin had "discovered" that the inner circle of Jewish doctors, who had guarded his health for twenty years, was now planning to poison him. These falsely accused dignitaries were imprisoned, to await a trial whose outcome was a foregone conclusion. Public sentiment bristled anew against the Jews. Substantiated reports were circulating that Stalin was planning to send all the Jews to Siberia.

During those mad days, *Purim* arrived, and I decided that we must not let the desperate situation break our spirit. For the first time in a long while, we made plans to celebrate the holiday in a large family circle. We invited Yisrael Freidman and a friend, who was a *shochet* and *mohel*, Reb Yaakov, and their families. Reb Berl, one of the Machnovke *Rebbe's Chassidim* also joined us. Altogether we were twenty-five men, women and children, celebrating the *Purim* feast in our apartment.

The gloom that hung in the air seemed more palpable than the cold gusts which blew in through our windows (our gentile neighbors had broken them the night before). At the meal, we spoke of the troubles and persecutions that had befallen Jews in the past, which seemed to be repeating themselves in our present time. I retold what the Iluy of Zevihl had declared during the famous Beilis blood libel in 1911.

"The heavens will not allow such abominable wickedness! In *Tehillim* (55:24) we read that those murderous treacherous men, 'they shall not live out half their days,' and our Sages explain that this refers to Doeg and Achitofel, the two chief advisors of King Shaul and King David, who wickedly turned against their masters. The obvious question arises: There were people far more wicked than these men, who were at least very learned men. Why were their lives cut short (when other wicked individuals lived to old age)? It is because G-d will not abide abominable lies and perversions against Jews.

"We also see this from the story of Navos the Yizraelite whom Achav's wife Ezevel had killed in order to inherit his vineyard. Eliyahu confronted him, 'You have murdered and also inherited? So says Hashem: In the place were the dogs licked the blood of Navos, the dogs will lick your blood. Hashem will wipe out all your descendants from Israel.' (*Melachim I* 21:19)

"Why did Achav deserve such a severe punishment for this misdeed, more than all his other sins? It is because Hashem will not tolerate the murder of a righteous man on the contrived charge that he is really wicked.'

I concluded this tale by saying that the accusations of murder against these doctors is as perverted as the charge against Beilis. Let us hope this is a sign of God's forthcoming salvation.

Suddenly two of the children jumped up from the table—my Moshe Mordechai and Yisrael's son Naftali, both five years old. They each put a hand on the other's shoulder and began to dance and sing! We were astonished at their spontaneous reaction, and it raised our spirits.

"Look at this!" Reb Berl called out. "If little children are dancing and singing, it is a sign that a miracle will happen to us!"

Early the next morning, we heard on the radio that Stalin was ill. This official announcement of his illness was universally understood to mean that he was already dead, for they never announced when a high Party member took ill.

This was a miracle like the original miracle of *Purim*!

The benefits of the tyrant's death were not long in coming. The doctors were freed, and with them thousands of innocent Jewish prisoners. Anti-Semitism once again was, relatively speaking, driven underground. All our people felt the relief. A few months later, when a daughter was born to us we named her Esther Malkah, after Queen Esther, in remembrance of this modern-day deliverance.

The smoldering embers of Jewish discontent, fanned during Stalin's years, did not burst into flame again until the 1960s. Then, Jews searching for meaning and expression of their special identity began to appear in the thousands at the *shuls* on holidays like *Simchas Torah*. (A *shul* was the only place they could assemble without a permit, since "everyone is free" to worship as they please in the Russian democracy.) Every year, Jewish boys and girls gathered at *shuls* to sing and dance in the streets; many found their partner in life from these meetings. There were cases where parents and children both left secretly, only to find that they had been going to the same destination.

Many young people were angry with their parents for not teaching them about Judaism. They formed secret study groups to learn about Judaism and the Hebrew language. Their new knowledge nourished the desire in them to leave Russia and go to Israel, where they could live as practicing Jews. These youths did not know that mixed dancing was forbidden; they were not truly informed about the Torah—how to pray, wear *tefillin* and observe all the *mitzvos*; many had not been circumcised. How could they have known? Who was there to teach them? And yet, these Jewish souls cried to be unfettered of Soviet ideology. They demanded to be returned to their Jewish heritage, which had been so tightly repressed for two generations.

20 THE JEWISH DIRECTOR

AMONG THE PRISONERS LET OUT AFTER STALIN'S death, was a young girl named Sarah. Her family had been caught trying to cross the border after the war. Her father, a famous *Rav*, had been tortured to death, and her ailing mother died soon after her release in 1953. Sarah had a brother who had remained in Uzbekistan after the war to continue learning Torah secretly, but she had no idea what had become of him. Fearing she might be imprisoned again (they frequently imprisoned former prisoners on new trumped-up charges), she traveled to Moscow hoping to blend into the large population. In order to start a new life without the stigma of her recent incarceration, she had forged a different name on her identification papers.

Sarah came to us in Moscow and asked for help in finding a job. Her situation was quite difficult. Besides the fact that she was religious and kept *Shabbos*, which was enough of a problem, she was also constantly worried that she would be recognized on the street. My wife and I decided that, even though we lived in one and a half rooms with seven children and my mother-in-law, we would bring her into our home, give her a machine that wove scarves and teach her how to use it. I would thread the warp, and she would work in the woof. By doing this, she would be able to earn a modest living.

By 1954, only special cases were allowed to work at home, under the direction of a factory. We asked the daughter of our landlord, a war widow with two children, to apply to a factory for a home job, one which the girl would do in her place. The widow agreed to do us this favor. Sarah worked several months in our house without attracting attention.

As time passed, though, she was afraid she would eventually be found out. I advised her to go to my factory and apply for a job. She did so and worked there for several years. Fortunately, she was never bothered on account of her *Shabbos* observance. At first she was probably not even taken for a Jew. Though Sarah is the name of the first of our founding matriarchs, it was rarely borne by any Jewish girl. Rather it was a common name for Tatar gentiles. She was very likely taken for a Tatar.

Several weeks passed. One Friday morning, I arrived to find the director waiting for me. I was worried, for he never came to work so early.

"This Friday," he told me grimly, "you're not going home early." (I always left three hours before *Shabbos*, so that I could arrive home in time.) "Today you're going to finish laying the warp for the machine that makes bed covers. Otherwise, the other workers will be left without work tomorrow."

"You know that today is Friday, and I must leave work early," I answered him earnestly. "I have never worked on *Shabbos*, and I never will."

He was insistent, and the whole day he stood at my side to make sure I did not slip away. He suggested that I go on working for three hours longer, right up to the minute *Shabbos* started, and as I could not then travel home, I should remain over *Shabbos*. I told him that if I failed to come home for *Shabbos*, my wife would be convinced

that the police had taken me into their custody and would immediately fall ill from grief. I strained every nerve to finish in time, but I
had only finished forty percent of the work when I saw it was time
for me to return home. The director began to pressure and threaten
me.

I put down the tool. "If so, good-bye," I told him. "You can fire me
if you want, but I will never agree to work on *Shabbos*, no matter
what."

I arrived home, not telling my wife, in order to spare her any
distress on *Shabbos*. On Sunday, I decided to go back to work and
see what happened.

I came as usual, and the guard opened up for me. Even if the guard
already knew that I was being dismissed, I anxiously said to myself, it
is not his job to tell me. I continued to work undisturbed. On
Monday, I came to work again, and no one said a thing. I continued
doing my job as though nothing had happened.

Shortly after Sarah was settled in her job, her brother came to
Moscow from Tashkent. He was overjoyed to find his sister alive and
well, and he, too, turned to me for advice in finding a job. He had also
changed his name and documents upon learning what had befallen
his father. I advised him to come to my factory.

"I'll teach you how to weave the warp of a loom," I encouraged
him. "Many other religious Jews have managed to keep *Shabbos* in
this profession, and with the help of Hashem, you will manage
alright too."

Heeding my words, he came regularly to the factory, where he sat
next to me at work, as I taught him the skills. This youth was truly
G-d-fearing; he kept all the *mitzvos* with exactitude and devotion.

The gentile workers sensed that he was religious, even though
they rarely saw him because he was alone with me most of the day.
He wore a *yarmulke*, but whenever he ate, he used to put his hat
over the *yarmulke*. The director of the factory soon heard about
this.

I had always tried to avoid the director, and most of the time, he
too, passed by my room. Now, suddenly, he called me to his room.

When I appeared, he said, "Listen here, the fact that you don't
work on *Shabbos* bothers me, but I had pity on you because I heard

you had many children. All this time, I have put up with your unlawful fanaticism. But now I want you to tell me who that youth is who comes with you every day? Do you know him personally?"

"If I didn't know him, would I have brought him here?" I told him. "He's an unfortunate young man who is not quite sound, an orphan from the war years who was wandering here and there. I had pity on him and decided to teach him a skill he is capable of learning. He is not incapacitated to the point that he will bungle simple work; you needn't fear he will ruin a machine. He's simply a good-natured child that I want to help. If it bothers you, though, I'll tell him not to come anymore."

"But why does he put on a hat on his cap when he eats? This disturbs the other workers."

"Why should you pay attention to what a mentally unbalanced person does?" I replied. "I told you he's not all there."

The director stood up.

"Don't be brazenfaced, Chazan!" he said bluntly. "I know that he's wearing two coverings while eating! (A *chassidic* custom based on *Kabbalah*.) He's doing it with full intelligence, and there can be no doubt that he's a *Chassid*!"

I did not answer and left. Then, one day, the director sent for me. When I came to his office, he began to speak candidly.

"Do you know how I figured out that your young friend was a *Chassid*? Because I myself was a *Chassid* of the Rebbe Rashab (Sholom Baer) of Lubavitch. I studied Torah from him for many years."

He then poured out his soul, telling me what had led him to his present situation. When I had come to his room, his head was uncovered, but when he mentioned the Rebbe Rashab he put on his hat.

A few weeks passed. We heard that the director had resigned and had turned over the factory to two young Jews. Months later, I met him in the Great Synagogue of Moscow. He had stopped shaving his beard. I also met him in the *mikveh* on a Friday. We always exchanged frank glances of recognition and greeting but uttered not a syllable. This was the norm because if anyone was arrested, others might be implicated.

At a later date, this same former director sent someone to me to order *shmurah matzos* for *Pesach*. I found out that he, in fact, once again had become a *Chassid*, fearing and observing Torah. His son, who lived in Bielorussia, also lived a Jewish life.

Now, my new Jewish director had been observing my young friend and likewise called me over, but for a reason that left me dumbfounded.

"Listen, Chazan," he said. "This young man who has been working with you seems to be religious. We have a girl in this factory who keeps *Shabbos*. What do you think about a match between them? They seem to suit each other. Why not?"

How could they know that the two were brother and sister? This risky information could not be revealed to a soul.

"I can't even suggest it to the boy," I quickly responded. "He doesn't make a good living and isn't in the best of health, either. The girl would never agree to a match like this, and I doubt anyway if the boy would be interested."

He was not satisfied with my excuses, though, and continued to pressure me until I agreed to propose the match. The next day, early in the morning, the director eagerly called me.

"Did you speak with him?"

"Certainly."

"And what did he say?"

"What I had surmised. He said the match didn't appeal to him at all."

"It can't be!" he exclaimed. "Listen, tell him I'll give him four thousand new rubles (the ruble had just been devalued at the rate of ten to one) to help him get started. I want to do something for the Jewish people."

I was astonished. This director was totally assimilated. All he knew about Judaism was that he was a Jew. It was hard to believe that he even identified with his fellow Jews, let alone wanted to help them.

"I spoke at length with the boy," I said, "but he didn't want to even hear about it. Try speaking to him yourself."

That well-meaning director began to pester my friend daily, until he could take no more and left. He was afraid that if it continued, they would eventually realize why he kept refusing so adamantly.

That same year, the factory was closed. Everyone had to look for another job. This was the winter of 1954. Soon afterwards, both the brother and sister got married, and in time, raised families. They eventually left Russia for Eretz Yisrael, where they merited to see their sons and sons-in-law as Torah scholars and G-d-fearing Jews, living and practicing the traditions for which their parents died.

21 SCHOOL PROBLEMS

EVEN IN A WASTELAND LIKE RUSSIA, IT WAS POSSIBLE for children to learn Torah and keep *mitzvos* if they really wished to do so. After my son Mordechai had learned *alef-beis* and how to *daven* in a *siddur*, we celebrated the beginning of his learning *Chumash* with a party. A few months later, he knew many *parshiyos* of the *Chumash*. I had instructed Reb David to begin teaching him *Gemara* by *Pesach* of 1954, when he was only six-and-a-half years old. My son Chaim Meir had begun to learn *alef-beis* at three and was already reading from the *siddur*. They studied for hours every day, and we were very proud of their progress.

As for my daughters, their formal learning did not go beyond reading and *davening* from a *siddur*, except for one to whom I taught *Chumash*, the *sedra* of each week. Also, my wife reviewed the *Tzenah Urenah*, the Yiddish explanation on the Torah, with them. More important in my eyes, however, was teaching them the laws that were essential for every Jew to know. They were proficient in the laws of *kashrus*, the holidays and prayer. I took them aside and I explained what problems to look for in a slaughtered chicken. I also demonstrated how to clean the chicken and how to *kasher* it, too.

As for myself, the pressing demands of my job did not permit me to learn as much as I wanted. I utilized every spare minute during the week, and on *Shabbos* and Holidays, to review with my children and to learn myself. During the years Stalin was alive, I never dared learn Torah on public vehicles. After his death, I began taking a *Gemara* with me to study while traveling.

September of 1952 was the beginning of our struggle over our children's education. Our daughters were fourteen, twelve and eight, but only Chaya Sarah, the twelve-year-old, had ever attended a Soviet school.

We had arranged her attendance in a school in distant Tarasovka in 1951-52, on the pretext that we were a large family and had no room for her in our apartment. She lived in Tarasovka with the aunt of one of the pupils of Reb David Honigman. The aunt bribed the teacher to accept her into the school though her home was four kilometers away. As she was not a strictly local child, her absence every *Shabbos* did not call for any action either. She might well have gone to her parents for that day.

In 1953, she attended a Workers' school, along with our oldest daughter Devorah. These schools were set up for youths who entered the labor force early and had not finished their formal education. The advantage for us was that school hours were only three mornings a week, Monday, Wednesday and Friday; thus, the problem of *Shabbos* observance was avoided.

For our eight-year-old Batsheva, however, the situation eventually became dire. This was brought to my attention in due time.

My landlord rented a small apartment to a new tenant, a typical Communist Jewish couple; they kept no *mitzvos* yet they spoke Yiddish. My mother-in-law saw her once hang up a *tallis*.

"What does your husband need that for since he never wears it?" she asked.

"Well he might go to *shul* some *Yom Kippur*, and anyway it will not hurt to have it when he comes to the end of his one hundred and twenty years."

Their daughter married a Jewish boy on army service who joined their home. He could not understand why my children did not go to school.

"They will grow up ignorant and incompetent barbarians," he ranted.

His wife and parents-in-law tried to quiet him down. "What business is it of yours? Don't you think they know what they are doing?"

"I just can't tolerate it! These kids are being ruined!" He threatened that he would go tell the municipality.

"My eldest is attending the Workers' school," I replied. "The next one is also going to enroll, now that she has a diploma from the school in Tarasovka. The third one, you are quite right, is going to start school. Thank you for taking this interest in us. You are quite right."

I was not worried that my children would be influenced by the schools. In my day, the anti-religious brainwashing was intensive and a major part of the curriculum. Now, however, the Communists had already won. They did not want to mention the idea of G-d even for the purpose of obliterating it, since the concept was so alien to most of the population! I therefore felt that school attendance at this time did not require the "death rather than submit" ruling my father-in-law promulgated in his day.

The problem now revolved around keeping *Shabbos*, which was a regular school day. Ever since Stalin's death, a slight spirit of liberality had been manifest amongst the authorities and Party members, who admitted that Stalin had unfairly terrorized huge segments of the population. I stood a better chance now than at any other time of having my religious practices and *Shabbos* observance tolerated by the school.

In the end, I decided that I would have to send Batsheva to school, but she would not go on *Shabbos*. I felt that Hashem, who had helped me so miraculously all these years, would surely continue to help me now.

Batsheva was eight when she began to attend school. It bothered the principal that such a beautiful and clever student would not conform to school rules. Her teachers began to pressure her to attend on *Shabbos*. They understood there was nothing to be gained by broaching the subject with her father, so they tried to trick Batsheva into stating that she wanted to attend but that her father would not permit it.

"No," she would answer. "I myself do not want to attend. I am religious, and I keep *Shabbos*."

Their steady attempts to convince her failed. One day, I returned home in the middle of the day and found my wife and mother-in-law weeping.

"What happened?" I asked.

"You received a summons from the school to come and see the principal!"

I went immediately to his office.

"Who are you?" he asked.

"Aaron Chazan."

"Ah, yes. I wanted to speak with you."

He brought me into his private office, where the vice principal and a woman were seated. He looked me over.

"I would like to know, why doesn't Batsheva come to school on Saturday?"

I was honest. "My wife and I are religious Jews, and we keep *Shabbos*. This is how we've educated our children all their lives, and this is why they don't want to go to school on *Shabbos*."

"No good, Chazan, no good," he said. "Tell me, do you work on *Shabbos*?"

"I do not."

"How does the factory permit this?"

"Some days, I work on the morning shift, and other days on the afternoon shift. The management isn't even aware that I observe *Shabbos*. I have never worked on *Shabbos* in my life and I never will."

He gave this some thought and then said, "Be that as it may, you are already an adult, and it's not my business to educate you. But you must convince your child to come to class on *Shabbos*, as all the rest of the children do."

"How can you even suggest that?" I exclaimed. "My children know that I'm an uncompromisingly religious Jew. Even if I agreed to do what you suggest, they would assume I went insane. Under the circumstances, would they listen to me?"

I ignored his demands, and Batsheva continued as before, not attending on *Shabbos*. But the principal did not give up. He came up with a ruse, trying to convince Batsheva to join the Pioneers, the Communist Children Organization. He conjectured that once she associated with children who were enthusiastic Communists, she would be persuaded to become like them. Batsheva's teacher was appointed to the task. She tried to pressure Batsheva into becoming a Pioneer.

At the end of one of the classes, the students were ordered to remain in their seats for a moment. The teacher called Batsheva to the front of the classroom while the eyes of all her classmates were riveted on her.

"You are an excellent student, Batsheva. Don't you think you deserve to be a Pioneer?"

"No."

"Why not?"

"Because I'm a religious Jew."

When she came home and told us of the encounter, we rejoiced at her strength of character, but I was worried that her answer was too blunt and might lead to repercussions. I kept my thoughts to myself, though. The next day, I was again called to the principal.

"Do any of your religious laws forbid one to be a Pioneer?" he asked.

"No, we have no law like that," I replied. "My daughter refused to join because the other students have told her she'll have to write on *Shabbos* when she becomes a Pioneer. Is that so?"

"No," he answered. "She can be a Pioneer even if she does not write on *Shabbos*."

"If joining the Pioneers," I said, "does not entail violating *Shabbos*, then I agree to have her registered as a Pioneer."

Now she "belonged" but it had no effect on her whatsoever.

Several times after this, the principal called Batsheva in and tried to persuade her to attend school on *Shabbos*. She was not afraid to reiterate that she believed in G-d and would never violate *Shabbos*. Her teachers went so far as to write insults about her on the bulletin board, and to reprimand her often in front of her classmates but she would not give in. For three years, Batsheva learned in this school, under mounting pressure, until we moved to Bolshevo.

22 WORKING IN MOSCOW

I COULD NOT FIND WORK THE FIRST HALF OF 1955, and I spent this time teaching my children. My son Avraham was born in March of 1955. In the summer, I found a job in a factory making plastic buckles for belts. I was hired through the help of a religious man named Zev Sirota. Ten or eleven years earlier, two brothers of Zev had been pupils of mine in Tashkent. Coming from a religious family, they appreciated my efforts to educate them. Twenty years later, in a visit to the Lubavitcher *Rebbe* in New York, a stranger came over and embraced me. "Don't you remember me?" he said. "You took me out of school and taught me Torah at your *cheder*!" It was Reuven Sirota, one of the two brothers!

Zev Sirota made buckles in the factory in a one-man department where he could control his own hours in order to keep *Shabbos*. They liked his work, and when they needed more buckles he proposed to bring along another "expert" who would take over the

169

machine for more hours after his working day. He brought me.

Zev knew that I would learn quickly how to turn this machine and then file off the sharp edges on the fast-revolving stone wheel. He did most of the machine work and left the filing to me, which I usually did after the two dozen workers were all gone.

One evening, near the end of 1956, I caught myself dozing off and my face fell forward almost up to the wheel-edge. Afterwards, I began to take more care. I made sure to nap before so I would be able to remain alert, but I never felt quite safe after that near disaster. A few months later, I left because of this persistent fear.

One evening, while still on this job, I had an unpleasant encounter with the railway police. Together with a crowd, I crossed the railway lines at an authorized crossing point. Then, still with the crowd, I walked on again for about a kilometer up to the station. Out of nowhere, a young man challenged me.

"You have unlawfully crossed the line here. Pay the fine."

"I crossed together with the crowd a kilometer back," I protested.

"I saw you cross here," he bellowed.

"You know I did nothing of the kind," I answered. "Why do you discriminate against me? Just because I'm a bearded Jew? This is the Week of Concord and Fellowship of the Nations. Can't we expect a measure of peace and fellowship from you? By Soviet law, anyway, there is no difference between one people and another."

"By me there is. I recognize the difference," he said sourly.

As I would not pay up, he took me into the office of the railway police. Seated in front of us was a policewoman, the red cap of her uniform on a side chair. This color, as it happens, indicated her rank and was not a Communist emblem. He reported me to her and she demanded I pay up. I told her that I crossed as one of a crowd a full kilometer earlier and that when I asked him why he was discriminating against me, he said that he could well tell the difference between a Jew and one of his own. I tried to point out to him that in this Week of Concord and Fellowship of the nations, of all times, he should display a better Soviet spirit.

She paid no attention to my moral stand on Soviet equality. She demanded my particulars, name, address and identity papers, also fifty rubles, a fine equal to a tenth of my monthly wages.

"I have no name," I replied. "I live in the street, and I have no money and no papers."

Her angry demands drew from me the name Avraham Moishevitch Chazan with only the surname true. The first name and the patronymic name (son of Moishe) only had the same initials as those of Aaron Mordechovitch (son of Mordechai). I also gave my address in Kliazma.

"You are only trying to twist your way out of paying the fine," she said insultingly.

She phoned the Kliazma police station. They did not know of an Avraham Moishevitch at all.

"So I will have no choice but to detain you," she said triumphantly.

"If you don't pay attention to my complaint of prejudice," I said, "I owe you no reply. I wish you would take me to court."

That made her more angry. She called in an officer with epaulets. He took me into his room and went over the story again. He ordered a young man to search me.

"Note that I forbid it!" I shouted back at them. "I have given no consent to be searched!"

"You will only get yourself a high fine and a prison sentence," the officer said calmly.

"I am not afraid of prison," I replied boldly. "I don't want to talk to any of you. I'll talk to a Soviet policeman who honors the Constitution."

They called in the policeman on the beat.

"For two years I have been working at the Bolshevik Collective Factory and you have seen me come and go daily," I said to him.

They phoned to the factory, and it was confirmed that Aaron Mordechovitch Chazan did work there. I explained to the senior officer that I had given the correct address, Lenin Street, and the correct surname and initials, but that I had to make a stand against this unconstitutional behavior.

"Be off now and we'll look into the matter," he replied, dismissing me.

The next day at the factory, they told me they were worried that I might have been caught with some of their goods unlawfully in my possession.

That same day, on the way home, I stopped at the Machnovker *Rebbe* and told him this story. He laughed at my performance. A few days later, I also told the story to Rabbi Eli Sandler.

"Why be so courageous?" he said. "It could have gotten you into no end of trouble."

There was truth to what he said, but nevertheless, I had felt that I had to stand up against their discrimination.

Elul, 2955, was an eventful time in my life. Months before, I had received an invitation to attend a *yahrzeit* assembly in Krasnostav with other survivors. I was eager to attend.

On August 24, 6 *Elul*, forty of us visited the patch of grass outside the remains of our town, where eight hundred and seventy of our townspeople were buried. It rent my heart to think that only a few feet from me lay the bodies of my martyred parents, brother and sister and their families. After years of so much suffering, they had met such a fate! All of us had some relatives there, and we wept and said the mourners *Kaddish* as well as *Kel Maleh Rachamim*.

Later, while we ate lunch, we exchanged news. I spoke to them about Judaism, and they were attentive. Batya, the same woman who had once wanted to take away our *shul*, was there, too. She now lived in Zevihl. I had not seen her or heard of her all this time. She amicably offered me cookies, which I refused, of course.

A friend took me aside, saying, "Don't you know? Batya is now a religious Jew. She keeps *kashrus* and *Shabbos* and even goes to *shul* to pray."

It was encouraging to learn that even someone like Batya, once a fanatical Communist, had returned to the faith of her fathers.

On the way home, I stopped in Slavita and met some people who had lived in Krasnostav in my day. While speaking with them, I tried to awaken their interest in Judaism, but they only mocked my words.

"Don't tell us about religion," they mocked.

"When will you ever come around and see the light, Aaron?" another said.

Those who had attended the *yahrzeit* assembly were the ones who felt intimately connected to their Jewish identity and destiny, but these others had become completely estranged from Judaism; over them the Communists had triumphed completely. It grieved me to think they would probably be lost to the Jewish people forever.

That *Elul* was an occasion of great happiness for us from another standpoint. We celebrated the wedding of our eldest daughter. Moshe, her *chasan*, was the brother of Yisrael Freidman's wife. He survived only because of miracles and special providence. After his release, he came to Moscow to look for his sister. Our Devorah had just become seventeen, and the match was made. We celebrated the wedding in our home, with over a hundred guests attending. It was truly a joyous occasion. The young couple settled near us.

Right before *Pesach* of 1956, I had my first encounter with the police. Over the years, I had arranged for a large quantity of wheat kernels to be sent in from Tashkent, which I used for baking *shemurah matzos*. Kliazma had a flour mill, and the grinder in charge was an old gentile. Every year, in exchange for a generous sum, he let us in to grind our wheat. That year they had closed down the mill, but the grinder agreed to allow us in for one day. He locked us inside, leaving open a small door in the back.

We were a crowd of about ten men, and we got right to work. Suddenly we heard voices outside and realized it was the police. Although the *shemurah matzos* were really for tens of families, we quickly decided that I, Reb Yaakov Orenstein and a thirteen-year-old boy named Moishe Heskel would say that the flour was ours and that the others had just come to watch. We divided the one hundred and twenty kilograms of wheat among us. I took fifty kilos for myself, and Reb Yaakov and the boy claimed thirty-five each for their families. This would give the impression that we were simply grinding the flour for our personal needs and not to make illegal profits on the black market. At that time, flour was only occasionally available, which made it a prime black market item, and black marketeering was a serious offense.

The police entered, and we told them our story. They locked the mill and brought us to the police station. When they checked and found out that we had large families and were impoverished, they let us go and even gave us back all the flour. So, that year, everyone had *shemurah matzos.*

In 1957, I finally found work buying up small quantities of old rags for a factory, which reprocessed them. My supervisor was Reb Moshe Zaichik, who now lives in Petach Tikvah, Israel. Zaichik himself kept *Shabbos* and educated his children to be G-d-fearing, observant Jews. Moreover, he excelled in giving charity and doing good deeds. His attitude was that no sacrifice was too great when it came to helping fellow Jews. Indeed, many of the Jews in the factory had gotten their jobs through his efforts. He arranged it so that I could keep *Shabbos* at my job without problems. They were very satisfied with me at this job, for I could be trusted not to waste their money. People who qualified for anything else would not have been interested in such work, but for me it was perfect; I sought no status, only to be able to keep *Shabbos*. I stayed on for eight full years, until we were able to leave Russia.

During my previous eleven years in Moscow, I had changed jobs about ten times; each time my *Shabbos* observance became too noticeable, I had to leave.

At this job there was another plus. The turnover was big and entailed a lot of work, thus my wife also became employed there, working half time.

But if my career worries had come to an end, my problems with the school system took their place.

At the end of the winter, our living conditions were desperate. We were still living in that crowded, freezing, one-and-a-half-room apartment, which took the heaviest toll on my mother-in-law, who was in her late seventies. It was senseless to remain, as the family was growing from year to year. Even though Devorah was now married and had her own home, she and her husband visited daily, frequently eating with us on *Shabbos*. To rent a larger apartment was impossible because no one would rent to a large family.

In 1957, the government gave us a plot of land in Bolshevo, a new district in the suburb of Kaliningrad. I borrowed large sums of money to build a five room house, three rooms for us and two for my daughter Devorah. Before *Pesach* of 1957, after seven years of living in Kliazma, we moved to the new house. With this move, too, I finally rid myself of all the school problems we were having with Batsheva.

Of course, I had to pay off my debts. Being an impoverished worker, this presented difficulties. I decided to make a special oven for baking *matzos* and stayed up nights for months before *Pesach*, baking the *matzos* with helpers. In this way, within a few years, I was able to finish paying what I owed. Fortunately, I was never caught making the *matzos*, or I would have faced the serious accusation of disseminating religious propaganda. When Chanah was born in May we were grateful that we could move to a larger dwelling.

23 SCHOOL PROBLEMS IN BOLSHEVO

WHEN WE CAME TO BOLSHEVO, I DID NOT ENROLL the children in school. As a large family in a new neighborhood, we were not unnoticed for long, however, and the school authorities began to pressure me to enroll the children. In the face of their threats, I had no choice but to enroll some of the children, the fewest that I could. I was not worried about the influence the school would have on them, knowing their strength of character, but I was worried about attendance on *Shabbos*. How long would they let me get away with it?

My policy was to hold out as long as I could, never sending them before eight years of age. Generally if I had to send a child, I sent a girl before a boy. This way the boys could learn Torah undisturbed as long as possible. Batsheva, who was now twelve, continued to attend school, but Chaim Meir, who was eight, did not attend. In 1958, Moshe Mordechai went to school. He was ten years old. Batya began to attend two years later, when she was nine, but Chaim Meir, who was older than she, did not begin until a year later.

My children's late start in school was never a problem. The older girls would teach the younger ones the basics of reading and math, so that by the time they joined their class, they were on the level of the other children and were even among the better ones in class.

Almost immediately, however, problems with Batsheva arose again. Her learning hours were in the afternoon, from one to six. We arranged for her to leave class early every Friday on the excuse that she underwent regular medical treatment. After a few months, the woman who was principal heard of her weekly Friday disappearance and began to wonder what kind of treatment had to be done weekly, particularly on Friday nights. Inquiring at the local clinic, she was told that no such patient appeared on their lists. She gave strict instructions to Batsheva's teacher not to let Batsheva go home that Friday before class was over.

The next day, Batsheva came home upset. Her teacher had told her that from then on, she would not be allowed to leave class early on Friday. I told her not to worry.

"I'll come and take you out of class," I assured her.

That Friday, I came to the school and asked one of the cleaners to call my daughter out. While I was waiting, the principal suddenly appeared. I amicably introduced myself.

"Yes," she said. "I wanted to speak with you. Wait a minute."

"Fine," I answered. "But I want my daughter to come with me."

When Batsheva came, I told her to go home immediately. She left, and the principal ushered me into her office. The vice principal and the senior counselor of the Pioneers joined us. The principal asked me why my daughter left class early every Friday. I told her the truth.

"Impossible for such a thing to be in a Soviet school!" she said emphatically.

"This is what we did when we lived in Kliazma, according to an agreement made between me and the principal," I replied. "You can phone him and check it out if you want."

"Where did the principal in Kliazma get permission to make his own rules?"

"I don't know, but it won't help to protest. My children, of their own volition, refuse to write on *Shabbos*. That's why they don't attend school on *Shabbos*."

"But she's a Pioneer!" she exclaimed.

"They accepted her into the group knowing that she wouldn't write on *Shabbos*."

"Look on the wall. Do you see that red flag? We received that mark of honor for your daughter's class, because of its excellent scholastic performance. Now, because of your daughter's behavior, they will take this flag away."

"Do you want to throw my daughter out of class?" I asked.

"No, but I am responsible for this school, and I don't want to suffer consequences because of you."

"I will bear the consequences. You can bring me to court if you want," I replied.

"I can now see that you belong to an underground movement against the authorities."

"The police can investigate that."

Our discussion was stormy; I vociferated my position and she realized I would not budge. We finished in mutual anger. In the end, I won. Batsheva continued to leave the class early on Friday for the rest of the year.

The principal, however, was not satisfied. She tried to talk Batsheva into coming on *Shabbos*. Batsheva refused. The principal exploded and told her angrily, "If so, go to Palestine!"

Batsheva quickly replied, "It is also good here for me."

Eventually, this principal was appointed regional education director and left our school, but the principal who took her place, also a woman, was even worse.

That winter we became grandparents, and half a year later, Yaakov was born to us in May. The following winter, we married off our second daughter. We found her *chasan* through mutual family ties. Our son-in-law's brother had married a religious girl from Bukovina (a province of Romania, annexed to Russia after World War II, in which a large number of religious Jews still lived). This girl had a well-regarded, eligible brother. Hundreds of friends joined us in celebrating the wedding.

In January, 1960, our Rivkah was born.

When we had moved to Bolshevo, I had found a new Torah teacher for my sons, Rav Israel Olidort. As he refused to be paid, I could not use him indefinitely, though I was very happy with his work. His was one of the three families who kept *Shabbos* in Odessa (as related earlier). I found another teacher, Reb Yaakov Lerner, a one-armed invalid. This handicap was in fact an advantage. If an official entered the house while he was there, we could always say, "We are giving our friend the invalid a meal." The Machnovke *Rebbe* helped me cover some of the cost of my sons' education while I paid the rest.

In 1958, Moshe Mordechai attended the Soviet schools in the morning, but studied *Gemara* after he returned home (at one o'clock) for the entire afternoon. My sons were always eager for their Jewish studies, competing with each other to excel. I emphasized studying the *Gemara* in depth and learning large portions of *Shulchan Aruch*. They also learned *Chumash* with Rashi every week. As time went on, I became filled with the satisfaction of knowing that each of my children was steadfast in his trust of G-d and practice of *mitzvos*.

In 1955, Batsheva and Moshe Mordechai came down with yellow jaundice, a serious illness, and had to be hospitalized. They refused to eat the hospital's cooked food. Batsheva, who was ten and more mature, secretly threw the food into a garbage can, but Moshe Mordechai, only eight, blatantly ignored the meals brought to his bed. When the nurses saw he wasn't eating, they gathered around him and tried to force open his mouth and push the spoon in, but he would not open his mouth. The doctor told me in alarm that if he didn't eat, he would not recover. Since visitors were not allowed in, all I could do was send him a note via the doctor, in Yiddish, in clear printed letters.

"You may eat," the note said. "It is kosher."

I thought this was preferable to telling him that he was allowed to eat because his life was in danger. But I could not fool him. He would not even listen to me. The entire six weeks he was at the hospital, he, as well as his sister, ate only fruit, uncooked vegetables and candies, until the doctors pronounced them in good enough health to be released.

When my son came out he said, "You know, you said it was kosher but how do you know? They simply chop the chickens' heads off."

I smiled with pride at his words.

My children taught and encouraged each other; they constantly talked about *kashrus*. Upon reaching the age of seven or eight, I made a point of teaching them *Chullin* (which centers on *kashrus* laws), first the *Mishnah* and later the *Gemara*. If anything happened to me they would know the rules of *shechitah* and *kashrus*. Furthermore, I taught both the girls and the boys how to examine the inner organs of a chicken.

I often pointed out to my children that my trials as a child, had been far greater than theirs. They grew up knowing that they were religious Jews and that they had nothing in common with everybody else. I, however, as a young child of eight, had my whole world overturned. All my religious friends became enemies who taunted and despised me.

I recounted to them an episode of my youth. Once, I observed how a bird escaped time after time when someone wanted to catch it. I had reflected then, "This is my situation. The bird knows full well that it has many enemies, yet it takes measures against the danger and does not surrender. We have many enemies who hope for our misfortune, but we must guard ourselves and not give in."

As my children grew older, each had to wage his own battles and undergo trials in school, on the street and at work, but not once did any of them waver. Despite the grinding poverty we suffered, my children shared my struggle and never complained. Perhaps their strength of character stemmed from their witnessing the suffering my wife and I took upon ourselves to preserve our Judaism. My children, no less than I, experienced countless miracles and escaped dangers. Until the day we were privileged to leave the bitter, blood-soaked Russian soil, we were oppressed for our faith.

One bright consolation we had at that time was the *melaveh malkahs*. My sons, my sons-in-law, my nephew Yisrael Freidman of Perlovka, and Israel Olidort with his son Motl and son-in-law Velvel Sirota and I gathered as one extended family and celebrated each *Motzei Shabbos*. It was no more than potatoes, herring and cake, but to us it was a heartwarming feast. The boys prepared a *siyum* in an order of *Mishnayos* each week. The boys were also examined on the *Gemara* they had learned, and the girls and small boys on the *Chumash*.

G-d was with us. Israel Olidort's grandchild, David, started school in 1966 at the age of seven. By then he was so unshakable in his faith that he stayed away *Shabbos* and left early on Fridays. One Friday, they kept him in, but he refused to write. They tormented him until he fainted, but he did not write! He now is a literary worker for the Lubavitcher *Rebbe*. He is one of a few whose task it is to memorize the *Rebbe's* Torah conversations on *Shabbos* and *Yom Tov* and thereafter write them down. These are printed as pamphlets and disseminated throughout the world.

24 UNDER ATTACK

ONE SUNDAY, IN APRIL OF 1960, A FRIEND BROUGHT me a newspaper that was printed in Mitishchi, the main city of our region. He showed me a letter to the editor, signed by the teachers of the school. "The Public Is Called to Arms!" the letter cried out.

The authors were calling on the public to arise and protest "what is going on in our hometown of Bolshevo. Children of the Chazan family learn in our school, but not on Saturday, for religious reasons. Their parents have so deeply indoctrinated them to believe in their religious nonsense that the children themselves claim, 'We uphold our religion of our own volition and will not transgress the *Shabbos*.'"

Further on, the letter accused, "And not only that, Saturday is set aside for teaching the children to help out at school and learn to love work, according to the new law. (This law was passed during

182

the Khrushchev administration.) Chazan's children ignore this law, too. This disturbs the unity of the whole class. Chazan had better realize that his children are not his private possession. They belong to the entire Soviet Nation. We must not permit such flagrant dereliction. We are calling upon the municipality and the factory where Chazan works to correct this serious breach." (See the entire text of this letter in the Appendix.)

This libellous letter, and more so the editorial comment that followed it, struck terror in our hearts. There was no doubt that the authorities would begin to follow up on us, and who could predict what the outcome would be?

"Did you read that letter in the papers?" well-meaning friends asked us that entire day.

"Things are really serious now; you had better think about whether you're doing the right thing!"

Such discouraging words only heightened our apprehension, but my family and I decided not to submit. On Monday, I traveled to my job at the kiosk of the old rags dump. When I arrived, I saw a note hanging on the door.

"Don't open the kiosk. Come straight to the office."

At the office, I did not know whom to see. I asked the clerks, "Why was I called here?" No one knew.

"Wait until the senior director will come," they advised.

A short time later, the director arrived, accompanied by the secretary of the Communist bureau. (Every industry had an office of the Communist Party to oversee the enterprise and evaluate the workers' productivity.) They ushered me into a room, and we sat down. The director took out a newspaper from a drawer.

"Did you read this?"

"Yes," I said.

"Is this true?"

"No."

"It's not true?"

"On Saturday the children do work around the school. But tell me, is the government really interested in getting work out of little children?"

"No, the children do work so that they will learn to love work and hate idleness. It also keeps them off the street after school hours."

"If that's the case," I told him, "my children work in the house twice as hard as the others do in school. I am busy at my job all day, my wife also. She is overloaded with running the house because I can't afford any help. Now, let me ask you. We have five small children who are in the house the entire day. Who will watch them? I have a garden in the yard; who will work it? We have a large family with many mouths to feed; who will stand in line for many hours at the markets and stores? (In Russia food can be bought only at centralized locations, servicing thousands of people. These locations are often located far from home. People wait on line for the stores to open and then to buy the groceries, which can take hours!) Only our older children can do this! They learn in school, they do their homework, they take care of the shopping, they tend the garden. Do you want them to do even more work than this? They have more work than any other children in Russia!"

"Okay, okay. Let's say you have a plausible excuse for your children's not working at school, but you don't permit your children to write on *Shabbos*. Instead, you train them to defy Communist ideals. I think you and your wife should be tried in court. I think your children should be taken to our institutions and brought up correctly."

His harsh words were not vain threats. The Communists had actually done this to members of an Orthodox Christian sect.

"My children must be religious," I said, "since they owe their life to religion."

"How is that?"

"How old are you?" I asked the director.

"I'm older than you."

"How many children do you have?"

"Two."

"Can you explain to me why you have only two children? What's the matter? Are you or your wife sick? A woman naturally gives birth every year or two, but it seems that you planned to have only two children so that you could live an easy, comfortable life. I could also have done that, but I am a religious man. Because of my religious convictions were they born, so they are dutybound to be observant."

I turned to the secretary of the party bureau.

"How many children do you have?" I asked.

He smiled sheepishly and said, "One daughter."

"Why only one?" I challenged him. "Don't you know that Stalin passed a law forbidding abortion? (This law was passed to help repopulate the country after its loss of twenty million citizens in World War II.) You're the one who is breaking the laws of the country, not me. You didn't have more children because you wanted to enjoy the pleasures of life, to go to the theaters and cinemas. Is that what you call loyalty to the Communist ideal? I am a simple, pious man. I have thrown my life into my children, and they are loyal citizens whose behavior is impeccable. You can verify this at their school and with my neighbors."

The director did not want to continue our discussion.

"We'll speak about it again at a later date," he murmured. "In the meantime you can go."

When I got up, he called to an official, "Change his day off from Saturday to Sunday."

"You may as well fire me then. I will never work on *Shabbos*."

This was not the first time I had unpleasant encounters with employers. Hashem helped me survive them all.

The director never spoke with me again, and I continued to work in the kiosk. When my supervisor heard of the confrontation, he was afraid I was becoming a problem worker and wanted to fire me, but I was able to keep my job because of the efforts of his deputy supervisor Reb Moshe Zaichik. His kindness on my behalf was just one of many acts he did for me and countless others.

In December, we celebrated our first *bar-mitzvah*, before a crowd of over a hundred guests. Moshe Mordechai decided to celebrate his *bar-mitzvah* by making a *siyum* on *Chullin*. I suggested a theme for his *bar-mitzvah* speech, which he developed by himself. He spoke for an hour, and no one could believe that a youth born and raised in Russia could be so knowledgeable. The Machnovke *Rebbe*, Rav Eli Sandler and all the prominent Torah scholars in Moscow were present. Some of them cried from the wonder of it.

It was no problem getting a pair of *tefillin* for him nor, for that matter, any Jewish book. The attic of the Great Synagogue contained hundreds of pairs of *tefillin* and thousands of books thrown away by the communized children of devout Jews. Others, alas, threw away such holy books as trash.

In 1960, I was able to switch Batsheva, who was fifteen years old at the time, to a Worker's School, and the problem of *Shabbos* was solved for her. But Moshe Mordechai, Chaim Meir and Batya were attending school, and Esther Malka began in 1961. None of them attended on *Shabbos*.

We had a religious friend from Lithuania, named Rav Bezalel, whose son-in-law and daughter had moved to Moscow. They now live in Jerusalem.

"I feel as if I am in Eretz Yisrael when I enter this house," he would say in excitement. "Come here, children. Let me hear what each of you has learned."

They would run to him, bursting to tell him a Jewish law or something from the *Chumash*. Three-year-old Yaakov would come running, too.

"What, Yaakov?" he exclaimed. "You also know something?"

"Of course," Yaakov would answer proudly. "I know that G-d has created the world!"

In May 1962, Chaim Meir celebrated his *bar-mitzvah*. He finished *Bava Metzia* and made a *siyum* for the occasion, which was attended by all the rabbis and our friends. Before his speech, he recited three pages of the *Gemara* by heart. Everyone had to admit that it was possible to raise a learned Jew in Russia.

25 CHILDREN OF VALOR

IN THE SPRING OF 1962, MY WIFE AND I WERE requested to come to the municipality. Upon arrival, we found the mayor and his councillors waiting. They told us grimly that they would not continue to sit with folded hands, while we made a tempest in the school.

"My children themselves won't go to school on *Shabbos*," I answered, "and I certainly won't force them. In fact, I'm quite pleased about it. If you want, you can try me in court. I'm not doing anything illegal. According to the law, we can practice our religion."

"Listen, Chazan," the mayor said jumping to his feet. "A mountain of guilt is hanging over your head. Watch out that this mountain doesn't collapse on you. A grave punishment awaits you, and your wife had better realize it, too. Well, we've warned you. Now go home and think carefully about your future."

We returned home with low spirits. The authorities loomed

before us in all their power. How could we think we would manage to escape them forever? Any day, they might come to take us away. We knew full well what they were capable of doing. I had heard stories from the one Jew in a thousand who had miraculously made it out of Siberia alive! He told unbelievable accounts of the horrors he had been subjected to. We prayed day and night to remain safe, but our fears never eased up.

This dread was compounded by our difficult financial state, since I would not engage in illegal barter or shoplifting from my factory, common practices among the Russian workers. If I ever fell into the Communists' hands, I resolved, it would be for the sake of Torah and *mitzvos*, not for unlawful material gain.

Our son Yitzchak began school in September, 1962. Two years later his teacher came up with a plan. She told him that his classmates would pick him up on *Shabbos* to take him to school. We did not know whether to believe her words, but on *Shabbos*, at eight in the morning, his whole class showed up, forty strong. It was a quarter of an hour before the *minyan* in my house was due to start. Two men were already there.

"Does Yitzchak Chazan live here?" asked a girl who was older than the rest. Apparently she had been put in charge of the operation. "We've come to take him to school".

"I'm going to call him," my daughter said and quickly closed the door.

She ran and informed me of the situation brewing outside. I put on my *tallis* and confronted the class. The *tallis* particularly caused a sensation among them.

"Where is Yitzchak?" a few of them began to hoot. "He has to come to school. Where is he hiding?"

No sooner did he hear the shouts than Yitzchak came out and faced his classmates.

"Today I rest," he said unflinchingly. "Today is our *Shabbos*. Tell the teacher I cannot come."

After this show of strength, his teacher left him alone.

One day, the principal asked me, "Why can't your children write on *Shabbos* and attend school? All the other Jews send their children to school on *Shabbos*, even the grandchildren of Rabbi Schleifer go on *Shabbos*! Who told you it's forbidden? Are you sure you know your own rules?"

I knew my rules very well, I assured her. It is clearly forbidden for children to write on *Shabbos*.

"Don't you find many Communists," I went on, "who don't obey the country's laws and willfully commit violations? In the same way, there are many Jews who transgress the Jewish laws, but I will not. I will never transgress the commands of the Torah."

Some time later, Reb Meir Yonik told me he had been visiting a neighbor and a friend of the principal was present. She told Reb Meir that the principal had gone to Rabbi Levin and asked him whether children could write on *Shabbos*. He had answered that they could. Now, this woman told my friend, the principal asked her to tell Chazan that he has no reason not to send his children to school on *Shabbos*.

Hearing this, I went straight to the Great Synagogue to speak with Rav Levin. I first met his secretary and told him the story.

"I never heard of such an incident," he said. "But wait. Rav Levin is expected here any minute. Ask him yourself."

As soon as Rav Levin walked in, I told him of the incident.

"This is an outright lie," he said. "Nobody asked me any such thing. And if they ever do ask me, I will tell them that the Torah forbids children to write on *Shabbos*."

Hearing this, I excused myself and went home.

In May, 1963, our youngest child Shoshana was born. Shortly after, in September, a crisis ensued that eventually led to our firm decision to emigrate from Russia.

One *Shabbos* morning, I was on the way home from *minyan* with my eldest son-in-law. (Every few weeks we changed the location of the *minyan*.) We stopped to visit our friend Reb Meir Yonik, whose son Berl had just begun to study *Chumash*. After spending some time there, we continued home. Reaching my street, I saw a policeman standing not far from our house.

"Do you think he's waiting for us?" I asked my son-in-law.

"Oh, these fears of yours!" he chided me. "That policeman is not interested in you."

As soon as I walked into our yard, Batya came to meet me.

"Don't go into the house!" she warned me. "Three men are there, to speak with you."

But it was too late to retrace my steps. The policeman stationed in the street was now coming to our gate.

Next to our house was a small *sukkah*. I went in and removed my *tallis* to avoid possible inquiries concerning where the unlawful reactionary religious assembly had been held. Finally, I entered the house.

The mayor of Bolshevo, the principal of the school and a third person were waiting for me. As a district comprising hundreds of thousands of people, it was rare indeed to get a personal visit from the mayor of Bolshevo. I took a seat with the three of them.

"Unpleasant guests have come to you," one of them said.

"Why unpleasant?" I protested. "It's a pleasure to meet the mayor and the principal of the school."

"Do you know why we've come?"

"No. How could I know?"

"You don't know?" he said, slightly exasperated. "What will be with your children?"

"What about them?"

"They don't go to school on Saturdays."

"That is nothing new. They don't want to write on *Shabbos*, and so they don't go to school on *Shabbos*."

"You must persuade them to come on Saturdays."

"I'm not an anti-religious propagandist. I'm a religious man. My children are in school every day. Let the school try to persuade them."

At that moment, Yitzchak, who was ten years old at the time, passed through the room. The mayor called him over.

"What do you believe in?" he asked the boy.

"In G-d."

"Do you really believe there is a G-d?"

"Of course!" he answered. "If one believes, then there is a G-d."

"And if one does not believe?"

"That's not even a question," he answered and ran out.

"Now you have seen for yourselves that my children are religious, even with no prompting from me," I told the mayor. "That's the way all my children are. They have absorbed the religious atmosphere of our house, and they themselves want to keep *mitzvos*."

The mayor turned to me again. "Let me make this clear. You have no choice. You must send your children to school on Saturday. It's my responsibility to see that children are present in school all the days they have class. Whether they write or not, does not interest me. That's her matter," he added, pointing at the principal.

"I cannot allow some children to be different from everybody else," the principal objected. "His children are stubborn. His daughter Batsheva stayed late a few times on Friday, but the moment it began to get dark, she put her pens away and refused to write. What will we do with them in school on Saturdays?"

The mayor only repeated that I had to send my children to school on *Shabbos* and that more than this he would not demand. He warned me, though, that if I did not send them to school the next Saturday, I would be tried in court.

Our conversation over, my visitors left. This time the threat was too serious to be ignored. The mayor indisputably meant business. He would take immediate measures against us if his demands were not met. I sat down with my children to discuss a plan of action. Our first decision was that we would never transgress *Shabbos*, no matter what the threat. In the end, we decided to accede partially to the mayor's demands. Every *Shabbos*, a different child would go to school, without taking his briefcase, pencils or notebooks.

The next *Shabbos* was *Rosh Hashanah*. My sons wanted to *daven* with a *minyan*, so Batya, who was twelve, spoke up.

"It seems that the lot has fallen on me. I'll go, but please wait until I come home, before you make *Kiddush*. May Hashem help me."

The next *Shabbos*, she left for school without her briefcase. We *davened* at Reb Moshe Zaichik's house, and all through the service, my daughter and the school loomed in front of my eyes. How was she faring? I was certain she wouldn't transgress *Shabbos*, because she was strong-minded, but how much would she have to undergo from her teachers and classmates and that rotten principal?

After prayers, we returned home and anxiously awaited her arrival. When she came in, the mental strain was visible on her face.

"Thank G-d, everything is alright," she said.

We made *Kiddush*, and then I asked her, "How did it go?"

"My first class was math," she said. "The teacher wrote an exercise on the board and asked me to come up and solve it. I walked to the board, and she said, 'Take the chalk and write the answer.' I told her, 'I am forbidden to write on *Shabbos*.' Hearing this, she began to scream at me and tried to force the chalk into my hand. But she saw I wouldn't take it. So she called the principal, who came with the vice-principal.

"Both of them ordered me, 'Take the chalk! Immediately! Do the problem!' But I repeated that on *Shabbos* I do not write.

"They stopped their shouting, and I stood silent. All the children in class were dumbstruck; they looked at me and the principal to see who would win. Suddenly, the mayor walked in. He towered over all of us.

" 'What's going on?' his voice boomed out. 'Did the Chazan girl show up?'

" 'There she is, standing next to the board,' my teacher spat out. 'Just look at her! She refuses to write. She is forbidden to write, she claims.'

"The mayor turned to me, and said, 'Why aren't you writing? You came to class to learn. You know we have no holiday today.'

" 'I am a religious Jew,' I replied, 'and today is our holy day. I cannot write.'

" 'Take the chalk and write!' he ordered me.

But I didn't move. Finally, he asked the teacher to show him my notebook. (I had left it in school on Friday.) He looked through it and saw that my marks during the week were very good. He took the chalk in his hand and said, 'Tell me how to do the problem and I'll write.'

"I did the problem out loud, and he wrote it down.

" 'Is this correct?' he asked the teacher.

" 'Yes,' she replied. 'But she did not write it!'

"He took my notebook and wrote a five on it. (This means 'very good' on the Russian scale of achievement.) Then he turned to the teacher and principal and said, 'Don't bother her anymore. Let her just sit and listen to the classes.' And he left.

"But this scene was repeated in every one of my classes!" Batya exclaimed. "My last class was Russian language, and the teacher is an anti-Semitic Ukrainian. She shrieked at me the whole time. All she did was abuse me, but thank G-d, I held up. I just didn't answer her. Suddenly, a middle aged man walked in, and everyone stood up for him.

" 'What's going on here?' he bellowed.

" 'There is a religious family in the neighborhood,' the teacher said with distaste, 'and the daughter refuses to write on their *Shabbos*. She says it's a holiday and she can't write. No matter how hard we try to convince her, she's just plain stubborn.'

"The man asked to see my notebook. After he looked through it, he told her, 'Let her sit and just listen to the classes.'

" 'What!' the teacher protested. 'Have you come to defend her?'

"The man answered, 'Comrade, I am your superior. I told you not to start up with her. Leave her alone.'

"After this class, I came home undisturbed."

We felt such joy at her strength of character! The younger children were jealous of Batya, and they enthusiastically began to boast how unflinching they would be when their turn came. With the help of G-d, the rest of *Rosh Hashanah* passed without incident.

From then on, we regularly sent one child to school on Saturdays—one *Shabbos* one of the girls and the next, one of the boys, except for Moshe Mordechai, the oldest boy who was due to leave school in another half year anyway. But they never wrote.

Chaim Meir attended, keeping his hands in his pockets all the time. Batya, Esther Malka and Yitzchak also went. Finally the pressure of the school administration eased for the children. Instead, they concentrated their efforts on me.

My wife and I received a notice to come to a parent-teacher meeting. We did not attend, but a gentile neighbor who was there, gave us a summary. The main topic of the evening was, "What should be done about the Chazan children who won't attend school on Saturday, and even if one does come, he doesn't write?"

The principal and teachers led the discussion. They strongly advocated prosecuting me in court and putting my children into the custody of a Soviet Institution. They called on the parents at the meeting to give their approval to this plan.

A Russian woman, one of our neighbors, rose and addressed the assembly.

"Would you explain to me what is so criminal about the fact that Chazan's children don't come to school one day a week?" she said. "I am their neighbor, and I see that on that day all the children are home. They are well-mannered and their behavior is irreproachable. Instead of prosecuting Chazan, you should prosecute those parents whose children don't show up at school many days a week, children who are loitering on the streets, committing thefts! Leave the Chazans alone! The rest of us should only have such fine children!"

26 THE FIRST DEPARTURE

WHILE LIVING IN MOSCOW, WE WERE FORTUNATE TO have non-Jewish neighbors who respected us and never said a word to the authorities, although they knew full well that I baked *matzos*, built a *sukkah* and frequently hosted a *minyan*. They saw that we arranged *bris milahs* and weddings for others and had large crowds participating in these activities. Certainly our neighbors had more than enough material at their disposal, but they never informed on us.

In the beginning of 1961, I sent Moshe Mordechai away to the only *yeshivah* that existed then in Russia, a small secret Chabad *yeshivah* in Samarkand. He traveled a few days by train, just as I had more than twenty years before. When his school questioned where he had gone, I said that he had left Moscow to attend a higher institution. Fortunately, they accepted this answer.

My mother-in-law, now eighty, was in no way incapacitated, and her spirits were strong. She decided that in the few years remaining for her, she wanted to see her other children, those who had left Russia years before. Although it was hazardous to apply for emigration, she felt that she had little to lose. What would they do, after all, to a woman in her eighties?

She submitted her application to OVIR, the department of emigration, citing the law that permits emigration for the reunification of families, and was granted her request immediately. After *Sukkos*, Yisrael Friedman and I saw her off at the airport en route to Israel via Vienna. The airport itself was swarming with government agents, so we did not dare say a word to her, or even to each other.

My righteous mother-in-law passed away in 1978 at the ripe age of ninety-six. She lived to see a fifth generation born and had the satisfaction of knowing that all of her descendants, from young until old, were following the path of G-d.

A few days before, we had gone to say farewell to Rav Eli Sandler, a Torah scholar with whom I was friendly. He was also on his way to Israel. It was the night after *Simchas Torah*, and at his house were a few other close friends. He illustrated his feeling that Jews were beginning to awaken to their heritage with the following story:

"Here in Moscow I knew a middle-aged Jew, a Jew like all others, who was the director of a factory. Suddenly, he made a complete change, he became punctilious in keeping *mitzvos*, grew a beard, wore *tzitzis*, went to the *mikveh* and ate *shmurah matzos* on *Pesach*. I couldn't figure out what had happened to him. While speaking with me one day, he told me what had led to his transformation.

" 'I was the director of a weaving factory,' he told me, 'and a young Jew who kept *Shabbos* began to work for me. This inconvenienced me. I always feared they would catch him working for me, but I took pity on him since he had a large family, and so, I kept silent.

" 'Once it happened that the weaving on the looms was almost completed. It was Friday, the day he always left early, but if he didn't lay the warp on a new loom, the workers would not be able to work the next day. The time had come to say something to him. I was waiting for him when he came in that morning. I pressured him to stay until he completed the work, promising that as long as he finished that loom he could just sit around on Saturday and didn't have to do any more work. But he refused. When the time came for him to leave, he threw down his work right in front of my eyes, and said, 'I will never work on *Shabbos*! You can fire me if you want!' Then he walked out. Now this made me think: Master of the World! Here is a young man, absolutely destitute, and yet he will undergo such a sacrifice for *Shabbos*! And I! I am already old and don't have to provide for anyone! I make a comfortable living, so why do I desecrate the *Shabbos*? Right then and there, I decided to leave my work, do *teshuvah* and become a proper Jew.' "

I listened to Rav Sandler's story but didn't say a word, although I knew I was that young man. I was too shy to claim the credit for inspiring the man's *teshuvah*.

The departure of Rav Sandler and my mother-in-law had a profound effect on me. Until then, it had been unthinkable to leave Russia. Even to apply for emigration was foolishly dangerous. But now I saw that they had applied and were granted their requests, and others who applied had also succeeded. The thought of emigrating began to take shape in my mind as well.

The situation concerning the children's schooling was increasingly thorny. The threats to bring me to court were becoming more frequent, and I knew that it was only a matter of time before they carried through with their threat. What, therefore, did I have to lose by applying to leave?

I decided to begin the battle to emigrate. May Hashem help me! I prayed more fervently than ever.

27 GROWING UP ISOLATED IN MOSCOW

(Batya Chazan continues the story:)

EVERYONE WONDERS HOW WE CHILDREN, GROWING up in Moscow, managed to resist the pressure of our classmates and teachers while remaining dedicated, unswerving Torah Jews.

I think the simplest answer is that, as we were growing up, there was a thick line of demarcation between us and everyone else. We were religious Jews. Nobody else had anything in common with us. As strange as it may sound, if you grow up knowing this, such an attitude becomes second nature.

But it was more than that. We knew that our ancestors had been great Torah scholars and *tzaddikim*, men who had awakened their people to new levels of devotion and attachment to G-d. As their descendants, how could we defile their memory by choosing a path other than the one they had taken? This pride in our lineage was infused in us at an early age, because of the living examples we saw in our parents and our grandmother. They felt these ideals and lived them, and it was inconceivable for us to even imagine being different.

Our grandmother's trust in God was immense. She lived with us in difficult conditions for years, but she never complained. Every day, she prayed heart-rending *tefillos* and said *Tehillim*. She carefully followed every detail of Jewish law. How well I remember her admonishing us not to let the steam of a meat pot escape while the tea kettle was nearby, lest the steam touch the *pareve* tea kettle and make it *fleishig*!

She was knowledgeable in *Chumash*, and even *Gemara*, from the days when her own sons were studying in the house, and she would listen to what they were reciting.

When my father was teaching my brothers *Gemara*, and they had difficulty understanding a passage, she would sometimes call out impatiently, "Blockheads!" and then proceed to elucidate the passage.

Our grandmother ruled the kitchen in our home, taking pride in her spotless pots and her general high order of cleanliness.

All through the years, we suffered poverty, but we never complained, because we knew how difficult it was for our father to make a living. He went from one job to another for the sake of keeping *Shabbos*. He was forced to work long hard hours the whole week, and there were days when we didn't even see him, unless we rose early. On the contrary, we were deeply impressed by his devotion and his frequent absences made us long for *Shabbos*, when we could all be together.

As lively as we were, our parents never hit us. Our mother is a quiet woman, exceedingly modest. I never saw a hair of her head. She had superhuman strength. She kept the home spotless, and washed the whole family's laundry by hand for hours each day. (We purchased a hand-cranked washing machine only after Yitzchak, the seventh child, was born in 1952.) When the teachers in school would conduct inspections to make sure the children's collars and clothes were clean and fingernails cut, they were amazed that we were always so clean, whereas children from small families were not. And in addition to her daily running of the house, every year or two there was a new baby. Moreover, we made many celebrations for others in our home. All in all, the work load my mother carried was immense.

Our mother taught us the *alef-beis* and how to *daven* from a *siddur*. We learned from her all the *Halachos* pertinent to us, and she loved to tell us stories from the *Chumash* and *Midrash* (which she knew from the Yiddish explanation of the *Chumash*).

My father was highly respected by all who knew him, even our gentile neighbors, because he was so honest and straightforward. When my sisters married, many people whom we did not even know came to the weddings because of their high regard for him. When the time came to marry off my sisters, he borrowed money from good-hearted people, and he always paid it back. As much as he could, he educated my brothers and also the sons of friends. He tried to encourage other Jews to observe the *mitzvos* as much as they could. He undertook to make *Bris Milahs* in our house, while we provided food for the celebration. He arranged Jewish weddings.

My parents kept an open house, and there were always people visiting or staying over. People came to us when they were on their way to Israel and had to stop in Moscow to arrange their papers. All anyone needed to do was knock on our door, and he was given a bed. We even had vagrants and abnormal people living with us at times, since there was no one we would refuse.

I was just a little girl when we were in Kliazma, but I'll never forget that one-room apartment. My father had built a small wall projecting from one side of the room, in order for my grandmother to sleep privately, with one of my sisters. Everyone else slept in the room itself. My father built a long wooden couch, although we couldn't afford a mattress, on which a few of the children slept. To this day, I can't figure out where we all slept. Finally, we moved to Bolshevo, where we lived spaciously—in three rooms. My father built a "cellar" which I found out, years later, was a *mikveh*.

Most of the time, we held a *minyan* in our house on *Shabbos* and occasionally on days the Torah was read, or on days of fasting. The only ones who ever came to the *minyan* were old men. One of the men who sometimes came asked my grandmother for her *Korban Mincha Siddur* when she left for Eretz Yisrael.

"I'll give it to you," she told him, "if you promise to *daven* three times every day."

He promised, and she gave him her *siddur*.

My father once sent me to call this man to come and be the tenth man for the *minyan*. When I got to his house, he was babysitting for his grandchild, wrapped in his *tallis*, and *davening* from his *siddur*, just as he had promised.

There was once an international industrial exhibition, and the girls in the family begged our father to let us attend. He agreed, on condition we spoke only Yiddish on the street.

While observing the Israeli exhibit, we raised our voices a bit in talking. One of the Israelis came over, surprised, and began to speak Hebrew with us but we didn't even know the word "*Shalom*." Finally, one of their men who knew Yiddish came and spoke with us. Telling him our names, we asked him to give regards to our relatives in Israel, which he promised to do. He gave us flags, a necklace and pins with a Jewish star on it. As if all I needed was to be found with Zionist propaganda! But we took the things anyway so as not to offend them.

We grew up happy and high-spirited. As all children do, we fought, but never outside the house. I was forever fighting with the brother just ahead of me. But there was no question that we all felt very close.

I was not worried about what the future held for me. My three sisters had all married husbands who felt the same way we did, but we knew that Russia was only a temporary way station. Every *simchah* we made would end with a heartfelt *lechayim*, "*Leshanah haba b'Yerushalayim*!" (Next year in Jerusalem!) We knew we would eventually leave, somehow, sometime.

Our experiences in school reinforced this feeling. My five years in school consisted of one trial after another. When I began going to school, I would leave early on Friday, just as my older sister and brother did. The teachers challenged me.

"Look, there are five other Jews in this class, and they stay in class and write! Why can't you?"

"Because I'm religious," I would reply. I had to repeat this answer countless times, because the teachers never let up.

When I began to attend on *Shabbos*, the teachers would discreetly put a pencil and paper on my desk, and whisper, "Go ahead. You can write, and we won't tell your father." But of course, I would not. I politely ignored them.

My classmates spurned me because I was different. There were five Jews in my class, but all those years, they never spoke with me. The only child I had any contact with was a tattletale whom the other kids despised. The rest of the kids called me *Zhidovka* (Russian equivalent of Jewess, with a derogatory connotation).

Because I came to school with dresses that covered my knees, they would jeer, "Here comes the priest!"

Because I wore stockings, a few asked, "Do you have some disease on your feet?"

Others asked out of curiosity, "Why do you wear them?"

"Because I like to," I would reply.

I had a physics teacher who used to call me *Fazan* (which means pheasant in Russian) instead of Chazan. She threw me out of class several times for no reason. Since I knew I stood out from the rest of the class, I was always careful not to give the teachers an opportunity to find fault with me. One teacher, a Jew, was particularly rotten. She gave me a failing mark every *Shabbos*, even though she never asked me a question.

I had a good voice and used to be part of the class choir. After I turned nine, though, I refused to sing with the others, coming up with a different excuse each time, until the teacher became exasperated with me.

Our dancing class was even worse. I wouldn't think of dancing with a boy, so each time it was, "my foot hurts," "I don't know this step," etc. They knew there was more to my refusal then these worn-out excuses, but they didn't know what to do with me.

My sister once had an attack of appendicitis, and was absent on *Shabbos*. Skeptical, the principal came personally to check up. Even when she saw my sister stretched out on a bed, sick with fever, she presumed the girl was just acting, until she heard some time later that my sister had been taken to the hospital and operated on.

There were some years that I attended school from one to seven every afternoon. On Friday, I would take my schoolbag to school and participate for two or three hours. When it started getting dark, I put my things away and stopped working.

My classmates would begin to mock, "Oh! Here come the stars! Look! She has to put her pencil away!"

One of my younger brothers or sisters would pick up my school-bag during the recess before it got dark, and I would just sit in class until school was over.

Like me, my brothers and sisters had little contact with their classmates. Avraham, however, had a non-Jewish classmate named Lushke who lived nearby and who liked him immensely. Lushke came every day after school and spent hours in our home. He even picked up some Yiddish, in which we would joke with him on occasion.

When we left Russia, he came the next day to visit only to find the house empty. His mother went to my married sister and asked, "Where is everybody?" Upon hearing that we left Russia, she began to weep.

"My son was just beginning to grow up decent," she wailed. "But now that the Chazans have left, I'm afraid he'll become a bum again!"

The undisputed thorn in our lives was school. But *Shabbos* and holidays made life joyful. Every week, we waited for *Shabbos* with anticipation. In one room we held the *minyan* Friday night. My father and all the boys and other men *davened* there. The girls were in the second room. My mother would watch the little ones, and the other girls would *daven*. Then we would take over watching the children, so that she could *daven*.

One reason our joy at the table was so great was because we could finally sit down with our father. My father and each one of the boys made *Kiddush* for himself and had his own two *challos*. My father would mention something on the week's Torah portion which would set off a lively discussion. We would close the windows, so no one could hear us singing *Shabbos* songs. How warm and close with each other we would feel, sitting around the table! To this day, I miss the specialness of *Shabbosim* in Russia.

Shabbos meals usually consisted of vegetable soup, a side dish of vegetables (usually potatoes) and fish. In the summer, we had sauerkraut. When we had a happy occasion to celebrate, we made a barrel full of pickles.

Every day, we made herring or salted fish. For *Shabbos*, we tried to have a more special dish. I remember often traveling to Moscow to get a fish for *Shabbos*. Many times I came home empty-handed after hours of waiting in line, because only *treif* fish were being sold. Only occasionally did we have chicken, and a few times, we even had a goose. On occasion, after the chicken was slaughtered, it was found to be *treif*. I can remember the tumult in our home and the effort we put into trying to find a gentile to buy the chicken from us.

Once we even had meat. One of my brothers and I went with my father late at night to a private home where a *shochet* was waiting with a calf. What tension we all felt while they checked its lungs to see if it would be kosher! Finally, at two in the morning, we walked home with the meat package under my father's arm. I was bleary-eyed and exhausted from the tension and late hour. My father had wanted us to accompany him, so that he would not look suspicious walking alone with a package in the middle of the night.

The one other treat we regularly had on *Shabbos* was *challah*. Only when a Russian holiday was coming up did they sell flour in the stores; otherwise it was unavailable. We would buy as much flour as we could, and then save it, using a little every week. How delicious were those tiny slices of *challah*! We almost never tasted cake or cookies, since we could not eat the *treif* baked goods in the stores, and whatever flour we had was used for the *challos*.

Besides *Shabbos* and *Yom Tov*, another special time was during times of saying *Selichos*. We looked forward to staying up late to say *Selichos* with a *minyan*. Usually, the *minyan* was in our house, but a few times we traveled to the Machnovke Rebbe and joined his *minyan*. We remained there until dawn when the trains began running, and then returned home.

On *Sukkos*, the whole family would eat in the *sukkah* which was built just off our house. By this time, the streets were already covered with snow, so the girls quickly ate a *kezayis* (the minimum amount of bread that constitutes a meal) and left. The men stayed longer and quickly finished the meal there. No one slept in the *sukkah* in the freezing weather, except for one old man my father had known in Tashkent named Reb Zalman Leib, who used to say,

"We must keep any *mitzvah* we can!" He would spend most of his day in front of a heater in that icebox *sukkah*.

We would make a *menorah* for *Chanukah* by digging a hole in a potato and filling it with oil. We lit the *menorah* by the door which faced our porch, so as not to be too conspicuous. We had a beautiful custom on *Chanukah*. Every other night, after candle lighting, we would go to the house of one of our close religious friends to celebrate and eat *latkes* together, once at Yisrael Freidman's, another time at the Oliderts and one night at our home. In that way, we maintained a relationship with all the other religious families and their children.

In the last few years, we also met at each other's homes after *Shabbos*. During these *melave malkahs*, the adults would test the children on the *Chumash* and *Gemara* they had learned during the week. All of us were eager to show off. We sang and were sometimes given little prizes. These gatherings were so special that even the youngest in the family refused to be left behind.

Late winter, we baked *matzos* for *Pesach* in a large oven. We did this only at night and every other day, to avoid suspicion. We had a few workers we could trust, who were supervised by my father. I remember my older brother and I once working for hours kneading the dough and baking *matzos*. My father rewarded us with a single orange, an expensive delicacy, for our labor. We were fortunate that our non-Jewish neighbors never informed on us, even though they could smell the *matzos* baking.

We would have wonderful *Pesach Sedarim*. This was the one time that we had only the family and no guests, because whoever celebrated *Pesach* preferred to do it in a family circle. We had special dishes for *Pesach*, and even a silver cup that added a glow to our table. Every boy had his own *Seder* plate. (My father did this for educational purposes.) Everyone read the *Haggadah*, and every so often we would stop and my father would expound on a point. All the children would ask the *Mah Nishtanah*.

In commenting on the various tribulations of the Egyptian enslavement, my father was not lacking present-day parallels. Our *Sedarim* usually ended at two or three in the morning, after all the songs. My father would sing one song to a tune he knew from his home. One brother would sing the Chabad tune to the same song, and another brother would come up with a third tune. Finally, my father would retire because he had to lead the *davening* and read the Torah the next day. But the rest of us, excited by the *Seder*, would stay up longer and talk.

We had to go to school on *Chol Hamoed*. On *Pesach*, we took only fruit for lunch. Of course we didn't dare take *matzoh*.

On *Shavuos* night, my father and the boys stayed up the entire night learning. Although we could not feel the joy of the holidays as part of a community, the holidays were nevertheless the highlights of our life. Our father would remind us that in other parts of the world, tens of thousands of Jews celebrated the festivals and kept Judaism as we did. We dreamed that we would live to practice Judaism openly someday, as Jews were doing elsewhere.

28 THE MAY NINTH CELEBRATION

(The author continues the story:)

IN THE WINTER OF 1964, AFTER DELIBERATION WITH my family, I applied to Obir for permission to emigrate. My hopes were not unfounded since relatives in Israel had already sent us invitations. Perhaps the law allowing the reunification of families would be extended to us. At the same time, my nephew Yisrael Freidman took the same risk of applying, and for similar reasons; he, too, found the pressures from school and work mounting.

In my letter to Obir, I delineated my family's difficult situation. We were a religious family, my children being as observant as me. It was impossible to live in Russia, I said, since we could not find kosher meat and milk, as our law requires. The children were always hungry; they were thin and weak, my pitiful wages not even enough to buy food for them. Since keeping *Shabbos* was a must, I not only could not get a decent job, but had to leave jobs countless times and begin looking anew. It was impossible to continue living under these circumstances, I told them. I could not get help since I have no relatives here. My family was killed in the war, and only in Israel do I have relatives of my wife who will help us. I am therefore asking Obir for permission to emigrate in order to live decent lives.

After a few months of waiting anxiously, we got a reply. Permission denied.

We did not let despondency get the better of us. Throughout 1965 we applied again and again, but with no success. The only outcome of this application was a visit from the mayor, who inquired why we wanted to leave. I explained my position clearly, and he could not refute the poverty he saw in our home.

In March of 1965, we celebrated Yitzchak's *bar-mitzvah*. Not wanting to be outdone by his brothers, he finished *Megillah* and made a *siyum*. After delivering an impressive discourse, he surprised even me with an unexpected conclusion.

"We find in the *Midrash Vayikra Rabba*," he explained to his audience, "a detailed account of how Chanania, Mishael and Azariah defied Nebuchadnezzar's command to worship his idol. These are the words of the *Midrash*, Nebuchadnezzar said to them, 'Did not Yirmiyahu say about the nation or country that will not serve Nebuchadnezzar, 'On that Nation will G-d visit the sword, famine and pestilence' (*Yirmiyahu* 27:8)? Either you fulfill the first part of this sentence (and obey my order to bow down to the idol) or I will fulfill the end of that sentence!'

"In the book of *Daniel*, their reaction is recorded. The three righteous men answered Nebuchadnezzar, 'We serve our G-d, and He can save us from the fiery furnace and from your hands' (*Daniel* 3:16). The *Midrash* explains that the three youths answered the king unflinchingly, 'When it comes to income and property taxes, you are king over us. But when it comes to worshipping God, then you, the Emperor Nebuchadnezzar, are the lowest of mankind; you and a dog are equal in our eyes!' "

Yitzchak raised his clenched hand above the crowd and repeated forcefully, "When it comes to denying G-d then you, Nebuchadnezzar, you and a dog are equal in our eyes!"

One of the guests was Reb Mordechai Chanzin. He had spent

twenty years in prison for propagandizing Zionism among his fellow students. There he heroically kept *Shabbos* and *kashrus* and suffered hard punishments. Later, he was appointed the secretary to Rabbi Levin. After Yitzchak's speech he emotionally burst into applause until he recalled that he was still in Russia. He stopped short.

Around this time, the newspaper *Pravda* published an article in which the philosopher Lord Russell of England accused Russia of forbidding freedom of religion to its Jews. The well-known renegade Aaron Vergelis responded by printing a searing vituperation in his Yiddish magazine *Heimland*. (Vergelis was a devoted Communist who had been imprisoned during the Stalin purges and was freed after Stalin died, but learned nothing all those years; he began to curry favor with the new ruling class and was allowed to publish a magazine in which he pursued a fanatical pro-Communist, anti-Judaism line.)

In his article, Vergelis cried out indignantly, "What do you have to do with Russian Jews? Who appointed you their spokesman? In Russia, no Jew is interested in being religious! The modern Russian Jew wants to integrate into Russian society, except perhaps, for some elderly people. Let the world know this."

This desecration of G-d's name cut into my heart. I soon found my opportunity to react. My friend Rabbi Heshl Horowitz told me on Friday when I came to the *mikveh*, that the *gabbai* of the Great Synagogue was planning an elaborate celebration in *shul* of the May Ninth Russian victory over Germany. The holiday, to be celebrated that Sunday, was a great day in Russia, and the *gabbai* wanted to show the diplomats and tourists that the Jews shared in the nation's rejoicing. But at the same time, the *gabbai* did not want the Jews to know of his plans for the celebrations so that no one would have an opportunity to bring children and show that Judaism was alive in Russia.

I had never taken the children to the Great Synagogue because I knew it would have angered the *gabbai*, who was in the employ of the government. He did not want young people or children to come, only the elderly regulars, so that the impression would be given that younger people were never drawn to the *shul*. As far as the future was concerned, there were no Jews in Russia. Through the years, the children had *davened* in the *minyan* in our home or the home of a friend, but when I heard of the upcoming event, I turned to my sons, and said, "Now is the time to make a *Kiddush Hashem*! We will all go to the Great Synagogue! When all the diplomats and tourists come to the celebration, they will see that even our little ones are devoted to the Torah!"

My children enthusiastically took up the suggestion. I approached my nephew Yisrael Freidman, who had ten children, and a few other friends proposing that they join us in the plan. They agreed willingly.

On Sunday, we brought our children to the Great Synagogue. At the front of the *shul* was the *aron*, containing the Torah scrolls. High voltage lights illuminated them and they glistened with the polished silver shields and crowns. Rav Levin's seat was to one side of it, and on the other side was a balcony for the Israeli Consuls and foreign guests, surrounded by a fence, to be certain they had no contact with the crowd. Even though there had been an effort to keep it secret and no one was invited, somehow everyone heard of it and the *shul* was filled to capacity by young and old.

Yisrael and I remained in the interior of the *shul*, pressed into the throng. Right before the afternoon prayer, we signalled our children to jump up on the stage between the *Rav* and the guests. We had given them *siddurim* to pray with, and instructed them to *daven* in a loud voice with the congregation.

Over twenty children, ranging from eight to seventeen, suddenly leaped up on the *bimah*, in full view of everyone, *siddurim* in hand. When the *gabbai* saw the children, he became hysterical. He tried to force them off, but the children resisted. He could not be violent, because everyone, including the foreign dignitaries, was watching the spectacle. In a constrained tone, the *gabbai* asked Rav Levin to order them off, but they ignored his request as well.

"Rav Levin, you just said this is not a theater but a *shul*," Yitzchak told him. "In a *shul*, one *davens*. That's what we came for."

"What are these Jewish brats doing here?" the *gabbai* blustered in an undertone. "I'll take them apart!"

But he could only stand there bristling. He was powerless to move them during the celebration.

"The Russians must have staged this!" my son heard one of the Consuls whispering.

"Are you listening to the children?" the second Consul replied. "They really are praying!"

The children turned out to be the main attraction for the guests and congregants, who could hardly believe that in the heart of Moscow there existed young children and youths who knew how to pray from a *siddur*. Throughout the celebration, cameras clicked and flashed, taking hundreds of pictures of this unbelievable event.

Something else unforeseen and moving was the spontaneous speech of a young engineer who had returned to Judaism. After praising the Red Army, he specifically praised the Jewish heroes who went on suicide missions, some of them two or three times.

"It is not as the anti-Semites are saying that the Jews fought the enemy from Tashkent (far away from the front). They offered mighty resistance at Moscow, Stalingrad and Leningrad. They have fought tyrants throughout the ages."

The *gabbai* passed him notes to stop, but he ignored them and spoke on. He spoke abut the greatness of the Jewish nation and the courage it had shown in all generations. As the most recent example, he cited the Israeli victory in the War of Independence. This speech profoundly affected the Russian Jews who heard it and added to the *Kiddush Hashem* of that day.

The assembly came to a close. We left the Great Synagogue with mixed feelings. We were glad we could show Jews in Moscow that there still existed Jews faithful to Torah. At the same time, though, our perpetual fear loomed before us. Perhaps now they would take revenge on us.

Time passed, and nothing happened. Instead, we heard that the *gabbai* had suffered a heart attack right after the celebration and was in the hospital for several weeks. We utilized his absence to repair the broken boiler system of the *mikveh*, something which he had forbidden.

We had had a skirmish with him two years previously, also over the *mikveh*. Approximately thirty families were using the *mikveh* every month, including some who traveled ten hours from Kharkov, spent the night in Moscow and returned home the next day. That summer, the *gabbai* began closing the boiler of the *mikveh* at six. By the time night fell at eleven, the water was cold, which caused great inconvenience. I immediately approached Rav Levin to find out what had happened. He referred me to the *gabbai*.

"You people are responsible for it," the *gabbai* snarled at me. "You immerse yourselves in the *mikveh* before prayer in the morning and ruin the taps of the water system."

"If so," I said, "close the *mikveh* in the morning, but not in the evening! And where are all the workers that maintain the Synagogue day to day? Why can't they see to this aspect of the building, too? If necessary, we'll help pay for any repairs. There's no justification for what you did!"

The *gabbai* reopened the *mikveh*, but two years later, the hot water pipes in the boiler broke down. This time, the *gabbai* refused to repair it, even at our expense. Now that he was convalescing in the hospital, Rav Levin gave permission. Organizing the repairs ourselves, we procured a boiler from a man in Torasovka, Leib Pinkas, who no longer needed it. Reb Shmuel Bishinsky, an engineer, volunteered to do the job. He did so quickly and professionally. But the time the *gabbai* returned from the hospital, the *mikveh* was once again operational.

29 ENROLLING IN THE YESHIVAH

IN SEPTEMBER OF 1965, MY GRANDSON BEGAN attending school. The year before, Avraham had also gone. When my youngest son Yaakov saw him go, he told me defiantly, "I will never attend school, no matter what!" He was six years old at the time.

In school, the gentiles would often nickname their Jewish classmates Abraham.

"Hey, Abraham, take the paper! Abraham come here!" they would hoot at the Jewish children.

But our Abraham would nonchalantly interrupt them, "Why do you call him Abraham? Call me Abraham. I'm Abraham! Go ahead!"

"We already know that," they would answer, annoyed. "You say what you are, but they don't; they change their names."

A neighbor told me that at a parent-teacher conference, one woman asked the principal, "What about Chazan's grandchild? Does *he* at least attend on *Shabbos*?"

"Him?" answered the principal. "He's even worse than his uncles!"

I was overjoyed to see that devotion to G-d and His Torah was continuing into the next generation.

At this time, all my energies were focused on leaving Russia. If we could not get the visas through conventional means, then I would try every avenue possible, even those that seemed illogical and doomed to failure. I hit upon an absurd scheme by which I hoped to arouse the attention of various government ministries.

Moscow had a *"yeshivah"* that the N.K.V.D. had officially asked Rabbi Shlomo Schleifer, the *Rav* of Moscow, to open. Under their supervision the *"yeshivah"* only served to camouflage their suppression of religion. Rabbi Schleifer took some young men, mostly from Uzbekistan and Georgia, and brought them to this so-called University or Seminar, in order to make them *shochetim, mohelim* and rabbis. The students had to be over eighteen years old, since it was prohibited to teach religion before that age.

How did Rabbi Schleifer find teachers or students? He looked for the few remaining religious Jews such as myself, and proposed for us to come to his *yeshivah*, promising us the same payment and food any Russian student gets. I refused, saying I was afraid to do this, lest they send me to Siberia as they did the other rabbis. One day, Rabbi Schleifer asked to see me.

"What are you doing now?" he asked me.

"I'm working," I replied.

"How are you in your observance of *Shabbos*?"

"Thank G-d, I'm not breaking *Shabbos*."

"How's that possible?"

"I'm working in various places with weavers. As there's not enough work for the whole week, my not working on *Shabbos* is not noticed."

"But you must know that the government is going to close down the small factories and open big ones instead, where they can have tighter control. When the day comes when you have to work in such a big establishment, what will you do? They won't let you have *Shabbos* off then."

"So what can I do about it? As a Jew I have to hope. There is no provision for the future. The One Above helped me so far, He'll go on helping me."

"Let me make a proposal to you that will ease your lot. I have an order from the government to open a rabbinical college and, as you have done a lot of learning Torah, you will be a very suitable member. You will only sit and learn and have no worry about *Shabbos*."

"I have a record as a worker for these past twenty years which I'd rather not lose, and secondly, you know what they have done with rabbis. My father was a *Rav* of a *shtetl* and in the end, he had three possibilities before him: to renounce the rabbinate in public; to escape and go underground; or to be sent off to Siberia. He decided to flee. I, as a young man due to become a rabbi, had three possibilities: to renounce publicly my father's ideals; to share his dire perils as a young entrant to the rabbinate; or to take on hard labor for five years to 'cleanse' and 'prove' myself as a citizen of the republic. I worked for five years, married and moved to Odessa, where I worked as a bookbinder of official documents in various places. Then, in the war years, I worked in Tashkent and eventually came to Moscow where I've continued to work. I've established a record as a workman. I can't, I must not get interested, after all this, to become a religious worker, which I've managed to avoid thus far."

"You no doubt think," he responded, "that those rabbis sent off to Siberia were condemned simply for being rabbis. But it was not so. Those sent off either dealt in foreign currency or interfered in politics. A rabbi who only learned Torah was left unmolested."

"I don't know of any such statistics. I do know that in my own family I had two brothers-in-law who did no harm of any kind. They were so far from politics that they did not even read any newspapers, but they were taken and done away with, leaving behind widows and orphans."

Rabbi Schleifer pondered for a while and then cited the Yiddish proverb, "When wood is chopped, splinters get broken off," by which he meant that the innocent get chopped down in hard times together with the guilty.

Since he was sitting in the room of his office in the Synagogue, and our conversation was being secretly taped, he could say nothing else. He conceded my point regarding the perils of the rabbinate. Finally he asked, "Well, will you come and join the *yeshivah*?"

"Let me discuss it with my wife," I replied.

The next week, he spoke to all the younger Torah students of Moscow, about fifteen men, and received the same answer from all of them. In other words, all of them refused to join the *yeshivah*.

Rabbi Schleifer opened the *yeshivah* with eighteen men, mostly young Sephardim from Georgia, as well as some middle-aged men.

At that time, a young *shochet* and a *mohel* from Dniepropetrovsk arrived in Moscow. We helped him enter the *yeshivah*, where he taught his crafts to others. He imbued his students with a spirit of devotion to the Torah. About fifteen to eighteen students mastered his crafts. Most of them now live in Eretz Yisrael.

After Rabbi Schleifer's passing in 1957, his place as the Rabbi of Moscow and head of the *yeshivah* went to Rabbi Levin.

Soon thereafter, the police insisted that the students be discharged from the *yeshivah* on the pretext that they had no permits to live in Moscow. In the end, only one person remained at the *yeshivah*. The synagogue had a kosher restaurant for the *yeshivah* students, which remained open as long as that person was enrolled.

Outwardly, the *yeshivah* still "existed" as window dressing for tourists. A visitor entering the synagogue was greeted by a sign: "The *yeshivah* affiliated with the Great Synagogue of Moscow is accepting applicants for the year 1963. Apply to Rav Y. L. Levin."

Although I refused to enter the *yeshivah*, I played along with this bluff. I went to Rabbi Levin and asked him to accept my children, ages eight, eleven, fourteen and sixteen, into his *yeshivah*. I did not mention eighteen-year-old Moshe Mordechai, who could legally attend, because sending my children was the farthest thing from my mind. I just wanted to create a stir in offices higher up.

"Don't you know that Soviet law forbids teaching religion to youths under eighteen?" he asked.

"The honorable *Rav* knows that I educate my children to observe Torah and *mitzvos*. Since my salary doesn't allow me to buy kosher meat or even butter, they are suffering from malnutrition. I'd like to enroll them in the *yeshivah* so at least they'll get a wholesome meal every day from the Synagogue's kosher kitchen." (Actually, we never ate meat from the Synagogue kitchen, because any meat we ate had to have no questions regarding its status.)

"But I'm not allowed to accept them at their age," he said. "If you want, go to the Ministry of Religious Affairs and tell them about your situation. Maybe they'll make an exception."

I asked the *Rav* for the address of the office, and he gave me their Moscow branch. At that time, there was a so-called kosher kitchen for the only remaining student of the *yeshivah*, who lived there with his wife and three grown children.

Rav Mordechai Chanzin, secretary to the *Rav*, advised me not to go to the Moscow branch but to the Central Office of the Ministry, where the real power lay. He told me to ask by name for Vice Minister Rozanov, the second highest official there. However, he asked me not to go until he himself had left for Israel.

Shortly thereafter, he left. The following day, I went to the Central Office of the Ministry of Religious Affairs. I took leave of my family, aware that I was doing something very dangerous. As I did not know how to get to that ministry, I took a taxi and told the driver to take me there. Since I was afraid I would be asked the purpose of my visit and possibly arrested for pestering high officials, I intended to tell him that Rabbi Levin had sent me to one of the departments but I had lost the slip of paper with the name. This was my excuse for not going to the Moscow region office of the ministry.

A guard was stationed outside the offices of Vice-Minister Rozanov.

When I asked to enter, he inquired, "Whom do you want?"

"Comrade Rozanov," I answered.

Surprised, the guard gave me a questioning look.

"What do you have to do with Comrade Rozanov?" he demanded.

"It's a secret," I said.

"Wait here," he told me and left. He entered the office, and soon returned. "Which nationality do you belong to? I'm sorry to ask, but the Ministry has different nationalities under its jurisdiction, and they want to know which one you belong to."

"I'm a Jew."

He brought me into the office and opened a door. I walked into the room, and he closed the door behind me. I was suddenly engulfed in total darkness. I did not bang on his door to keep it open so that I might see, but resignedly, despairingly, stepped forward, feeling each step to make sure I was not falling into a cellar. I bumped into a man whom I heard approaching me. Was this strange set-up made to check out newcomers and potential foes?

"Whom do you want?" he asked.

"Comrade Rozanov," I repeated.

He opened the door to a small room that was full of books and files, apparently the Ministry's archives. At the head of a table sat Comrade Rozanov. A long bench was near his table.

"Sit down," he said. "Where are you from?"

"From Bolshevo," I replied. "I pray in the Synagogue of Rav Levin."

"I know him. What do you want from me?"

"I'm a religious Jew. I have educated my children to be religious and they eat only kosher meat. My paltry wages, however, are insufficient to pay the high cost of such meat for them. I decided that since Rav Levin's *yeshivah* gives kosher meat to its students, I'd like to enroll my children there."

"Why did you come to me? Go to Rav Levin!"

"He does not want to accept them."

"Why not?"

"Because they're younger than eighteen years."

"Well, that is the law. It is forbidden to instruct religion to youths who are under eighteen."

"But who else would attend a *yeshivah*," I persisted, "if not my children? The purpose of such an institute is to train rabbis for the Jews. My children are educated to be religious. They don't write on *Shabbos* in their school, and they eat only kosher food. Do you really think that youths raised on the principles of atheism would want to study at a *yeshivah* and become rabbis? After all, what is the goal of a *yeshivah*? What kind of rabbis would they become?"

"Why are you standing in the way of your children?" he asked. "Let them learn like all other children."

"But I told you, they are different from other children."

Rozanov did not know what to say. He acted as I had known he would, refusing to violate the law for my sake. I asked him to write out his refusal for me, so that I would have an excuse to try to reach the Minister of Religious Affairs himself. But he would not do this.

"It is not our policy to write out things of this nature," he answered curtly. "If needed, we have a phone. Goodbye!"

As I was leaving the building, the thought of his sharp words made me nervous. I kept thinking, would the N.K.V.D. pick me up here for an investigation? But this apprehension was empty, and I left the building without disturbance.

From the Central Office, I went by bus to the Moscow branch of the Ministry of Religious Affairs, as Rav Chanzin had advised me. I knew the way and had no need to ask directions. It was an old-style Moscow house near the main Synagogue. At the head of the department was a man called Lishenkov. There was no guard at the door and no anteroom to the office, where he sat all alone. He received me in a friendly manner and unceremoniously listened to my request to enroll my sons in Rav Levin's *yeshivah*. I also told him I had met with the Deputy Minister Rozanov, which astonished him.

"They let you in to see Rozanov? What did he tell you?"

"He told me that this matter was not under his office's jurisdiction, which is why I have come to you, Comrade Lishenkov. I want you to allow Rav Levin to accept my children to his *yeshivah*."

. There was regular contact between him and Rav Levin. The confirmation that Rav Levin was to give me later, that my children were not allowed by religion to write on *Shabbos*, came after receiving permission to do so from Lishenkov.

An amicable person, Lishenkov asked me in a friendly tone, "Tell me, Comrade Chazan, why can't you behave like all the other Jews who educate their children under the existing conditions of our Soviet homeland? They live undisturbed lives. Why do you make such problems for yourself? You made a request to go to Israel and they refused, so why make matters complicated for you and your children if you want to remain in Russia?"

"Comrade Lishenkov," I replied. "Aren't there Communists who act contrary to the laws of Communism?"

He nodded.

"In the same way, there are Jews who act contrary to the laws of Judaism," I continued. "But my wife and I are different. We are faithful to our religion and have raised our children in that spirit. I am a loyal citizen who has never done anything against the Government. You yourself know that keeping our religion is within the bounds of Soviet law. But our situation is such that our children have to suffer because they refuse to write in school on *Shabbos*. They're malnourished because they refuse to eat anything forbidden by our religion. My wages are insufficient to buy kosher meat for them. I have applied to OVIR to let me emigrate to Israel, where I have relatives who can help me. All the relatives that I had in Russia were murdered by the Nazis. But OVIR, for no reason, refuses to let us go. So, I have no choice but to put my children in the *yeshivah*, so that they won't starve. Please allow Rav Levin to accept them to his *yeshivah* in spite of their young age."

"I cannot violate Soviet law," he replied. "But go and speak with Rav Levin. Maybe he can open up a school in Yiddish especially for little children."

"What?" I said excitedly. "It's possible to open up an elementary school for young children? This is excellent!"

Lishenkov hastened to add, "I didn't say it's permitted. I just said try to speak to Rav Levin about it."

"Goodbye," I said warmly. "And thanks!"

I knew of course that this offer was merely a put-off, the kind of cynical joke in which Russian officials delight. I figured though, that if I did not follow up his suggestion, he would always be able to push me off by claiming, "If you didn't listen to my advice, don't bother coming to me again." Furthermore, I wanted to incense prominent officials with my obstinate efforts, so that my case would become known. Often, the local officials gave a flat refusal and shoved a case aside. On the other hand, if my case became public, there would be a better chance that they would want to get rid of me and allow me to emigrate.

I knew, also, that my actions might bring me into greater danger and might achieve the opposite result. Many friends advised me not to start up with these unprincipled officials.

"There's no telling what they might do to you," one friend cautioned me. He was a famous professor of medicine who knew both the Babylonian and Jerusalem Talmud by heart. I got to know him when I came to him with a medical problem. He was pleased to meet a Talmudic scholar with whom he could discuss learning. Upon hearing my name, he told me he had also known my father when he had gone underground and came to Moscow in the Thirties.

He took me into a small rabbinic study and said, "Your father was also here. By the time he left, the whole caseful of books was out on the table."

He also told me that whenever Rabbi Schleifer could not locate a dictum in the Talmud, he would phone him. This professor devotedly attended his patients day and night. In his boyhood, he studied in the Chafetz Chaim's *yeshivah*. One night, he recalled, he felt that someone was moving about in the dormitory. Waking up, he saw that it was the Chafetz Chaim himself, coming to see that, in the cold of winter, all the boys were properly covered. In one of his books, he kept a few letters in which the Chafetz Chaim addressed him when still in his teens, as "the rabbi, the genius."

"You're putting a knife to your throat, and endangering your entire family," he warned me.

Still, I decided to carry on.

I went to Rav Levin and told him Lishenkov's suggestion. He laughed and said, "Don't you know we are not permitted to make a religious school?"

I would have to think of a new plan, but I would not give up so quickly.

30 INSIDE NATIONAL HEADQUARTERS

THE NEXT STEP IN MY DARING PLAN WAS TO TRY TO reach other members of the Politburo. My goal this time was the Secretary of the Communist Party, Suslov, who held one of the highest positions in the country. In September, 1965, I wrote him a letter, detailing my family situation and asking to meet with him or his deputy. I mentioned that I had applied to OVIR many times but that each time I was refused. To make sure the letter reached its destination, I wrote "Confidential" on the envelope.

I went to Party headquarters in Moscow and handed my letter to one of the officials. She gave me a phone number, telling me to call in a few days to get my answer. When I called back, they told me my letter had been sent to the local branch of the Party in Moscow. I called up the branch and was told that my letter was sent to the branch in my region. I realized that this run-around would last forever, so I called Party headquarters to try again. The official gave me the same answer that I had received when I called the first time.

"My letter was addressed to the Secretary of the Party and was marked Confidential," I told her boldly. How dare you send it anywhere else!"

"Comrade Chazan," she told me. "Everyone knows your secret. You want a visa to go to Israel. This is not the concern of the Party. You should speak to OVIR."

"OVIR refused to give me the visa," I replied, "without bothering to check out the facts of my case. We should have received special consideration since I have always been a loyal citizen and my wife was even conferred a Heroic Mother. (After the war, Stalin awarded this title to women who had ten or more children. His motive was to encourage population growth. Nevertheless, in all Moscow, there were only a few women with this distinction.) But we are just ignored! You are our leaders. Why can't we complain to you about an office that won't even check out a vital matter involving a large family? To whom should I go for justice, the King of Persia? It seems to me that Party headquarters is unquestionably the proper place to bring our complaints. And another thing," I went on. "Why can't I come and speak personally with my leaders? Why don't you give me the Minister's address? Why is everything done by telephone? Tell me when and where Comrade Suslov will be in, and I will come and speak with him personally about my pressing problem."

"Okay, Comrade Chazan," the official softened and said. "Write another letter to this address, and I'll pass it on to the man you want. Call back in three days."

I followed her instructions, and telephoned back.

"Your letter was delivered to the right place to be read before the Party Secretary Suslov," I was told. Phone back in a few days."

When I called this time, I was told that Suslov's deputy, Comrade Zakusin, would receive me the following morning. My hopes were lifted. Things were moving. The next morning, I came to Party headquarters with my wife. From the lobby I rang up Zakusin's office to let him know of our arrival.

"Who are you?" he asked.

"I am Aaron Chazan. I have an appointment with you this morning."

"Oh, you do? About what?"

"About an emigration visa to Israel."

"That's not our affair. Go to OVIR."

"I have already applied to OVIR many times. They keep telling me that they'll check out our case. But we still have not heard anything positive. I want to ask you to intercede with them."

"How many years have you lived in Moscow?" he asked.

"Nineteen."

"Well, if you have had patience for nineteen years, you can wait a little longer. Goodbye!" And he hung up.

I put down the buzzing receiver, discouraged. The trip to Party headquarters had been in vain. We left the building and went to buy some provisions that were not available in Bolshevo. We bought ten to twelve one kilogram loaves of black bread, butter and groats.

As we were leaving, I reconsidered and told my wife, "You phone him and tell him that we were promised a meeting with him, and he must keep his promise. Tell him you're a Heroic Mother and that you came especially to meet him, even though you have great difficulty in walking. Your words will carry more weight. Tell him your husband does not speak Russian very well and therefore didn't quite grasp what he was saying."

My wife called. She spoke as I had advised, and he yielded. He came down thirty to forty minutes later, entered a room and sent a message to us to come in. We wished to leave our handbags outside the door, but the caretaker said, "Not my responsibility," so we took them in with us. Zakusin passed his eyes over them.

"The stores here are full of goods of every kind," I said, flattering him. (In fact, they were badly stocked, and people had to stand in long lines.) "But most of it is of no use to us because we can only eat kosher food."

"Where do you live?" he muttered.

"In Bolshevo."

"Bolshevo happens to be known to me. I've been there recently. They are laying gas pipes there."

"Yes, they are laying them but they say it will cost a lot of money." A pause.

"Well, look here," he said. You are religious people so you have it difficult, but your children don't have to follow your ways. Take my case. My parents had me christened. So what of it? They remained religious, and I am a Communist."

"But we have an obligation to bring a boy into the Covenant and to give a full religious upbringing to the young. Your parents brought you up as they saw fit. We're bringing up our children as we see fit. We have much more than just baptism, and the Soviet Constitution allows it all. Comrade Zakusin," I went on, "I know we are interrupting your busy schedule. We don't want to waste your time. We only want to describe to you personally our impossible existence because we observe *Shabbos* and eat only kosher food. We have no option but to emigrate."

He asked us to explain what kosher food was. I obliged. "The meat needs to be kosher and the milk needs to be kosher. It is not within our means to buy these."

"So what do you get to eat? Children need to eat, and you yourselves must also eat."

"Once a week, for the day of rest on Saturday, which is *Shabbos*, we treat ourselves to something better. The day before we go to the market and buy a chicken of about one-and-a-half kilos, the price of which is seven rubles, and we go to a *shochet*, a butcher of kosher meat."

"Where is it killed?"

"Not far from here, on the other side of Nogina Square. In the Great Synagogue on Archipova Street, there's a *shochet* on duty who slaughters for anyone who brings a chicken."

"Does one pay for this?"

"No. It is done for no charge."

"And are the feathers plucked?"

"Yes, the same *shochet* does this as well. To do all this and get back home to Bolshevo takes up to eight hours, all for just one chicken, and this has to be divided among fifteen people! We do not have the money to buy the kosher meat and milk which are more expensive."

"So what do you get to eat?"

"My wages suffice only to buy vegetables during the week. Our children are weak and hungry," I continued. "They are browbeaten in school daily because they won't write on *Shabbos*. The teachers constantly berate them. I myself cannot hold a job with decent pay because I keep *Shabbos*."

"Do you have any married children?" he asked.

"Three of my daughters are married."

"Are their husbands religious?"

"Yes."

"Tell me, where did you find your first son-in-law?"

"My son-in-law is not from Russia. He is one of the Romanian refugees. He was an orphan brought up religiously, and he came to pray in the Synagogue."

"How did he get to you?"

"Naturally, I also came to the Synagogue because I'm a religious man, and so we understandably got acquainted. He said he was aged twenty-six and would like to settle down with a religious girl. After seeing him several times, I liked him and said I had a daughter aged eighteen, and as there were no religious young men in Moscow, I asked him to come to our house so that we could get to know each other better. He was pleased to accept my invitation, and I gave him my address. He came and we got well acquainted. My wife and I realized that he was a very serious young man, and the two young people approved of each other. So the match came about."

"And where did you get the second son-in-law?"

"Also through the Synagogue. He is also not Russian but from Bukovina, from a religious family. While passing through Moscow, he came to pray at the Synagogue. He finished his army service and was seeking to get married. So in a similar manner we got close and the match came about."

He did not inquire regarding my third son-in-law.

"I see that your Synagogue is like our club. That's where we meet and marry." He was silent. Then he told me matter of factly, "You seem to be under the impression that everyone in Israel is religious. That's a complete misconception. Israel is a thoroughly secular state."

"Our relatives live in Bnei Brak, a religious city, and that's where we would settle, too."

Our discussion continued for an hour in a friendly spirit. At the end of our meeting, Zakusin said, "It had nothing to do with me but I'll ask OVIR to reconsider your request."

I began to beg him to put pressure on OVIR, but he firmly replied, "I have no authority to give orders. I can only request. And this I have promised to do.

31 THE BOARD FOR EDUCATIONAL MATTERS

IN SEPTEMBER OF 1964, I HAD TAKEN CHAIM MEIR out of school and sent him to work in a factory for four hours a day. He was too young to work according to the law, and the Jewish director of the factory had gone out on a limb to do me this favor. Like many others I encountered, he wanted to help a religious Jew. I wanted to send both Chaim Meir and Batya to a Workers' School, which did not have sessions on *Shabbos*, but having a job in a factory wasn't enough to qualify. I also had to receive permission from their school principal, the woman who accused me of being anti-Communist and was constantly looking for ways to bring me to court. Why would she agree to my plan, especially when she knew my motives? I decided on a most radical plan, one that would prove that my actions were in consonance with Communist law.

I went one day to Rav Levin and submitted a hand-written request in Hebrew for a confirmation that Jewish law forbids children to do work on *Shabbos*.

Rav Levin read my note and began to tremble.

"I'm afraid that I cannot give this confirmation without permission from the Office of Religious Affairs," he said. "But give me your note so that I can show it to them."

He asked his secretary to translate it into Russian, and I left. It took Rav Levin over a week to "transmit" my letter. Each time I asked, he said he had forgotten. His secretary then told me what day the *Rav* usually went to the Ministry. I followed Rav Levin into the bus and gave him the translated copy of my letter (which the Secretary had given me when he translated it into Russian). Although it was not easy for the *Rav* to ask for permission to give me such a letter, I insisted.

To our amazement, they allowed him to give me the necessary confirmation. Once I had it in my possession, I went straight to the school and showed it to the principal.

"Here is proof," I told her, "that I am a completely loyal Russian citizen. Even the Minister of Religious Affairs, who authorized Rav Levin to write this note, agrees that my children should not write on *Shabbos*."

"Good," she replied evasively. "We'll send you to the Regional Board on Educational Matters. Maybe, they'll permit you to send your children to a Worker's School."

This is the text of the letter I sent and the confirmation I received:

To the esteemed Rabbi, Rabbi Y.L. Levin:

I, Aaron Chazan, and my wife Leah, were educated in rabbinical homes to keep *Shabbos, kashrus* and all the *mitzvos* of the Torah. We have educated our children to keep the Torah's laws exactly as we do. This is why they do not write in school on *Shabbos*. The school administration accuses us of being counterrevolutionaries and has threatened to bring charges against us in court. I have told the principal that we are sincere and not insubordinate to the Government. We are merely religious Jews who study and observe our laws, which forbid us and our children to desecrate the *Shabbos*. I would like the illustrious Rabbi to give us a confirmation that

Jews, including little children, are forbidden to desecrate the *Shabbos* as is written in the Torah, "You, your son and your daughter shall not work on the *Shabbos*," which includes little children. Since the Holidays are also approaching, as is the new school year, I am fearful lest they bring my case to court. Therefore, please give me the necessary confirmation. We trust that G-d, the G-d of our holy parents, who were martyred for His Holy Name and for observing His commandments, will keep us from stumbling in those very things for which our parents underwent so much suffering.

Yours truly,
Aaron, son of Rav Mordechai Chazan, of blessed memory,
Leah, daughter of Rav Zusia Freidman, of blessed memory.

This is the confirmation we received a short while later:

To Rav Aaron Chazan:
The fourth of the Ten Commandments is the prohibition for a Jew to desecrate the *Shabbos*. The *Mechilta* defines this prohibition as applying also to little children. This prohibition extends to *Rosh Hashanah, Yom Kippur, Succos, Pesach* and *Shavuos* for twenty-four hours.

Rabbi Y. L. Levin, *Rosh Yeshivah*.

I presented my request to the school, and it was transferred to the Regional Board on Educational matters, Department of Child Delinquency. This board dealt with requests for early withdrawal from school, which were made generally for juvenile delinquents or youths incapable of advanced study. I was given an appointment to appear in Kaliningrad before the board at two o'clock on *Erev Yom Kippur*.

I came at the designated hour, but was called in at 3:30. During my wait, I saw people going in and out in rapid succession.

"When is it my turn?', I asked. "How much longer do I have to wait?"

"All the other cases are easy to decide, so they are being seen right

230

away," they told me. "Your case, however, is very serious, so we were given instructions to keep you waiting until your mayor arrives."

Finally, I was called. I entered the room where over thirty people were seated. All the principals of schools in our region were there, headed by the ex-principal of the school Batsheva had attended in Bolshevo, Mrs. Tichomirova (the same name as that of the counsel for the Prosecution in the Beilis case in 1911), now promoted to Director of Education for the region. Also present was the mayor, who presided over the group.

I told them that everyone has the right to educate his children as he wishes with regard to keeping religion, according to the laws of the country. Furthermore, when the father of a big family does not earn enough to feed his children, he may send a son or daughter aged fourteen to fifteen out to work for four hours a day, in order to help with the family income. To allow them to go on with the school subjects, there are special schools for working people where they can get an education by coming three days a week from eight in the morning till one and in the evenings.

The mayor expressed the opinion that they should be allowed to work and attend a Workers' School, but the principal of my children's school stood up and protested.

"Comrade Mayor," she began in a crisp tone. "Chazan's true motive for taking his children out of school is not to contribute to the family's sustenance but to enable them to keep *Shabbos*. All his children learn in my school, and not one will write on *Shabbos*. We have invested strenuous efforts to persuade the children to write on *Shabbos*, but they continue to rebel. One is not permitted to bring up children the way Chazan does, even his own Chief Rabbi does not bring up his children this way. They study in the school and arrive on *Shabbos* and *Yom Tov*. You, Chazan, have no permission to bring them up according to your private wishes."

My fear was that they would send my case to the juvenile delinquent children's section of the education office. There, my case would be judged like the Christian sects who are altogether against the Government. The children would be remanded to Communist institutions and the parents put into prison. Indeed, they threatened

231

me and my family with this. The principal who had been in Bolshevo before her supported her accusation.

"I remember this Chazan very well, though he does not remember me," she said. "Every Friday afternoon, he used to come and take his daughter Batsheva out of class early so she could pray with him. He must be made to understand that Rav Levin's confirmation carries weight in Palestine, not in Soviet Russia!"

"And I remember you well," I called out in disgust. "All I'm asking for are decent living conditions, which I can't have unless my son and daughter help out!"

But the two principals had convinced the mayor, and he changed his tone.

"If that is Chazan's motive, we have to hold him to the full stringency of the law," he said. I suggest that if his children won't write this next *Shabbos*, we will impose on him a monetary fine of twenty rubles, and if they persist in rebelling the following week, we will arraign him in court. He and his wife will find their rightful place in prison, where they will work to pay for the upkeep of their children who will be placed in Soviet institutions."

My heart was gripped by icy fingers when I heard his menacing words. There was no doubt he would fulfill his threat. But suddenly the words of our sages flashed through my mind, "Even at a time of danger, a man should not alter the rabbinic manner of his rank" (*Sanhedrin* 92b). Trembling, I advanced right up to the table.

"What!" I shouted. "Are you planning to set up an Inquisition in Russia? The Christian fanatics in Spain seized children from their Jewish parents, and that's what you are planning to do, too? Just this past week I was in the National Headquarters of the Communist Party to tell them about the religious needs of my children and myself. I didn't hear from them the kind of threats I'm getting over here!"

My emotional outburst dumfounded the assembly. Finally, the principal turned to the committee and said, "What's to be the result?"

"He can go home now," the mayor replied. "We will speak with him another time."

I went out shaking with fear. Would they imprison me? I took the electric train home and arrived in Bolshevo close to five. I quickly ate the final meal before *Yom Kippur*, since *Kol Nidrei* was at six.

I was afraid the police would come for me that night. When the worshippers arrived, I told them what had happened that day, and my worries of an impending arrest.

"Maybe we should pray in someone else's house, so that none of you suffer consequences because of me," I suggested.

The other worshippers would not agree. They stayed in the house and prayed along with me, the men in one room, the women in a different room. Reb Chaim Lazar Gurevitch, a Lubavitcher *Chassid*, had been appointed the *baal tefillah* and was already wearing his *kittel*.

"Perhaps," he suggested, "I should not lead the service then. Just in case we have visitors."

"Okay," I said. "You don't have to. I'll lead."

He had good reason to feel apprehensive. For the "crime" of teaching children he had served seven out of a ten-year sentence in prison. Since no books of any kind were allowed in prison, he used to say *Tehillim* as well as all his prayers by heart. A great scholar, he was also able to review his Torah and *Chassidus* by heart. He therefore took off his *kittel* just in case. I decided that despite the tension I would not let my spirit fall. I put on my *kittel* and led *Kol Nidrei* for over forty people. My sons helped me sing the prayers.

My fears, thankfully, had been groundless. *Yom Kippur* passed uneventfully, as did *Sukkos*. The school administration, however, did not leave me alone. After *Sukkos*, I received an urgent summons to come to the Municipality. As soon as I arrived, they ushered me into the mayor's office, where I was introduced to the deputy mayor, a lawyer by profession.

"Why don't your children go to school on Saturday?" he said harshly.

"They do go."

"Is this what you call going?" He raised his voice and banged the table. "They are spreading anti-Soviet propaganda by showing all the other children that they don't write on *Shabbos*. I will sue you in court. You are committing a serious crime by spreading anti-Soviet propaganda, and you will get a well deserved punishment!"

"What have I done wrong?" I replied indignantly. "I did not want my children to go to school on *Shabbos*, but the mayor, who is sitting right here, gave me no choice. He himself agreed that they do not have to write on *Shabbos*." I raised my voice now, too. "What propaganda are you accusing me of spreading? Do you mean to say that Jews in Russia cannot keep their religion? *Shabbos* is very important to us. In every generation our fathers let themselves be killed rather than transgress *Shabbos*. This dedication to our day of rest is our heritage." I jumped up from my seat, shouting, "What do you want from me? My whole family was killed by the Nazis and now you want to kill me, too!"

He also rose and shouted back at me. We kept outshouting each other until the secretary of the council walked in.

"Everyone can hear the clamor outside!" she said. "Quiet!"

The mayor turned to me.

"Listen, Chazan," he said. "In our country there are Christians, Moslems and Jews, and each one has his own day of rest. The Christians keep it on Sunday, the Moslems keep it on Friday, and the Jews on Saturday. Can the Government make three days of rest a week? They therefore instituted a general day of rest for everyone — Sunday. You have to understand this and obey the law."

"Please tell me, Comrade," I said, "why they appointed Sunday as the day of rest. In consideration of whom? Why didn't they make the day of rest on Monday or Tuesday? Apparently, they wanted to be considerate of the deep feelings of the Russian people for their religious traditions. Why isn't this same consideration extended to the Jews?"

The mayor now tried a different approach. "Comrade Chazan, you are a simple laborer. Tell me, do you want your children to end up doing the same kind of simple work that you do? If you allow your children to write on Saturday, they'll be able to attend a university and learn a distinguished profession. Otherwise, they'll just be simple workers."

"I've always been taught that labor in Communist Russia is honorable; now I hear from you that it's degrading to be a laborer. Tell me who works at a job? Dogs? No, only men! Work is work, whatever it is. I see nothing shameful in doing any honest work. I don't care if my

sons will be laborers. It's more important to me that they keep
Shabbos!"

Our conversation ended, and they let me go.

A month later, I was watching the children in the house, while my
wife was at the doctor. A teacher from school appeared and told me
to come to the parent's assembly that was called for that hour. I
explained that there was no one else to watch the children and
therefore I could not come.

"I advise you for your own good to come to the assembly," she
warned me. "They're discussing your case, and the final vote may
have serious implications for you."

I went to the assembly, which had a full turnout of parents. At first,
they discussed what to do with some delinquent students. Then I
was asked to come to the rostrum. The chairman of the assembly
launched into an account of how I was leading my children astray
from the glorious Communist ideal. After hearing this tirade which
was padded with insults and emotionally charged accusations, the
parents were bristling.

When he finished his speech, the chairman called out in a loud
voice, "Whoever is in favor of bringing Chazan to court, raise your
hand!"

All hands went up.

"Against?"

Not one hand.

"How do you feel about the vote of the assembly?" the principal of
the school asked me.

"How do I feel?" I thundered, so that every person in the room
could hear me. "How did I feel when the Nazis killed millions of my
brothers, when they shot them down in pits and burned them alive,
when they gassed them to death and tortured them limb by limb?
That's how I feel now!"

The hall was silent. Finally, one teacher remarked, "But Comrade
Chazan, the Nazis murdered Jews, whereas we want to befriend
them."

"Oh, thank you!" I scoffed. "I am a Jew and I want to remain a Jew.
I will never forsake *Shabbos* or do anything against my Jewish
tradition."

The meeting ended, and I went home. That was the last attack I suffered from the school administration. By the time they sent me a letter threatening to bring me to court, I had already left for Israel. But my difficult times were not over.

32 COMING HOME

THE WONDERFUL NEWS ARRIVED FOR YISRAEL Friedman and his family that *Chanukah*! He was finally granted his exit visa, and with joy and good wishes we saw them off. My determination to get those longed-for visas now increased a hundredfold.

A few days after Yisrael left, I went to *daven* in the Great Synagogue. After the prayers, I began speaking with a friend, Reb Zev Sirota. The *gabbai* walked by us, stopped a second and continued. Then he walked back to us and gave me a questioning look.

"What's with you?" he said. "Didn't you travel to Israel?"

"No," I answered.

"Aren't you Friedman from Perlovka?"

"No, I'm Chazan from Bolshevo."

"Why didn't you go to Israel?"

"They won't let me."

"Don't worry, they will," he said and left.

I was puzzled. Did he have something to do with Yisrael Fried-man's visa?

A short time later, I heard that the *gabbai* was boasting to his friends that he had gotten an exit visa in order to get rid of a religious Jew. When I asked Rav Levin if this was true, he told me he, too, had heard the *gabbai* say it.

"Why don't you ask him yourself?" he suggested.

I approached the *gabbai* and told him I heard he had helped a religious Jew get his exit visa. Could he do me that favor as well? He promised to do what he could. It was silly, though, to rely on the *gabbai* alone.

Three months had passed since Zakusin from the Communist Party Headquarters had promised to speak with OVIR, and still no answer. I phoned Zakusin again, and he referred me to the N.K.V.D., where my file was being held. I kept calling them, but was pushed off every time for two months.

In the end, I was told bluntly, "If OVIR refused you, you have some nerve bothering another office before a whole year has passed!" This was the law.

Once again, I phoned Zakusin.

"How is it possible that when I told the official from the N.K.V.D. that you had referred me to him, he pushed me off?" I complained.

Zakusin was noncommittal. "We are unauthorized to revoke the decisions of the Ministry of the Interior," he said.

"But what can I do now?" I pleaded.

"Try writing to Kosygin or the Foreign Ministry. And now I must ask you not to bother me again. Do you understand? We are finished, Comrade Chazan. Goodbye!"

I wrote a letter to Kosygin but received no reply. I did not know where else to turn. I was becoming more and more anxious as each month went by. My oldest son had just turned eighteen and would soon be called to the army. Would I never leave this land?

On the *Erev Shabbos* before *Pesach*, some distinguished visitors paid me a surprise visit—the mayor, the regional Director of Education and another man whom I did not recognize. They asked numerous questions about my living conditions.

"We are ready to give you a house with five rooms," they finally said. "The house you are in now you can give to your daughters after the necessary repairs have been made. We will also allow you to buy a cow, so you'll have milk for your children. We will even pay the expenses for them attending a convalescent home, so their health will improve."

Each of my daughters was struggling in a one-room apartment woefully inadequate for her growing family. Their seeming generosity, though, would not relieve our situation.

"My children cannot eat the non-kosher food in your convalescent homes," I told them. "Having a cow will barely make a dent in providing for the needs of my large family, and you haven't said a word about how my children will be free of the daily browbeating they get in school."

I firmly refused their offer.

"How are you willing to go to a capitalist country and forsake your Motherland?" the Educational Director pressed me. "Really, how can you make such an disloyal move?"

I thought quickly for a reply to that loaded question. "All my relatives were murdered by the Nazis, and their bodies thrown into a death pit!" (In Russian, *rodina*, homeland, is similar to *rodnia*, relatives. I pretended to have misunderstood what he said.) "My parents, brother, sister and their families were wiped out together with the entire town! To whom should I be loyal to? To a pile of corpses?"

The three men exchanged glances. They said goodbye and left.

Right after this meeting, I traveled to the Great Synagogue to immerse myself in the *mikveh*. The *gabbai* told me that Rav Levin wanted to speak with me during the *Chol Hamoed Pesach*.

I visited the *Rav* a few days later. He told me that he had been called to the local branch of the Ministry of Religious Affairs and reprimanded for giving me a confirmation that according to Jewish law my children were prohibited to write on *Shabbos*. He protested by saying that they were the ones who had permitted him to write it. They dropped the subject but brought up a new one.

"We see that Chazan accepts your authority, so we want you to influence him to give up his plans to go to Israel," they said. "He claims that his family is large and his living conditions are impossible. Well, we are prepared to give him a bigger house and a chance to make better wages. We don't really care if Chazan himself travels, but it's a pity that his children should fall into the hands of a capitalist country."

"Well," Rav Levin concluded. "What shall I tell them?"

"I really think," I replied, "that the *Rav* is clever enough and doesn't need any advice from me on how to answer. But if I were in his place, I would say, Chazan only turns to me in matters dealing with Jewish law. Outside of that, for instance in the matter of traveling to Israel, he does what he wants."

August arrived. I had sent another letter to Kosygin, months before, again with no reply. Suddenly, I received a letter from the Office of the Premier that I should apply to OVIR concerning my request. I assumed this was the result of a letter our relatives in Israel had written to Kosygin.

On Wednesday August 3, 1966, I took my wife and a few of our skinniest children to OVIR. In the waiting room, there were also many tourists. I asked the secretary to let us in to the director, but she refused. I began to shout, and my children yelled along with me.

"We want to meet the director! We want to meet the director!"

A secretary came out from one of the offices and, observing the scene we were making in front of the tourists, brought us in to the director.

"Don't make such a disturbance!" she admonished us.

I finally came face to face with the director, Razantzov.

"Who are you?" he asked me.

"I'm Aaron Chazan from Bolshevo."

"Aha! This is the one who applied countless times to OVIR, wrote several letters to Premier Kosygin, visited the National Communist Party Headquarters, went to Suslov, to Brezhnev, to President Podgorny, to every place possible, and still they're not letting you go. I'm sorry, comrade. There is nothing further to do at this point. They just won't let you go to Israel. You'll never get permission. Just give up because nothing will help."

I jumped up and screamed in despair, "What! You won't let us go to our relatives? We have to die here? We have no way of living here.

Look at our children. They're weak and sickly. They're starving, because they can't get meat or milk here that's kosher! What do you want? That we die of starvation? Why don't you let us unite with our relatives, who will help us get food?"

"I can't give you one," he said. "My superiors won't allow it."

"Who are your superiors? Give me their address!"

He wrote down on a piece of paper, "Pitrovka 38."

"Which office is this?" I asked.

"You've been living in Moscow for twenty years and you don't know which office is at Pitrovka 38?"

It was the headquarters of the N.K.V.D. which of course I knew, but I wanted him to write it down in order to have indisputable proof that OVIR had sent me to them.

A young clerk sitting next to the director added, "Over there you won't be talking so high and mighty!"

I took the piece of paper and was about to go.

"Wait a minute," Razantzov suddenly called to us. "You say you need kosher food for your children and can't afford it? Go to the Great Synagogue. They'll help you out."

I knew the malicious intent behind his words, but I played along with him. I went straight to the *gabbai* of the Great Synagogue.

"OVIR said you would help us out," I told him. "Give me money to buy kosher food!"

The *gabbai* guffawed. "Since when do we have a fund to provide kosher food to poor families?" He looked at me as if I had gone mad, but I insisted he write me a letter that they were unable to supply me with kosher food.

The next morning, I went with my wife to Pitrovka 38. We were received by a woman. I showed her the note that Razantzov had given us and repeated all my complaints.

"Did Razantzov refuse your request?" she asked.

"Not only did he, but so did every office I went to!"

"Write down your complaints again and also that Razantzov won't give you the exit visa."

I did as she instructed and gave her the letter.

"When will I get an answer?"

"In a few days," she replied.

We went home filled with hope. That *Shabbos* was *Shabbos Chazon*, the *Shabbos* before a nine day period of mourning, culminating with the fast of *Tisha B'Av*. This period commemorates the destruction of the two Temples in Jerusalem. My son-in-law led the morning prayers at our home. Right before *Mussaf*, Yitzchak could not hold back and began to hum the end of *Kaddish* in a festive tune.

"Is that proper?" the other worshippers criticized him. "In the nine days period of mourning you're singing *Yom Tov* tunes?"

He didn't explain why he was so lighthearted, since we had kept secret the details of our efforts to get a visa.

Sunday morning the postcard arrived from the N.K.V.D.—granting our visa!

Our joy knew no bounds, but we told almost no one, just in case. On the postcard was written the day we were to appear at OVIR to arrange our papers. When I showed up, the official remarked acidly, "Do you think we'll let everyone go? You can only take the younger ones with you!"

I was struck with fear. Would they keep Moshe Mordechai back for army service or the children already in working school? My lip trembled as I asked her what she meant. The official told me that OVIR had rejected our married daughters' applications, which they had submitted together with mine. They would have to remain behind, but the children living with me were permitted to go.

The thought of going without my older daughters was painful, but it was senseless to remain behind because of them. I had to save whomever I could. I wrote out the papers, and within a few weeks our passports were ready.

My anxiety for my married daughters was only alleviated when the first was allowed to leave three months later, the second, six months later, and the third, just over a year after we had left.

The plane that traveled once a month to Vienna was booked until after *Sukkos*. We did not want to wait an extra minute. We chose instead an exhausting two-day journey by train through Poland, Czechoslovakia and Austria. We left Moscow Sunday night with pounding hearts, and when we finally rolled into Vienna on Tuesday morning, our spirits had not dampened a bit. Besides my meager belongings and many books, I had taken with me three Torah scrolls, wrapped up within each other, which I had hidden in the corner of a crate.

At the airport in Israel, hundreds came to greet us. My mother-in-law and Yisrael Friedman were there. My wife's brothers and sisters-in-law, whom we hadn't seen for twenty years, and their children and grandchildren gave us a grand welcome. Countless friends from years back also showed up.

Joining the family circle in Israel, it struck me how the unswerving devotion which Reb Zusia had taught his children had paid off. Not a single one of his hundreds of grandchildren and great-grandchildren had left the fold. All of them learned Torah and scrupulously kept *mitzvos*. My righteous mother-in-law passed away in 1978 at the age of ninety-six. She lived to see a fifth generation born and had the satisfaction of knowing that every single one of her descendants was following the path of G-d.

Appendix: Translation of a letter that appeared in Pravda, Mitshini Region, on April 9, 1960.

Dear Editor,

We are asking you to publicize this letter to stir up the public against parents who are sabotaging their children's Communist heritage with their religious drivel. These parents educate their children to feel they are holier than everyone else and they don't respect our principles of honest work and communal living. The religious rituals practiced by the family not only harm the children but also disturb the routine of the school. These are the facts concerning the education that the four Chazan children of our school are subjected to in their home. These children also observe these religious rituals and do not attend on Saturday. As a result, their achievement is impaired, and the study and discipline of the entire class is disturbed.

On Saturdays, students work to thoroughly clean the building of the school. Chazan's children have no part in this. As a result, they are developing egotistical character traits. Their subversive education has struck deep roots in their conscience; these children do not attribute their absence from school to their parents' orders, but they themselves declare, "We are strictly religious and cannot transgress our religious law."

M. Michailova V. Sharimov
Teachers in Public School No. 1 in Bolshevo.

left: Rav Aaron Chazan in Russia

below: Rav Chazan (right rear) with Russian children in Eretz Yisrael

Rav Zusia Friedman, Rav of Odessa and
Rav Chazan's brother-in-law

Rav Yaakov Friedman, Rav in Kiev and Rav
Chazan's brother-in-law

The Chazan and Friedman families in Moscow

above: Rav Yosef Kozlik and his son

left: Rav Avraham Friedman, Rav of Odessa and Rav Chazan's brother-in-law

Rav Sholom Schachna, Rav in Berditchev and Rav Chazan's brother-in-law

GLOSSARY

All words are Hebrew
unless otherwise indicated.

alef-beis: Hebrew alphabet
aliyah (aliyos pl.): the calling up of a worshipper to recite a
    blessing on a portion of the Torah reading in the Synagogue
aron: the holy ark in the Synagogue that contains the Torah scrolls
baal tefillah: leader of prayer
baalei batim: householders
bar-mitzvah: the age of thirteen at which a Jewish youth becomes
    obligated to observe the commandments of the Torah
beis midrash: place of study
bimah: podium in center of Synagogue
Birchas Hamazon: grace after meals
bachur (bachurim pl.): an unmarried boy

bris milah: circumcision

berachah (berachos pl.): blessing

challah (challos pl.): a special bread served in honor of *Shabbos*

Chanukah: holiday commemorating the victory of Jews over the Greeks, symbolized by the miracle of the *menorah* in which a small flask of oil burned for eight days

chavrusa: a study partner

chazan (chazanim pl.): cantor

cheder (chadorim pl.): religious elementary school for boys

Chillul Hashem: desecration of G-d's Name

Chillul Shabbos: desecration of the Sabbath

Chol Hamoed: intermediate days between the first and last days of *Sukkos* and *Pesach*, when work is partially permitted

chasan: engaged or newly-married young man

Chullin: the Talmudic tractate pertaining to the ritual food laws

Chumash: the Five Books of Moses (Pentateuch)

chupah: wedding canopy or the wedding ceremony itself

chutzpah: gall

daven (Yiddish): to pray

erev: eve, the day preceding

esrog: the citron fruit which is required to perform one of the *mitzvos* of *Sukkos*

fleishig (Yiddish): meat, as opposed to dairy

gabbai (gabbaim, pl.): synagogue official

gartl: belt put on prior to prayer

Haggadah: text recited on the first two nights of *Pesach*

hakafos: the ritual of circling the Synagogue while carrying the Torah scrolls, on the Holiday of *Simchas Torah*

Halachah (Halachic adj.): the definitive body of Jewish law; also, each individual law

Hashem (lit. the Name): the popular appellation for G-d

hatoras nedarim: *Halachic* release from vows, usually made on the eve of *Yom Kippur*

illuy: genius

Kabbalah: metaphysical Jewish study of the Creation and existence of the Universe and its relationship to Godliness

Kaddish: mourner's prayer

kashrus: Jewish dietary laws

kav (kabin pl.): a liquid measure, approximating 2.2 liters or 1-1/3 quarts

kehillah: united Jewish community

Kiddush (Kiddushim pl.): benediction recited on wine on *Shabbos*; also repast offered to worshippers after morning services on *Shabbos* and Holidays

Kiddush Hashem: sanctification of G-d's Name

kittel: traditional white robe, worn the first night of *Pesach* and during *Yom Kippur* services

Kol Nidrei: the moving prayer which begins the *Yom Kippur* evening service

kolkhoz (Russian): agricultural commune

kosher: food fit for consumption under Jewish dietary laws (see *kashrus*); colloquially, anything that is fit

kulak (Russian): wealthy land-owners

latkes (Yiddish): potato pancakes, a traditional *Chanukah* dish

Lechayim: lit. to life; a toast

lulav: palm branch, used to perform one of the *mitzvos* of *Sukkos*

maggid: preacher

Mah Nishtanah: the four questions asked by the youngest child on the first night of *Pesach*, the *Seder* night, which introduces the retelling of the Exodus

marror: bitter herbs eaten at *Pesach Seder*

maskil: Jew who advocated integration and assimilation into gentile society and culture

matzoh (matzos pl.): unleavened bread eaten on *Pesach* in place of yeast bread

mechutanim: parents of one's son or daughter-in-law; relative by marriage

melamed (melamdim pl.): teacher of young boys

Melaveh Malka: meal after the conclusion of *Shabbos*

menorah: an eight branched candelabra lit on *Chanukah*

metzitzah: sucking; part of the rite of *bris milah*

Midrash (Midrashim pl.): collection of early rabbinic interpretations and homilies on the Bible

mikveh: a body of water for ritual purification

Minchah: afternoon prayers

minyan: quorum of ten male Jews, required for communal prayer

Mishnayos: portions of the *Mishnah*, the brief codification of Jewish oral law, completed in third century C.E.

mitzvah (mitzvos pl.): any obligation commanded by Torah or the Sages. Also, colloquially, any good deed

mohel: Jewish functionary who performs circumcision

Motzei Shabbos: the night following the Sabbath; Saturday night

muktzah: objects not to be handled on *Shabbos*

Mussaf: "additional" prayer recited on a festival

nigun: tune

Parshas Hashavua: portion of the Torah for the week's reading

Parshiyos: sections of the Torah

pareve: food that is neither meat nor dairy

Pesach: Passover, the eight-day festival of the Exodus (seven days in Israel) that occurs in March or April

peyos: side-curls; according to Torah law, a man's hair may not be shaved at the earbone but may only be trimmed there

Poskim: qualified arbiters of *Halachic* questions

Rabbonim (pl.): see Rav

Rav (Rabbonim pl.): a rabbi

Reb: an amiable and respectful title preceding the name of any Jew in direct address

Rebbe: 1. a schoolteacher 2. a Rabbi in his capacity as one's personal spiritual advisor or teacher 3. the leader of a group of *Chassidim*

Rosh Chodesh: the beginning of a new lunar month

Rosh Hashanah: the beginning of the Jewish year which is the Day of Judgment

Rosh Yeshivah: Talmudic scholar who heads the *yeshivah*

Seder (Sedorim pl.): the first two nights of *Pesach* (the first night only in Israel) when one recites the *Haggadah* and has a feast

Sedrah: one of the weekly *Chumash* portions (see *Parshas Hashavua*)

Sefardim (Sefardic adj.): Jews whose medieval ancestors lived in Spain

Sefiras Haomer: period extending from the second day of *Pesach*

until *Shavuos* during which each of the forty-nine days leading up to *Shavuos* are counted

seudah: festive meal corresponding to a particular religious occasion

sefer (seforim pl.): book, usually connoting one of Jewish or religious content

Sefer Torah (Sifrei Torah pl.): Torah Scroll(s)

Selichos: penitential prayers said during the month of *Elul* and on the days between *Rosh Hashanah* and *Yom Kippur*

Semichah: rabbinical ordination conferred by a recognized rabbinical authority that qualifies one to decide Jewish Law

Shabbos (Shabbosim pl.): the Jewish Sabbath that lasts from sundown on Friday to after dark on Saturday

Shacharis: daily morning prayers

Shailah: *Halachic* query

Shavuos: two-day festival (one day in Israel), occurring fifty days after *Pesach*, commemorating the giving of the Torah.

shechitah: the laws pertaining to ritual slaughter of animals according to Jewish law, which renders their meat kosher

shecht: the act of slaughtering (see *shechita*)

shidduch: a match, for the purpose of marriage

shiur (shiurim pl.): a lecture or class on a Jewish topic

Shema (also Shema Yisrael): the fundamental Jewish declaration of G-d's oneness

Shemini Atzeres: the one-day festival immediately after *Sukkos*; outside Israel it is followed by *Simchas Torah*, the Festival of Rejoicing over the Torah; in Israel the two days are combined

Shemurah Matzos: *matzoh* made from wheat that was guarded from the time of harvesting

shochet (shochetim pl.): ritual slaughterer (see also *shechitah*)

shofar: ram's horn; an important feature of *Rosh Hashanah* services is blowing the *shofar*

shtiebel (Yiddish): small synagogue, the members of which are usually closely interconnected

shul (Yiddish): colloquial for synagogue

siddur (siddurim pl.): prayerbook

simchah: joy; a celebration

Simchas Torah: the festival of rejoicing over the Torah, which concludes the festival of *Sukkos* (see also *Shemini Atzeres*)

siyum: celebration in honor of completing the study of a *Mesechta* of the Talmud

sukkah: temporary booth erected for seven days, in fulfillment of one of the *mitzvos* of *Sukkos*

Sukkos: seven-day Feast of Tabernacles

tallis (talleisim pl.): prayer shawl

tallis katan: four-cornered garment with tassels customary for a Jew to wear every day

Talmid Chacham: Torah Scholar

Tefillah (Tefillos pl.): prayer

tefillin: phylacteries

Tehillim: the Book of Psalms

tekios: *shofar* blasts (see *shofar*)

Teshuvah: repentance

Tisha B'Av: the ninth day of the month of *Av*, a day of fasting and mourning

Torah: the five books of Moses, the written law given to the Jewish people on Mount Sinai in 1312 B.C.E.

treif: not kosher, forbidden for Jews to eat

tzaddik (tzaddikim pl.): righteous man

Tze'enah Ure'enah: the popular Yiddish book of homilies written on the Bible

tzitzis: the tassels on the *tallis katan*

viduy: confession or confessional prayer

yahrzeit (Yiddish): anniversary date of a death

yeshivah (yeshivos pl.): academy or study hall where young men study the Torah and Talmud intensively under the direction of a renowned Torah scholar (the *Rosh Yeshivah*)

yeshivah ketanah: a *yeshivah* for Jewish boys in their teens

Yiras Shamayim: fear of Heaven; piety

Yom Kippur: day of repentance, a fast day. *Yom Kippur* concludes the period of introspection and repentance which begins with the month of *Elul* and includes *Rosh Hashanah*

Yom Tov: one of the six yearly holidays when work is prohibited (*Rosh Hashanah, Yom Kippur, Sukkos, Shemini Atzeres* and *Simchas Torah, Pesach, Shavuos*)

Yamim Nora'im: Days of Awe, referring to the festivals in the month of *Tishrei*, beginning with *Rosh Hashanah*

zemiros: traditional Jewish songs